# Dolphin Melody

Tui Allen

Published by Tuiscope
www.tuiscope.co.nz

ISBN: 978-1-7386-2270-2




Tuiscope
251 Kempthorne Road
Jacks Bay
Russell
Northland 0272
New Zealand

# DEDICATION

To Mieke Nova Tasman Dawes.
May she never know a world without dolphins

.

*Carried in the midnight silk*
*Of starry currents in the seas,*
*I listen to the rising wind*
*That sings to you of galaxies.*

Ripple

# CONTENTS

# MĀORI AND DOLPHIN VOCABULARY

Faraway readers may be unfamiliar with the occasional Māori vocabulary used in this story. Additionally, some ancient dolphin terms will be new to everyone. The following list might be helpful:

- **Aotearoa** – New Zealand
- **Ipipiri** – The Bay of Islands,
- **Te Tai Tokerau** – Northland, New Zealand
- **Motu** – island.
  Often used as part of a longer name, as in *Moturoa* (long island) or *Motukauri* (island of kauri trees).
- **Koru Maelstrom** – The dolphin's name for the Milky Way galaxy.
  This term blends English and Māori to best capture the dolphin concept of the galaxy as a storm of stars spinning like a whirlpool or spiral.
- **Waka** – boat, canoe or kayak
- **Koha** – gift
- **Eunivore** – "beautiful eater," such as orcas who avoid warm-blooded prey and strive to eat without causing suffering or waste. It might also apply to a human who eats with ethics and environmental concerns in mind, striving to minimize harm.
- **Malivore** – "cruel eater," like rogue orcas who eat dolphins alive, indifferent to the suffering they cause.
- **Azure** – Earth, named by dolphins after the planet's striking azure (blue) colour.

# ACKNOWLEDGMENTS

- To the dolphins of Ipipiri, for their help and inspiration in the creation of this story. They heard my thoughts, took my kayak into their physical and spiritual slipstream and showed me the beauty of these waters I share with them. If not for them, this story would have been set far from here and would not have been the same.
- To my beta readers - Jeannie McLean and Shauna Bickley.
- To all the other members of the infamous "Rogues" critique group who helped along the way, with critical assistance of text and cover design.
- To Barbara Else for her assessment of the second draft.
- To Judith White for her edit of the third draft.
- To my newest critique group, the Russell Writers, who listened and responded so patiently at our small but friendly meetings, one of which was even held afloat in Ipipiri waters.
- To my daughter Heather for her help with sound-tech advice and for the original music she creates, which inspires my musical stories.
- To my Jeff, who supports me constantly in so many ways, despite all the hassles, expense, grumpiness, absent-mindedness and moodiness that probably comes with any such creative mission.

# 1 - HINEMOANA, THE IMMORTAL OCEAN

I breathe.
My blood circulates.
I grow.
I think.
I give life, to the trillions who are born to me daily.
I move about, sometimes more slowly than a summer cloud, sometimes too fast to see. And sometimes I lie still and watch.
I'm young, I know – only around four billion years old. There are oceans on other planets older by eons. Yes, we oceans of the universe know more about each other than you might guess. We're like the dolphins, who sing to their friends on other worlds.
There's one old ocean out there in the stars, who's three times older and larger than I. She has monsters in her that would scare the megalodon to jellyfish! She tells me I lack maturity. But what could she learn in her twelve billion years that I couldn't learn in my four? I know all I need to know.
So yes, I'm alive, but I'm also immortal. Instead of having life after life like you mortals do, always forgetting the previous existences, I have only one that drones on forever. If I didn't have countless playmates, immortality would bore me to death.
But you, my children, have revved up my planet. All details of your myriad lives fill my spirit always, revealing a million stories.
I want to tell you one of them.
This story began among humans and dolphins in Aotearoa. They call me Hinemoana there. Let that be the name you know me by.

## 2 - BORN IN OCEAN MIND

How she longed for freedom to move and stretch all her new muscles. She tried to flick her fins, but they were trapped to her sides, by the enclosing body of her mother, Aria. Wordless thoughts streamed back and forth between mother and daughter, as they had for much of the pregnancy.

'Help me mother!'

'Not long now little one,' said Aria.

'I'm so frightened.'

'Relax! Let it happen. There's nothing to fear.'

Time slowed while the baby edged along the birth canal.

The pressure became unbearable. Squeezing. Squeezing.

Then it was over. Her fins flicked outwards, released at last. So, this was light! They'd warned her about it, but still it frightened her! Huge shapes moving about in so much space! The surface shimmered above her. Someone pushed her through it, into more light – dazzling, blinding. The breeze swept a million blue ripples dancing and singing against her skin. And the cold – the searing cold!

She stared around at the ocean, the sky above it, the dolphins she'd heard but never seen, the newness of everything.

'Mother!' she wailed. 'It's too bright. Too cold.'

Her mother and aunties kept her at the surface.

'Breathe!' they coaxed. 'Breathe! Breathe!'

She understood nothing.

'What's happening?'

'You've just been born,' said Aria. 'Remember what I taught you before you were born?'

The baby's mind went blank. 'No, I don't,' she said.

'Breathe! Breathe!' they urged again.

'How?'

'The exercises I taught you,' said Aria. 'Remember step one? Step two? To help you breathe. You'll die if you don't. Do them now. Concentrate!'

She blocked out the brand-new world around her and focussed inwards. How did it go now?

Step one: She compressed her lungs as she'd practised, forcing residual amniotic fluid from her blowhole. It trickled warm on the air-exposed skin of her head.

Step two: She reversed the action, expanding her lungs. Air from the atmosphere exploded inwards.

'Ouch! What happened?'

She wanted to return to where it was warm and safe. But she swam on, while the oxygen infused her blood, energising her.

Those around her breathed again also. They'd stopped while they waited for her to start. The adults caressed her until she calmed from the shock of the first air invasion – then they encouraged her to try again.

'I don't want to! I don't like it!'

'You must! Your life depends on it.'

For the second time, she gathered her courage and breathed again. But now, the in-flash of air was expected. Within half an hour she'd learnt not to fear it. Soon, they hardly needed to remind her. It was as though she'd always breathed.

Her marvellous fins and tail-flukes pressed the water, feeling its lift and fall, reading the sideways push of the current, powering her over and under, and through the waves. Her tiny flukes smacked the surface and sent the spray flying.

But Aria continued to ask, now and then, 'Are you breathing enough?'

Among the birth pod were her older siblings – the astronomer Antares, and the poet Zeta. She'd spoken to them often before birth. Now she could see them at last with her eye-vision, as they danced to entertain her, and caressed her with their pectoral fins.

'Mother! Mother! I'm still cold!' she wailed.

'Don't worry!' soothed Aria. 'Remember I warned you of this too before you were born. It will help if you take milk from me now.'

There was too much to learn. Would milk be as scary as air had been?

'Where? How?'

The aunties guided her to her first milk. It was creamy on her tongue, thick and sweet like syrup. Its heat warmed her.

The birth pod moved homewards now, away towards the Ipipiri

School, picking up speed. The baby struggled to keep up until Zeta taught her how to ride Aria's wake.

She tumbled into place, felt the pull of her mother's slipstream steadying her, carrying her. She began to learn the pattern of swooping curves, down through the cool green and up into the dazzle for a quick breath.

Bounce up breathe, bounce down, swoop swoop.

Bounce up breathe, bounce down, swoop swoop.

She kept at it, until soon she'd perfected the rhythm she would live by.

The activity completed the warming of her little body.

'The water is perfect. Why did I think it was cold?'

Her fins and flukes celebrated. 'I'm dancing,' she cried. 'Free at last! Does the ocean ever end, Mother?'

'It's not infinite dear, but Azure is a vast sphere, and the sea covers most of it. You could swim forever around. But the sea is nowhere bottomless. There's always a barrier somewhere below. Beware of shallow waters.'

At first, she had seen few colours. But as her aura prepared to expand for the first time, it revealed every spirit-colour that exists, including many that you humans cannot see.

The Ipipiri School came to meet the birth pod. Dozens of dolphins, bringing the intellectual chaos of the dolphin idea-sphere. Aunties, friends, and well-meaning acquaintances, all pestering.

'What name will you give her, Aria?'

'A name!' thought Aria, 'I must find one quickly.' She scanned her daughter with eyesight, mindsight and soundsight, seeking inspiration.

The baby stared about her. So many dolphins! Their thoughtstreams spun everywhere, sometimes from one dolphin to another, sometimes from one to many. Some ideas flew out and back to distant pods in other schools, far out to sea. The silent hurricane buffeted her from every direction.

'Mother, what's all that thought noise?'

'It's just the idea-sphere. You'll get used to it soon.'

The idea-sphere! Gossip, calculation, cogitation, deliberation, speculation, abstraction, estimation, gossip again, rationalization, reflection, viewpoint, fact, fancy, and more gossip, tumbling in fragrant clouds of colour and texture. There were memories, poems, hypotheses, prophecies, lunacies and conspiracies, schemes, fantasies, stories, theories, arguments, overtures, undertones, and afterthoughts. All invisible yet glittering like the shards of light rippling down from the surface above.

Her brain wobbled.

'It's too much,' she said. 'I'll look and listen instead.'

She blocked all thoughtstreams except those from her mother. Immediately she noticed the wind hurling spray in long white streaks from the crests of waves.

I could hear that before I was born, she thought. Now I know what it looks like.

She began matching up everything she could see around her with the sounds that went with it. With all the chaos now blocked, the physical sounds untangled. The heartbeats of the pod around her, a skitter of rain on the ocean's surface, the flutter of wind in the feathers of a bird, the clicks and squeaks of the dolphins and the spattering, rushing, and rippling of the sea mingling with the wind.

Something boomed far away. Time passed. It boomed again.

She listened, mystified.

'What was that sound, Mother?'

'The beating heart of a great whale,' replied Aria. 'The slower the beat, the deeper he hunts.'

'The sounds make patterns,' she said. They go high low, fast slow.'

'Like a melody,' said Aria. 'So that's your name – Melody!'

'Melody!' echoed the other dolphins and they welcomed her, by her new name, to the ocean.

But Melody had blocked them all, so she didn't hear. She was still too busy listening.

Zeta and Antares danced proudly around her, enjoying the celebration of the naming of their new-born sister.

A cry rang through the dolphins' mindscape. 'Music!'

Others took up the call: 'Music! Music for Melody!'

The idea-sphere calmed. The chaos stilled. A silent anticipation grew. Aria urged her baby to re-open her closed mind. Melody obeyed and she too heard the new hush from the ideasphere. Then came a few thoughtstreamed sounds, in beautiful patterns. Silent music twirled along the horizon, boomed up from the deep and plummeted from the zenith. Songs blew from mind to mind, without a sound, unlimited by instrument or voice, some older than Aotearoa itself and others as young as the day.

Melody floated so deep in the music that she forgot to manage her new body. Aria had to lift her back to the surface and remind her to breathe again.

The music consumes her, thought Aria.

'Perhaps Melody, you will become a musician yourself one day,' she said.

Melody roused herself. 'A musician?'

'Musicians create thought sounds like these we hear now,' replied Aria.

'Yes,' said Melody. 'Of course, I will be a musician.'

'It seems I named you well,' said her mother.


As Melody listened to her first music, her aura began to reveal itself – to the dolphins and to anyone else with the spirit-vision to observe it. Her aura glowed magenta, flaring to purple at the edges, but a thousand fainter hues pulsed, soft and opalescent, suggesting possibilities undreamed.


Melody's home waters near Aotearoa were in the same part of the Pacific where Ripple lived, over twenty million years ago. My oceans flourished back then. The seas were like crystal. They rang with natural sounds, untapped music and imagined silences – no wonder they'd inspired Ripple to the greatest moment of creativity in the history of this galaxy – our planet's finest hour.

Twenty million years! Where then were scattered only a few small islands, now stretched the long and crooked coastline of an island bigger than all the old ones put together. And south of it another, even bigger. Two huge islands and hundreds of smaller ones – the giant archipelago of Aotearoa.

This land had risen from the ocean floor, so few millions of years ago that it was within dolphin recorded history. In fact, the pyrotechnics of that rising made some of the most spectacular passages ever stored in the brain-banks of cetacean historians.

And it is in these waters and along the north-eastern stretches of these so-new coastlines that Melody's story played out.

# 3 - MARINE CURATOR

In the open sea, a few hours swim east of Ipipiri, the dolphin Libran worked at his vocation.

A distant storm had set the sea heaving but there was no wind here, so the swells were large but glassy. Libran floated alone. Smooth patterns of sunlight and sea echoed the markings on his skin. The only sound was a 'pouff' whenever he breathed.

A young giant petrel, flying her pelagic routes, inspected him, hoping for carrion. Disturbed by her shadow, Libran smacked the water with his tail. She flew off, snapping her beak in disappointment.

He returned to his remote conversation with a group of dolphins swimming further east, just out of his sight, but within easy reach of his thoughts. Unlike human astronauts who take their bodies with them, these were practising astronomers, trained to journey in space without their physical bodies. They'd just returned from astral voyages in the Toi Galaxy. Among them was Melody's brother, Antares, one of their best, despite his youth.

'Did you get much?' asked Libran.

'Sixty-five items,' replied Antares.

'What kind?'

'We have dozens of static artworks and many mobile genres.'

'From several worlds or just one?'

'All from the planet Raima, orbiting a double star on the outer edge of Toi.'

'Nice place?'

'Beautiful! No surprise it's rich in visual arts.'

'Intriguing. I'm ready to receive. Go ahead.'

'This first one's called Moondance. It's a flat image, made by a species with excellent hearing, for a species with no hearing at all.'

The dolphins began transmitting the material. Land, sea, and skyscapes from a world unimaginably far, poured into Libran's brain. They included pictures, sculptures, and visual stories, some frozen to capture a moment and others in natural or stylised motion.

He received them one after another, filing them away in his mind, taking no time to enjoy them for now.

Once he had them all, Libran thanked the astral travellers, then turned away west towards the coast in search of good hunting and company. Within minutes, the hills of Ipipiri and its offshore islands came into view and grew as he approached. As he swam, he focused on the artworks, and only now took time to appreciate them.

The one called Moondance impressed him the most – a rectangular image showing a misty landscape at night, with many fantastic species, all dancing in worship of the three Raiman moons, then visible in their sky. Each moon was a different shade of silver. The largest was pinkish, the smallest glowed white like the moon of Azure and the third shone softly blue. Created for a deaf species, this painting was silent, but its brushstrokes suggested rhythms, melodies, and chords. How could anyone breathe so much music and movement into a painting that had no sound? Libran saluted the genius of the faraway artist.

At his home pod he shared some material with interested dolphins. His task was to ensure all these artworks would exist forever in the glowing networks of Ocean Mind.

Libran's return to the pods of the Ipipiri School sent the scuttlebutt rippling along the thought-waves of his home waters.

'Libran has new art from a planet called Raima.'

The news leapt from dolphin to dolphin and from pod to pod, first within the Ipipiri School and then on to the pods of other schools in remote parts of the oceans. It blew from species to species too – the great whales quickly sent their own curators to meet Libran. He passed the works into the limitless vaults of their memories so they could be easily shared among whale-kind, and whale-kind were only too happy to share them further.

The news of Libran's arrival reached Melody. Her pod hunted close to his, so she sneaked across to peek at the celebrated one who was sharing the artworks with all who wished to see. Libran's body was well-shaped and there was power in his fins and flukes. But it was the shimmer of intellect glittering through the flare in his golden aura that stopped her breath. What would it feel like to swim into the glow of that aura?

Over the next few days, she watched him working with the crowds now seeking him out. He networked with many species; common dolphins, bottlenose, friendly orcas, and whales, some of whom had travelled far. A pod of rogue orcas wanted to receive the material. He would be safe swimming among them, while he was delivering the treasures. But they were malivores, ones who sometimes preyed upon warm blood. To snub them, and to keep others safe, he chose to deliver at long range.

Melody wanted to receive some art directly from Libran. Others, more trained in the visual arts, had the right to claim his time before she did, so she waited until the first rush was over before daring to approach him.

The sun was almost setting when she saw him alone at last. She placed herself nearby but respectfully clear of his slipstream. Her aura was withdrawn and tense, only flaring slightly at times with the colours of her mysterious spirit; his more relaxed, flickering around him like golden mist. But as we would expect of any two dolphins meeting for the first time, the two auras remained politely separate. There was no aural mingling.

Libran was tired after days of constant attention. He noticed Melody's arrival and would have preferred solitude just then. His quick scan of her intellect detected no sign of education in the visual arts nor any affinity for it. Such a young sprat too, he thought. He veiled his impatience.

'What kind of Raiman artworks would you like to see, child?' he asked.

'Something simple please. I don't know much about art.'

At least she admitted it, he thought.

'Then I'll show you just one - my special favourite.'

He thoughtstreamed the Moondance painting into her mind. There was a pause while she processed the image. Then her aura expanded, streamers of transparent colours lighting the sea and flaming from the tips of her flukes and pectoral fins.

It was not the beauty of the image itself, nor even the idea of the incredible journey it had taken to reach her. Something else had touched her.

She spoke at last. 'It's silent but . . . there's music in it!'

He glanced at her sharply. 'Bravo! Well spotted.'

The pair swam on, while Melody studied the image.

'Do you think there are musicians on Raima?' she asked.

'Most Raiman artworks have real music attached. Very few are silent like this one. I'm told it was made for a deaf species. Do you have a vocation planned, child?'

'I hope to become a musician.'

'Have you yet created music?'

How she wished he had not asked her that question.

'Not yet.'

To her relief he did not laugh at her.

'What do you do with your time while you wait to become a musician?'

'I study the music of Ripple and Rikoriko and all the best music that's been made since Ripple's day.'

'You could make no better preparation.'

'I try to make new songs but they're never new enough to be truly my own.'

'Keep trying. Your time will come.'

Now, as the half-grown female and the fully-grown young male swam on together, there was the tiniest mingling at the edges of the two auras.

Melody returned to her own family and often viewed the painting while dreaming of the music of Raima. Libran dominated her thoughts from that time, and she kept herself aware of his location in the school.

Libran gave Melody a little thought from time to time, noticing her sleek young form when he glimpsed her hunting with her pod.

Don't be ridiculous, he told himself, pushing her out of his mind. There were plenty of fully-grown females of far greater interest to him.

Time however, passed and Melody's fixation did not diminish. She collected every bit of scuttlebutt about him.

'Have you heard what Libran has for us now?' she asked her older sister Zeta.

'I'm sure I'm about to learn,' sighed Zeta.

'Moving images from another Toian planet where they use the fires from the star of their world to create designs in flame.'

'Hardly relevant to our oceans on Azure,' said Zeta.

'But he also has some from under the ice of Europa in our own star system. Might that be more relevant?'

'I'm sure anything Libran curates, is relevant to you, Melody.'

Big brother Antares teased her. 'Melody's in loooooove,' he crooned.

'Shut up you two,' she said. 'He might hear you.'

Twice in the following months she approached Libran to ask for other Toian treasures. The first time he complied but thought little of it. The next time, she came with thoughts less veiled, and he glimpsed her infatuation. She wasn't the silliest of his fans and she was beautiful in shape and sweet enough in nature, but was this young unknown female worth his attention?

Or was he being conceited, to think her beneath him? He couldn't decide, so he thought of other things.

# 4 - MURDEROUS BLADES

Melody's pod swam beyond the surf at the bay known to humans as Elliot, just south of Ipipiri. It was sunny and many humans were enjoying the water.

'Mother, what are those knobbly-shaped creatures in the surf?' asked Melody.

'They're humans,' explained Aria, 'and like many land animals, they can swim. Humans even enjoy it. Read their thoughtstreams and you'll see.'

'Can I talk to them?'

'No, dear. They're sentient but they don't use the normal communication methods in use throughout the developed universe. They're worth watching all the same.'

Melody did watch. She saw a mother and father playing with their two children in the shallows. The babies enjoyed the dazzle of water fizzing and frothing around them. The parents held them tight, keeping them safe.

They love each other like dolphins do, thought Melody.

She saw adult humans on hard fish-shaped objects, catching waves and riding them to shore. Melody rode a wave or two alongside them and read their elation as they soared across the face of wave, using its energy to create speed.

'They're so like us,' she said to Aria.

'Yes,' said Aria. 'They're both like and unlike. They breathe air like we do, have warm blood and warm hearts like ours, yet humans are different. Beware of them.'

But Melody saw nothing that day to give her any fear of humans. She saw only their love, laughter, and friendship, heard only their shouts of joy at the sight of her. They made her feel special. She swam closer to enjoy their awe.

One day Melody, Aria, Zeta, Antares and six other dolphins were out in the islands, hunting between Moturua and Motuarohia when they heard a harsh metallic roaring. Two small boats dashed towards them from the direction of Moturua.

Melody was curious. She leapt to observe them. The volume increased as the boats approached. When the humans on the boat saw the pod they shrieked and jumped about, strangely over-excited, as if they'd been whiffing puffer-fish toxins.

Because of the noise, the dolphins hardly knew which was up, down, east, or west. The shells of the boats were hard, the blades of the propellers more vicious than the teeth of any shark. The people on the boat screamed more loudly.

'Don't let them touch you!' cried Aria.

The sea was a mad confusion of fins, noise, flying foam and spinning metal.

'Look, look! There's a little one. It's soo cute!'

One boat came too close, running through the pod. Melody dived but not in time. The sea was exploding! She felt a blow and tasted her own blood in the water.

The boats charged away to the west.

Her sense of direction began to return as the noise faded but where had the world gone?

She forgot to breathe, began to sink.

'Mother! Help me!'

By the time Aria arrived with the rest of the pod they found Melody sinking and trailing blood from a minor cut to the dorsal fin. They pushed her back to the surface and sent sound pulses to her lungs to stimulate her to breathe.

She slowly returned to full consciousness. The pod circled around her. Aria, Zeta and Antares stayed close to comfort her.

Then they heard the boats returning, human voices shouting.

'Hey! There are the dolphins again!'

'Where's the little one? Get closer. I want a photo.'

The two boats roared around them, swerving unpredictably. The cacophony of shouting and confusion was worse than before.

'Stay together' screamed Aria.

'There it is! The little one. The little one!'

The dolphins scattered. The boats closed in, one either side of Melody. Some of the humans leaned over the side, pointing small rectangular objects at her. Only Aria managed to stay with her in the chaos, using her eyes to find her daughter. Melody leapt to escape one boat, but her leap took her too close to the other. The driver veered off, turning his stern with its whirling propellers towards her. Aria threw herself at Melody and pushed her to safety, but the propeller blades sliced through Aria's caudal peduncle, severing her tail. The tail spun slowly down through the clear water, trailing blood, growing smaller and smaller until it disappeared in the deep. The image stayed with Melody for the rest of her life.

'You hit one of them!'

'Oops! I did too. Look at the blood.'

'You cut off its fucken tail, idiot. You're not supposed to harm them.'

'It'll die now – it won't be able to swim.'

'We might as well eat it then. Can you eat dolphin? It's just a fish isn't it?'

'My Dad'll never let us use his boat again, if we come in with half a dolphin.'

'We could get in trouble over this. There are rules about boats near dolphins. Don't tell anyone. Right?'

They turned back to the island in a much more subdued manner.


The pod worked together to help Aria. She was able to keep herself afloat by using her pectoral fins, but without a tail she couldn't make headway. She used her own muscle power to close off some of the blood vessels to reduce the bleeding. Sharks had smelled blood in the water and began gathering. The pod quickly drove them away and stayed close to the bleeding Aria. The sharks knew better than to push their luck around so many strong dolphins.

Aria's condition worsened, her flesh dehydrating. The others called for help and dolphins from nearby pods arrived bringing near-liquid jellies to feed her. As Aria recovered from the first shock, she looked into her future and understood that it was possible for her life to continue. This wound might heal. Other dolphins would feed her, working day and night to protect her. They'd sacrifice their own freedom to nurse her through life.

But a dolphin could not grow a new tail as an octopus can regenerate one of its eight minions. To live without a tail was to lose the speed and dazzle of the life that she loved. She would become a burden on the pod. Her older children were independent already and even Melody was now old enough to survive without a mother.

For Aria it was an easy decision.

'Swim away,' she told them all. 'I wish to leave Azure.'

The others tried to dissuade her, but she insisted, and they understood.

She gave her children her love and urged them to go with the pod and not to look back. Aria's eyes followed them as they swam away.

I did well for the oceans, to produce those three, she thought.

Melody obeyed the order not to look back, but she was joined to her mother in spirit, and she felt everything.

Without a tail, Aria could not evade the sharks that came so soon to finish her. Melody felt every bite that ripped her mother's flesh, every crunch of tooth on bone. She felt the blood draining from Aria's veins and then the merciful fading of her pain as the spirit of Aria seeped away, vanishing from the ocean never to return.

The sharks only helped my mother, thought Melody. It was the humans who really killed her.

Her memory returned to the only other time she'd encountered humans – in the surf at Elliot Bay.

Aria's message echoed in her brain: Humans are different. Beware of them.

Antares and Zeta supported their little sister during the ordeal and swam close on either side of her for many days afterwards, trying to fill the void.

But Melody thought often of those screaming intoxicated humans.

'I hate them. I hate them. I hate them!' she said.

'Don't think like that,' said Zeta. 'They didn't mean to hurt her.'

## 5 - INTERSTELLAR MUSIC

One clear night with no moon to dim the full brilliance of the stars, Melody swam away from Zeta and Antares.

'Don't follow,' she said, 'I need solitude for now.' They let her go but kept guard from afar.

Melody looked outwards and inwards in space, forwards and backwards in time and thought of her lost mother.

Where are you now?

No sound came to her. No warm voice of Aria. But gradually, Melody's mind relaxed, and suddenly she was aware that everything was guiding her. The stars wheeled above, guiding her. The sun lay out of sight on the far side of Azure, guiding her. Aria guided her, from the happy past. The sea guided her too, by caressing her beautiful form with its softest waters.

Time passed. She swam on, keeping the pod in view to the west and the open sea to the east. Now, at last, something moved deep inside her. It grew and swelled outwards in waves. Then her mind began to work as it never had before.

Rhythms. Notes. Aria.

Her aura flamed, shimmering with transparent colour.

She shaped the rhythms and notes into patterns of Aria. Ideas rushed in – poetry, questions, longings. They all danced together, weaving themselves into music. Through the mind of Melody, a brand-new song arrived on Azure.

The song was Melody's prayer for her mother. Nothing like it had existed before. It was her own first song, Live on Beyond the Sun.

The song attracted more attention from divine entities of the universe than it did here on planet Azure. As a prayer, it was answered, even before it was made. Aria did live on beyond the sun! For a time, she soared in the hereafter as pure spirit, enjoying the temporary restoration of Past Life Memory that existed between lives. She thought over the life she'd just escaped. and discovered old friends from previous lives who happened to be sharing the same release time. There were wild spirits among them. It was quite a party! But once her time of rest was up, the powers of the universe sentenced her to new life on a kinder world, and yes it was far beyond her old sun.

Meanwhile back on Azure, Aria's offspring had to get along without their mother and she herself had trained them well for this.

Live On comforted Zeta and Antares. The three siblings did not spread it around Ocean Mind, wanting to keep it private and sacred to themselves. But they could not prevent it being adopted by divine musicians all over the universe.

Though the song was unknown to most dolphins, it made a powerful start to Melody's vocation.

'But still I hate the humans who caused our mother's death,' she said to Zeta. 'And I hate their noisy boats.'

'I told you before,' replied her sister, 'hating is bad for you.'

Again, Melody ignored her.


Two years after the arrival of the Raiman treasures, ten dolphin musicians swam in the contest composition zone, a day's swim northeast of Ipipiri. The day was grey and stormy. They worked with mental barricades in place, allowing no music to escape beyond their own brains. But inside each mind, musical compositions flowered, inspiring all the colour of the cosmic nebulae to shine in their auras as they worked.

A small crowd of dolphins now gathered at a respectful distance. Libran was among them, enchanted by the shimmering spectacle of the auras.

One dolphin held an annoyed pufferfish in his mouth. He passed it carefully to the next dolphin in his pod who passed it on in turn. Each dolphin squeezed the fish, releasing just enough of its toxic but mind-altering substance to enhance their mood. Once they were all as high as hunting gannets, they let the fish escape. It swam off in a huff.

Libran did not touch the drug. One of the contestants had caught his attention – a female who felt somehow familiar to him. Was it that young Melody who'd sensed the music in the silent Raiman artwork? So, she'd achieved her desired vocation then. He was not surprised. And she was no longer a child. Her aura was spectacular.

The musicians composed in a grey ocean, drawing ideas from the rush of the wind, the hissing spray, the shrieking of the birds who rode the storm. Even the sounds caused by the flow of air and water around the fins and flukes of their own bodies suggested rhythms and textures to include. Sometimes they dived, seeking inspiration from life pulses in the depths; or leapt skywards to harvest vibrations from the stars wheeling invisibly above the storm-clouds, which themselves contributed thunder, lightning, and grandeur to their song-spinning. Sometimes they moved in time to the music as they created it; sometimes they lay like logs at the surface, with all the action taking place in mind only.

Melody danced as she worked, leaping, gyrating, swooping like a bird, so absorbed in her task that she was unaware that he was among the crowd of watchers.

But now that Libran had noticed her, her physical grace and the flare of her aura mesmerised him. Its myriad colours flamed and danced, its intensity outshining all others.

As Melody worked, a vibration in the water allowed her to sense the presence of Libran among the watching dolphins. It revived her memory of the Moondance image, which had come so far across the cosmos. An echo of the painted music shivered through the oceans of Azure and resonated in her mind. She threaded it into her composition, recognising it at once as the missing strand her music sought. She merged it with her other notes and chords, until the new sound created a spiritual flightpath that would carry her song to the only target she dreamed of.

When the contest time was up, a call went out to let the main school know. Dolphins rocketed in from every direction. Within half an hour the crowd had trebled in size.

One by one, each musician crowd-streamed their new song to the audience. The listening dolphins moved in time to the melodies and at the end of each performance they slapped the water with flukes and flippers, applauding.

Melody was the youngest and least-known of the contestants, so her song was last to be heard.

As the first gentle chords whispered across their internal silences, the audience was almost motionless, flukes unmoving, pectoral fins swirling slowly, holding position. They listened to sounds that blew into them like a breeze from another world. They began moving, lightly at first, but building in power and speed as the rhythms, melodies, and harmonies spiralled them away until every fibre of their bodies danced in celebration.

When the closing notes died away, there was a moment of stunned silence and then an eruption of noise and spray as dolphins tried to send the ocean skywards in tribute.

Melody won the contest – and many hearts, including the one she most desired.

'I watched you at work,' Libran said later, 'and I knew your song would win before I heard it.'

'How did you know?'

'Your aura outshone every other in the contest zone. At times it seemed you were on fire.'

And so, Melody's song ended his indecision. He wished her to hunt at his side. In Ripple's day, love inspired music and music inspired love, and now, right here in her own life, the same was happening. His love meant more to her than all the fame her victory might bring.

Once all the accolades were over, Libran and Melody swam east and began a pairing that seemed unlikely to fade in the lifetime of either. At first, she was shy and bedazzled by him, hardly daring to share thoughtstreams, but his obvious respect soon convinced her that he saw her as an equal in all but age. Both knew even that would matter less as time passed.


When the results of the contest entered the scuttlebutt, Melody's winning song spread from dolphin to pod to school, and on beyond dolphins to whales and birds, and other beings of the sea. Melody's brother, the astral travelling astronomer, Antares, was one of the first to carry her song to distant worlds. He told her of the thoughtstreamed conversations that followed the song everywhere.

'From where came this new music?'

'From the planet Azure.'

'Who there created it?'

'A dolphin of their southern seas, well-named Melody.'

'How perfect. A dolphin of southern Azure, like Ripple herself of the ancient times.'

Ripple? Unbelievable! But it was true. As her song travelled on through the galaxies, Antares now often heard his sister's name associated with their revered ancestor, who began it all so long ago. She who shed the first light at the very dawn of music in the universe.

And when the song arrived at last on the world of Raima, the beings there wondered at the echo of familiarity in music from so far. They placed the song in their hearts, among their most beloved.

But the song rippled on further still. Dolphins are among the few species in the physical realms whose music is loved also among the divine, and The Powers had adopted music from Melody before, though not even she herself knew it.

## 6 - TAKEN BY THE WIND

In Samoa, there once lived a beautiful human called Natia who loved me with all her heart. In return, I linked my spirit to hers and followed her across the sea when she sailed away south with Tawera to his home in Aotearoa where he taught her to know me as Hinemoana. Their daughter, Manaia, was born there. Natia was always a part of my world, and now Manaia was too.

It was a short scamper to the beach from their house on the end of the Te Wahapu Peninsula, near Kororareka in Ipipiri. Manaia played in the sea every day, flashing about like a mermaid. Sometimes she swam underwater, holding her breath as long as possible, hair streaming behind her. And sometimes after sunset, she sneaked away and swam in the dark. That was the best time because the sea felt different at night - like velvet on her skin.

Manaia's golden eyes focused mostly on the wonders of all the plants and animals of her marine world. She often strolled in the shallows, in the company of a big ray who glided beside her. The local rays were curious, and as fearless of her as she was of them. Her eyes drank in the fluttering movements of the stingrays and the sweeping wingbeats of the eagle rays. She almost heard the music they danced to. Later she drew them, sometimes with their physical colours and sometimes with colours so brilliant, it made me wonder if she was like the dolphins who saw the spirit colours of auras.

One day she found two dead eagle rays on the beach. One was triple the size of the other as though they were mother and child. She froze. She caught a whiff and knew it was too late to save them. She ran home and asked Tawera why they were there.

'It's bycatch,' he said.

'What's bycatch?'

'When a fisherman finds a species in his net he doesn't want.'

'So, he kills my friends.'

'If we want to eat fish, we have to accept bycatch.'

'Then I won't eat fish.'

And she didn't, ever again.

Manaia was nine years old when she discovered a useful patch of bare earth in the grass between the beach and their old beach house. In the stillness of that summer morning, she smoothed the black earth, pressed it firm with her hands, and cleared the edges to define an irregular-shaped "canvas" framed by grass. She collected twigs from bushes, trees, and flowers, broke them into different lengths and positioned them to outline two broad pohutukawa trees and one tall pine. Beside the trees she defined three sweeping horizontal spaces to hold grass, sand, and sea. She created a large circle in the sky for the sun. She stood back to assess the design and was happy with what she saw.

I'll colour it, she thought.

She raced off to make a multi-coloured collection of leaves, bark, and petals. She sat cross-legged before the twig-drawing, but a breath of wind passed like a warning, scattering some of her petals.

Manaia cried to the wind, 'Tāwhiri-mātea! Don't steal my colours!'

She held her breath and waited, to be sure he had listened, before returning the colours to their correct piles. Tāwhiri obeyed, but only for now, and only because he was curious to see what she'd create.

Using torn-up leaves she made the trees dark green, building their trunks with real bark. She filled the turf areas with torn grass. Real sand sifted between her fingers to make the beach. Her "sea" was soon brimming with deep blue hydrangea petals. She scattered petals from the paler-blue hydrangea to fill the sky and used white petals for clouds. The colours gripped her. But she needed yellow. She spotted buttercups and ran to gather them. They almost drowned her with their brilliance as she coloured the sun with them.

Way brighter than my yellow paint, she thought.

Her buttercup sun poured blessings over land and sea. But still something was missing. Manaia ran to the front of the house, checked to make sure her mother wasn't looking, and stole a few petals from Natia's precious red rose. She scuttled back to her "drawing," tore the petals into tiny pieces, then sprinkled them on the two pohutukawa trees, casting them into summer flower.

Natia called Manaia to lunch. The real sun now shone through the window as they ate together, lighting the two dark heads. Natia's Chinese mother had put the silk into her hair and her father's Samoan blood had added a dusky beauty to her delicate face. Manaia's hair was as fine and as black as her mother's except for the glint of fiery red where the sunlight caught it, courtesy of some flame-haired ancestor of her father. Tawera had Viking blood as well as Māori.

While Manaia was inside eating, Tāwhiri-mātea stirred. His easterly sea-breeze freshened. It filled the sails of a small boat and sent it scurrying across my newly ruffled surface. Then it blew across Manaia's artwork. I watched the green flecks lift and fly away. I saw the petals, blue and red and brilliant yellow, tossing in the arms of that thieving wind until nothing was left but a few bare twigs, scattered like bones on the dark earth. But the art was not lost. I had seen it through Manaia's eyes and streamed it to a marine curator, who would protect it well. Manaia ran outside later to find all her colours gone. Tāwhiri laughed and lifted her hair and tried to steal that too but it was well attached to Manaia's head.

*

By the time she was fifteen, builder Tawera had covered the walls of Manaia's room with shelves. She filled them with bones, shells, pieces of wood and dozens of stones, some awaiting the touch of her brush and others already painted in all her sunlit colours.

Tāwhiri-mātea was sad that she no longer made art that his winds could easily steal.

'Stones are the bones of the earth,' said Manaia, and stones were her most common canvas.

She walked for miles along the beaches and coasts of Ipipiri and always carried a bag for stones and anything else that she could take home to paint later.

Natia gathered small pieces of brightly patterned fabric, which she stitched together into a patchwork shoulder bag. She cross-stitched the words, 'Manaia's Taonga' onto strong plain fabric and used it to line and reinforce the bag's interior. She sewed padded pockets near the top where Manaia could keep delicate items like bones or shells safe from damage by heavy stones. Manaia carried her treasure bag everywhere and it rarely came home empty.

'Coming home with me next month?' asked Natia one day.

'Mum! Samoa? Can I really?'

'Your dad's working so it'll just be the two of us.'

'Yay! I can get coral to paint, and Samoan stones and shells, maybe whale bones.'

# 7 - BLOOD IN THE SEA

She'd been in Samoa a week, and the constant roar of the ocean pounding the nearby reef had already become part of the silence. Manaia sat on the floor in the shade of the beach fale, painting stones. This was the last day of her childhood. But she didn't know that.

Later she remembered how happy she'd been that morning, surrounded by stones and shells of so many sizes, her biggest worry being what to paint on the next one. While awaiting their turn to become her canvasses, the stones helped stop the wind from blowing away the newspapers she'd spread to protect the handwoven floor-mats from paint spills. The trade winds lifted her hair, cooling her skin in the tropical heat. Breeze and heat dried the paint faster than she liked, so she worked quickly, racing to beat it. Her brushes flickered in and out of the water, then into their paint trays, flying across the smooth stone surfaces. Stars, flowers, birds, lizards, shells, leaves, fish, feathers, raindrops, and sunbeams were all flung to life by Manaia's brush as it released the light bright colours she loved so much. A banquet of wet paint surrounded her, but Manaia allowed no speck to fall on the protective newspapers, nor to smirch her own busy fingers.

Manaia and Natia were staying with Natia's Samoan half-brother and his wife in their coastal home on the island of Savai'i. That afternoon, Natia gave Manaia a list and sent her on an errand. Manaia swallowed her disappointment at having to put her paints away, and ran with a tote bag to the shop a few kilometres along the island's coast road. She bought what she needed and set off for home in the hot sun. The bag was heavy now and she no longer ran.

The bag grew heavier as she walked. The heat increased in the stretches of road sheltered from the breeze by vegetation. Green, green, nothing but green. Oh! But there was a white flower, and there was a red one, and a yellow. She imagined a forest with the colours reversed so only the flowers were green and the leaves had all the other colours. She must paint it like that one day.

She hurried to reach the more open stretches of road, where sea-breezes and blueness would cool her. She was sweating so much. The occasional car passed. The weight of the bag made ditches in the palm of her hand, so she moved it from hand to hand, rubbing her shorts each time to help the circulation return. She plodded along, still ten minutes from home, thirsty and impatient for the errand to be over.

A car slowed alongside, and a man leaned through the open window. He was alone in the car. A big man – solidly built. She glanced up and thought he looked familiar. Was this her uncle's friend – the one who visited last week? She wasn't sure.

'Want a lift?' The man spoke English. That was lucky. Her Samoan was minimal. Her mother had warned her of stranger-danger, but if this was a friend of the family, it might be rude to refuse.

'Do you know my uncle?' she asked.

'He was in my class at school.'

Manaia entered the car. The man drove on for a hundred metres, then turned onto a rough track leading towards the interior of the island. It led only into bush and scrub, where no-one lived. She could smell the man's breath, strange and sharp. An empty whiskey bottle lay on the floor. Her uncle's friends were strict churchgoers and non-drinkers. The man no longer looked familiar. Suddenly Manaia knew she'd made a big mistake.

'I have to go home now.'

'I'll take you home soon.'

'No! Now. Let me out now!'

He pulled over into a clearing and stopped the car. She twisted the door handle, wanting to run away. His hand shot out and grabbed her. She struggled but he was too strong. He hauled her out of the car as though she were a dog, ripped off her light shorts, pressed one meaty paw over her mouth to smother her screaming.

The ground was hard and stony. Sharp shells cut into her. The skin on her back and everything everywhere ripped apart, tearing and bleeding, his sweat and stink in her face, a monster worse than a beast. She would never never never…

Get away! Don't do this to me. Let-me-go-let-me-go-let-me-go!

Five minutes later, childhood was lost to Manaia.

He finished and wilted heavily upon her. She twisted away, grabbed her shorts and ran into the thick scrub, paused, listening, heard no pursuit, pulled the shorts on, and ran back down to the sea, which sparkled in the sun just like any other day.

She felt something sticky, looked down and red! red! She ran into the blue of the sea and swam hard, stopped swimming to rub at the red still sticking to her legs, trying to clean herself all over, soaking up the healing blueness to drive away the red.

She kept an eye on the land, on the lookout for the monster. His car reappeared and stopped. She froze in the water. He got out and peered both ways along the road. She submerged slowly slowly, trying to avoid ripples in case he looked at the sea. She stayed down, holding her breath, then releasing it bubble by bubble, making her air supply last, thankful for the hours she'd spent swimming underwater, training for this moment. When she could stay down no longer, she surfaced and saw the car driving back towards the shop. Her face felt sore where his hand had crushed it. She rubbed the bruises in the water to cool them.

She raced towards home, needing the sea again, even though she'd only just left it. She wanted only to swim and feel nothing touching her skin but healing seawater, to stay out there forever.

She rushed through the house, slowing down just enough to tell her mother something bad had happened and she'd lost the shopping. But Natia saw the blood seeping through her wet clothes and caught Manaia's horror like a contagion. She followed her daughter out of the house, onto the grass, past the beach fale where Manaia had painted stones that very morning. Natia stopped at the edge of the water. Manaia ran on ahead of her, into the sea. Only there in the clean blue might she forget things that happened on land. She swam and swam and when she looked ashore, she saw her mother there watching her, calling her.

She tried to blank her mind to everything but the feel of the sea on her skin, and the rippling patterns the sunlight made shining down onto the sandy bottom as she glided over it, and the bubbles passing her eyes, and the rhythm. Right arm up and over – reach forward, pull back. Left arm up and over – reach forward, pull back. Hand pressing the water, flutter of hand and flutter of foot. The sea-light was smooth across her torn skin, its lines lifting and falling as the waves supported her. She closed her eyes against the glitter and prayed never to return to land.

She did not see the two large dark shadows approaching underwater. The cuts on her back were still bleeding. One of the shadows circled, attracted by the blood. The other followed closely.

Alerted by the change in the movement of the water against her skin, she opened her eyes just as both shadows closed in. For the second time in an hour, Manaia screamed. A hit. A blow to her leg and a flash of pain. More blood in the water. A confusion of large, finned bodies thrashing beside her. Then two shadows skimming away underwater. She screamed again, kept screaming, turned, and raced landwards, trailing a new cloud of her own blood, this time coming from her leg. She did not look back for fear of what might be following her. When her feet touched the sand, she tried to run, surprised she still had two legs to walk on.

'Shark! Mum! Shark!'

But Natia ignored the warning. She was already thigh-deep, fully dressed, on her way out to help Manaia ashore.

'It wasn't a shark, dear. I saw it. It was a dolphin. It was swimming behind you, but it came up close, just before you shouted.'

Manaia showed her the bite mark on her leg. Blood flowed from the cuts of many teeth.

'It was a shark, Mum. I thought I saw two. But maybe the other one was a dolphin. It must have chased the shark away. Why would it do that?'

'Nobody knows why, but dolphins have saved people from sharks before.'

Natia was not the only person to have heard the screaming. In moments, friends and relatives surrounded them. A neighbour with a car took them to a clinic where staff assessed the leg wound and applied dressings. Manaia's shock aroused no suspicion since the cause was obvious. Only later when they were alone did Natia and Manaia talk.

'I was going out to you but when I saw the dolphin I stopped. I thought he would calm you better than I could. I didn't know there was a shark.'

'I didn't know there was a dolphin.'

'Do you want to tell me what happened?'

'A shark bit me.'

'Before that.'

'No,' said Manaia, 'I don't want to talk about that.'

'Is it as bad as I think?'

'Worse.'

'Who was it? How did he catch you?'

'I don't know him. I thought he was a friend of Uncle's, so I got in his car. But he was a monster. I just wanted to swim. To get clean.'

'Manaia, this horror will pass. I think I know what you intended when you swam out to sea. What happened to you is bad, but nothing is that bad. I promise you. But look at your poor back, all cut and scratched.'

'There were sharp shells on the ground.'

'I'll tear that man into tiny pieces with my bare hands if I ever catch him.'

'You never hurt anyone, Mum.'

'Manaia believe me, I would just love to hurt him.'

'I'll never speak to any man ever again,' said Manaia.

'Don't say that. Not all men are monsters. One day you'll meet one who's kind and gentle.'

Natia told the police what had happened. They asked what clothing Manaia was wearing at the time. Manaia had worn shorts that day, as she always did in Aotearoa in summer. The policeman rolled his eyes to hear this. Natia did not allow Manaia to wear shorts again, nor walk alone.

Manaia's life was split in two. Before and after.

She chose a large stone to make a painting. She had prepared it in the before-time but would paint it in the after – a split-life stone. The surface was beautiful, smooth like young skin, hard as glass, primed to snowy whiteness. She flooded the surface with purest blue, then charged the wet paint with a hotshot of red, then watched the two colours do battle. Red advanced, blue retreated, then rallied and attacked. Red streaked through the blue and blue exploded into red. The opposing forces blended at last.

'Blue and red still make purple,' she thought, 'just as they did before.' She added more colours, waited until the paint dried, chose her finest brush and painted a tracery of black across the surface, and the black ignited the other colours, energising them. Why had she never used black before? She tried dull black, glossy black and dark charcoal grey.

Manaia painted more than ever, leaving no moment vacant to think about anything else but the designs she created on the stones. Her pictures included sharks and dolphins, teeth and fins and curving flukes. She would have spent a lot of time swimming too, if the ocean had not failed her. She waded in the shallows sometimes to cool down, but it was not the same.

She told herself it wouldn't happen again, had only happened once because of the blood. But when she tried to swim, imagined shadows drove her ashore.

Night times were the hardest. Lying awake on her sleeping mat, face down because the cuts on her back still hurt. The shark was helpful then. She preferred that memory to the other one.

The bruises on her face and body bloomed like poisonous flowers over the next few days. Natia's eyes followed her everywhere, holding on with all her power to keep Manaia on the surface of the planet.

Even as the bruises faded, Manaia's cover-up clothing, her fear of walking alone and her new distrust of the sea made the rest of her Samoan holiday feel like a jail sentence.

Two weeks later they returned home to Aotearoa. Manaia could not talk to Tawera about what had happened and begged her mother not to tell him either. Natia complied for the first few weeks.

'Want to come fishing with me today, Manaia?'

'Thanks Dad. I want to work on my stones today.'

'Waste weather like this? How about Elliot Bay then? Take the surfboards?'

'I just want to get a few more done. Might try and sell some at the market.'

'Okay. I guess good beach weather is good painting weather too. I'll paint the carport.'

'Sorry Dad.'

Later, alone with Natia, he said, 'It's not like Manaia to turn down surfing. She's different since she got back.'

'That shark gave her one hell of a fright, Tawera. Made her scared of the water. She'll get over it.'

'Jeez Natia. It gives me the shivers every time I think about it. When I see those marks on her leg, I think we're lucky to still have her. No wonder she's changed. But I want my little girl back.'

'Give her time,' said Natia.

# 8 - URURANGI ECLIPSED

Melody's sister Zeta and Zeta's daughter Elethea swam close all the time, now that new life was growing within Melody. When Zeta used her ultra-sound to check the developing baby, Elethea listened and watched. Then she too scanned Melody. Soon she was as expert at reading the health of the baby, as Zeta was.

Elethea was eager to meet her new cousin and already talked to him. He soon grew to fill the space he had, and the less room he had the more he wanted to move.

'When can I get out of here? My tail is squished under.'

'Not long now.' Zeta reassured him, 'Have patience.'

'Once I could move my fins. Now they're pinned tight.'

'Rest now,' said Melody, 'while you still can. Once you're born, you'll swim so far, you'll want to stop and rest again.'

'I just want to stretch my flukes,' he whined, 'I don't want to wait.'

Melody sent him tranquillising chords.

He calmed, but now he wanted pictures.

'What can you see out there now, Mother?' he asked.

She sent him a sound picture of the arm of Koru stretched across the sky, like a glowing river sprinkled with stars.

'Soon you'll see it with your own eyes and ears.'

'Do stars have names?'

'Of course! Dolphins have named stars since they first began visiting them, millions of years ago. Many dolphins are named after stars, including your own uncle, Antares.'

'I hope you give me a star name, Mother.'

'We'll see. Now sleep.'

She continued rocking him with lullabies and musical visions of starlit skies as she rolled along, over and under the waves. Cocooned inside her, he drifted to sleep in the cadence of her movement and song.

After this, Melody hoped to find a star-name that might suit him and looked often to the star Ururangi in Matariki – the Pleiades.

'Remember it's unlucky to name your baby before he's born,' warned Zeta.

'If he were female, I'd call him Aria. I wish my mother could be alive to see him.'

'But he's male, Melody . . . and she's gone.'

'Ururangi is only a possible name,' said Melody, but in her heart she'd already chosen.

Water adepts in the main school warned of pollutants in the usual birthing waters, so Melody decided to give birth further out to sea. Prey would be harder to find, but the others would hunt for her.


Matariki was visible in the north, as always at that time of the spring pre-dawn, but its star Ururangi disappeared just as the baby was born.

While Melody gazed skywards, bewildered, her firstborn wallowed helplessly in the cold sea.

'What's wrong with my sister?' thought Zeta. 'She's ignoring her own baby!'

Melody stared at the sky in confusion. She leapt and splashed down again, flying higher than expected in her newly restored lightness. Everything else was at it should be on the ocean. A breeze ruffled the surface, but the night had not a cloud anywhere that might obscure a star.

What strange syzygy had caused this? she wondered. Was it an asteroid occultation? Was there a huge piece of space debris eclipsing Ururangi? Or was it some fault of her own eyes?

She took it as a sign, not to choose that name. Even when Ururangi re-appeared moments later, she did not change her mind. Some omens were too plain to ignore.

Zeta herself took on the job of stimulating her nephew to his first unwilling breath, succeeding at last.

'Wake up Melody! Help your baby,' she said.

Melody returned to Azure at last.

'Sorry!' she said. 'Something weird just happened.'

'That's for sure,' replied Zeta, not speaking of stars.

To Zeta's relief, Melody at last discovered the miracle of new life beside her and there he was, swimming free at last.

'He's beautiful,' she said, 'and he's breathing already!'

'No thanks to you,' grumbled Zeta.

The coldness of the water frightened the newborn at first, as expected. Zeta and Elethea guided him to Melody's milk, and they all laughed at his relief when the milk drenched him with warmth and energy.

Libran and Antares were nearby but out of sight, with a group of dolphins patrolling the waters in case of predators drawn by the birthblood. Melody thoughtstreamed to Libran: 'He's perfect! Thank-you for giving him to me.'

But to Zeta she said, 'What do I call him? How can I face the school with a nameless baby?'

This opportunity jolted Zeta from her usual calm. She offered dozens of ideas at first, mostly names of characters in the thousands of poems she stored in her brain.

'Stop Zeta! You're only confusing me.'

While Melody searched the universe for the perfect name, Zeta shared traditional baby poems with the nameless one and Elethea.

Human poetry creates images with words, but dolphin poetry goes straight to the images.

Zeta, a poet by vocation, created one to amuse her new nephew.

A human verbal translation might read:

Mother spins on a milky wave,
Singing a midnight tune.
Rainbows tickle her flickery flukes,
and fling her over the moon.

Whenever poem-Melody flew over the moon, the nameless one and Elethea rocked with glee. They replayed the poem again and again, laughing so hard that Zeta wanted to ask Melody to make a simple tune for the poem-images. It wouldn't be the first time the sisters had merged the poetry of one with the music of the other.

'But I'll wait until she's over this naming crisis,' thought Zeta.

On the day of the birth, dozens of bottlenoses and hundreds of common dolphins came by to congratulate her, to ask her son's name.

'What? No name yet? But he's hours old already.'

'He's your first. So why not call him Tahi?'

'How about an action name? Maybe Dash or Dart or Crackerjack.'

'Too common. Give him a thinking name like Fathom or Oracle or Dream.'

'Weather names are way better. Call him Storm or Squall or Nimbus.'

'Not if he grows up to be an astronomer. Choose a space name like Comet or Neb or Starfire.'

'My aunty names all hers after famous dolphins like Ripple or Rigel or Libran.'

'Shut up all of you! I think she wants to find a star name for this baby.'

'Well, there are plenty of those. What's the problem? Just pick one for Hine's sake.'

Finally, Melody asked Libran to keep them all away until she'd made her choice.

So, after that first day, Zeta, Elethea, Libran, Melody, and the baby, swam as a separate pod, but close enough to the main school for protection if they needed it. The baby recovered quickly from the birth and fed well from the start.

How he loved the ocean he was born into, the freedom it gave him, the way the shifting surface split the world in two, keeping all the glitter and speed in the air above, and all the serenity and mystery below. He followed his mother's every move, sticking to her slipstream as though he would never leave, and nor did she want him to. He was her constant shadow. Perhaps that was why finally, four full days after his birth, she settled on Ātārangi – shadow. It seemed so perfect at the time, so like that other name she'd wanted. For those first few weeks he hardly left her side.

Oh! If only he'd stayed there, close in her slipstream, her happy shadow always.

Melody belly-flopped to amuse her son, sending sheets of spray foaming over his head. Ātārangi used his flukes to try to whack it back to her. She leapt into the wind, and he leapt too, tasting it and feeling the strange emptiness of air on his skin. He wondered how birds could stay up in it. She explained about their hollow bones, their magical feathers, the wings that command the air as a dolphin's flukes rule the seas.

Melody dived to hunt, and he rode in her slipstream, snapping at the little fish, sometimes catching one for himself. After every success he spun in the air, holding it, triumphant, to show her. She laughed, delighting in his simple pleasure.

One day Melody and Ātārangi entered Maunganui Bay on the north-western side of the Rākaumangamanga, the long peninsula guarding the easternmost end of Ipipiri. Ātārangi explored the many crevices in the rocks on the edges of the cove. Weeds swayed in the currents that washed the rocks.

They entered an archway. Hanging rock blotted out the sky above them, but underwater lay a fantasy world.

The passage was full of fish, abundant with all kinds of life – jewel anemones, sponges, ascidians, bryozoans, and soft corals – all covering the walls and the large boulders on the bottom with their vibrant colours. All the fish seemed to know the two dolphins weren't hunting just now. At the surface darted dozens of blue maomao, demoiselles, snapper and trevally, while below them swam schools of pink maomao. Giant stingrays glided in the strong current and she spotted one very large kingfish. Everywhere she looked was new vibrancy, new life, a thousand feeding mouths and beating hearts.

They saw a spotted moray eel with his body draped through grey pillow sponges on one wall. This one was shy at first, but Melody was gentle with him and soon the eel was curling his body lovingly around them both. He explored their heads and fins, even "tasting" their skin with his needle-toothed jaws, never leaving a scratch.

They reached the end and re-entered sunlit waters.

Then Ātārangi found the eyes. They stared out from the blackness of a cavity in the rock and tried to drill holes through his brain. He darted back to Melody for reassurance.

'Mother, I found some eyes!' he squeaked. 'Scary ones!'

'How could eyes be scary, dear?'

'They could see forever.'

'What animal owned them?'

'It was . . . like a brain with eyes. Just one big brain.'

A brain with eyes that could see forever? It had to be an octopus. This could be fun.

'Take me there.'

Together they returned to the spot. With Melody alongside him, Ātārangi had the courage to stare straight into the see-forever eyes. They were ginger with horizontal black pupils. The brain surrounding them was like a nest of resting sea-snakes, but these were simply the eight arms attached to the octopus's mantle, each with its own personality and brain. The octopus called them her "minions," because they lived only to serve her. Her minions provided her many hours of stimulating conversation, and although she might not have admitted it, a couple of them were smarter than she was herself. And that was saying something.

The octopus assessed the young dolphin and, seeing no menace, her minions moved, slowly slithering into a squirming mass. The surface of her body morphed into a speckly gold – her curiosity colour. One minion stretched out long and thin, touched the dolphin's skin and withdrew immediately. Ātārangi saw it coming, saw the suckers underneath, felt them tasting his cheek, light as an air-bubble. He flinched but stayed where he was, staring at the octopus. Both beings survived the first touch without losing eye contact. The tangling of the minions mesmerised him.

'Tangles,' he said.

'Perfect,' said Melody. 'Let's call her Tangles.'

A thoughtstream from Tangles arrived in his brain: 'What are you?'

'A dolphin,' he replied. 'I'm a warm-blooded mammal.'

'You felt cold to me.'

'You only touched my skin. I'm warm inside.'

'Let me try again.'

'Wait. We need to breathe.'

The two dolphins surfaced, breathed, and returned to Tangles who was now happy to see them back.

Melody received a private thoughtstream from the octopus.

'Is your young friend important to you?'

'Of course. He's my son.'

'Make sure he enjoys every moment of his life.'

The comment puzzled Melody. Why had it been private only to her? Why would she need such advice from an octopus?

'Why wouldn't I?' she said, 'but thank-you anyway.'

Tangles now reached out to Ātārangi with two minions, and he allowed her to explore the skin of his face, giggling at the tickle of her roving suckers. Minion by minion she draped herself over him until she was like seaweed wrapped around a rock.

'It's true. Your heat is coming through. It feels like sunshine. Does it hurt to be so warm?

'Course not. I'm meant to be warm.'

Ātārangi swam around Maunganui Bay with Tangles riding just in front of his dorsal fin. Then she squirmed all the way to his tail.

'Not on my tail,' he said. 'It slows me down too much.'

She finally settled just behind his dorsal, with two minions gripping the fin and two more around his body, keeping her secure. That left four free to explore the passing world. The two dolphins swam out of Maunganui Cove, taking Tangles on the journey of her life, swimming to the end of Rākaumangamanga and circling the three islands at the end of the peninsula. A wide high tunnel cut straight through the island of Motukokako. They swam into it. Dark rocks soared high around them, blocking the sky. It was creepy for Ātārangi, even for so short a time. Melody hunted as they swam, bringing fish and shrimps for Tangles to feast on. Never had the octopus enjoyed such a party.

Ātārangi took milk from Melody.

The octopus thoughtscreamed, 'What are you doing!'

'Calm down Tangles,' said Ātārangi. 'It's normal for mammals.'

'It's horrible. Does it hurt her?'

'Not at all.'

'You should learn to eat fish.'

'I'm learning already. One day I'll eat more fish than you.'

'Do dolphins eat octopus?' asked Tangles.

'I don't know. Mother, do we?'

'Some dolphins do,' said Melody. 'Not me.'

'Why?'

'You can't talk to someone once you've eaten them.' She swam close to Ātārangi and allowed Tangles to transfer herself minion by minion from his back to hers so she could take her turn at carrying him.

'Besides, live octopuses can help dolphins, so I'd never harm one.'

'How do they help us?'

'Their minions are clever.'

'True,' said Tangles. 'Watch this.'

She began to show off, pulling stones and shells out of tiny cracks in the rock, walking along on the bottom like a legged animal, breaking open bivalves by gripping them and twisting the shells in opposite directions. She sneaked up on an open oyster and dropped a pebble between the two shells. The oyster could not close properly with the pebble in it, so she ate it with ease.

'Bring me a crab.'

Ātārangi dashed off and came back with one. She picked up a stone with two minions and smacked the unlucky crab with it, breaking its shell. Then she ate the flesh inside.

'I used to drill into crabs with my beak,' she told him, 'But a stone is much quicker.'

She tied seaweed into a ring, and he swam into it and wore it like a necklace. Then she plaited kelp around his caudal peduncle for a tail bracelet. Ātārangi turned himself almost in half trying to see his new decoration and sashayed about to show it off. It soon annoyed him and he made Tangles untie her own knots.

Different colours and textures swept over her skin as she matched herself to any background. She morphed shape too, mimicking a flatfish, then a rock, a sea-slug, an anemone, a bunch of seaweed. He thoughtstreamed a picture of a land-flower and she mimicked it.

'You got the size wrong though,' he laughed. 'You're too big for most flowers.'

'Who cares what a land-flower looks like,' she grumbled.

Tangles capped all by picking up sixteen stones, two on each minion. She began juggling them. She sat perfectly relaxed, in a mini-storm of whirling stones, the tips of her minions just twitching enough to keep them all spinning around her at once.

'How do you do that?' asked Ātārangi.

'Easy. Each arm only has two stones to watch. Works fine until they all start squabbling.'

She'd hardly spoken the words when one minion dropped a stone, spoiling the pattern. Another minion angrily whacked the negligent one with a stone. It lashed back, helped by its neighbour, but the angry one also had helpers and in no time a big punch-up was going on between all eight of them. It took Tangles some effort to get them under control. The dolphins' laughter vibrated all over the bay. Melody memorised the whole performance and later she made up a children's song about the juggling octopus and her squabbling minions. Teacher dolphins all over Azure added it to their class song lists.

At last, they took Tangles to her hole to rest and swam away to find the pod.

Later, Melody told her sister about the private message the octopus had given her.

'Why would an octopus say that to me?'

Zeta looked troubled. 'Some octopuses just know things,' she said. 'But it can't hurt to take her advice.'

For many days the sisters watched Ātārangi closer than ever, as he laughed and played with his mother, his cousin Elethea, and any other dolphin who was willing. As far as Melody could see he was enjoying every moment of his life, just as Tangles had advised. They often returned to Maunganui Bay to take Tangles for joyrides and to introduce her to their friends.

Melody's pod hunted the eastern side of the passage between Motuarohia and Moturua. Tangles squirmed on Ātārangi's back. The dolphins had found her a big crab. She was picking out the flesh from its broken shell.

A kilometre and a half away, on the western side of the passage, the human musician, Rōreka, paddled his yellow kayak. He glided along, crooning as he peered into the depths. He hadn't noticed the dolphins, but they'd seen him.

'Stay here,' said Melody to the pod. 'Keep Ātārangi with you. I'll go alone and call you if it's safe.'

She swam towards the kayak, approaching from behind. On this boat, there was no engine noise, no whirling propeller like the one that had killed her mother. The man propelled it with a long tool, finned at each end, powered by his own hands. He had nothing that could harm a dolphin.

But all the same, she stopped breathing, for secrecy.

The kayak glided, silent as a stingray. She followed, just beneath the surface, making no disturbance, listening to his thoughtstreams. He was thinking in sounds, concentrating hard, as though this was his vocation. The weird humming sounds he made matched infantile melodies in his thoughtstreams. Was he making music?

She knew about the primitive human music but had never met a human who shared her own calling. The human voice had possibilities, but the tunes! Nothing so unfledged could ever fly. She stayed listening, amused and appalled, for ten minutes in silence. She began to need air, and because she perceived no threat from him, she breathed.

He knew that sound. His song collapsed. He turned and spotted her.

'A dolphin! And much closer than 300 metres.'

He was smack in the middle of the new dolphin safe zone. He stopped paddling to abide by the new rules.

She read his delight at the sight of her.

'He's like the surfers at Elliot Bay,' she thought.

She called in the pod.

'This is a human,' she explained to Ātārangi, 'This one is no danger to you, but humans killed your beautiful grandmother. Beware of them.'

'Oh my God!' said Rōreka aloud. 'There's a baby dolphin wearing an octopus!'

Tangles dropped her crab, unfinished. She stared, mesmerised, at the man in the kayak. Her ginger eyes shimmered, and their rectangular pupils contracted.

'This is the one,' she said.

She pointed at Rōreka with one of her minions.

'The one?' said Melody.

Tangles directed her reply to Melody alone.

'The one for you,' she said.

For me? thought Melody. What did she need a human for? She hoped she didn't have to teach him better songs.

Then Tangles switched the full force of the see-forever eyes from Rōreka to Melody.

'Perhaps you do,' she said and did not break her gaze until Ātārangi submerged with her.

Octopuses puzzle me, thought Melody but she stared at Rōreka to make sure she would remember him if she saw him again. Rōreka gaped. Never had he been so close to a group of wild beings. Ātārangi re-surfaced with Tangles. Rōreka's smile widened at the sight of them.

'Why does he show us all his silly human teeth?' asked Ātārangi. 'Is he trying to look scary?'

'Humans show their teeth when they're happy,' explained his mother.

The pod spent half an hour playing around Rōreka, dragging him in their slipstream, rolling over beside him to look up at him, jumping and splashing nearby until he was drenched. Zeta's daughter Elethea caught a fish and sky-jumped holding it, to show it off. She offered it to Rōreka, but he didn't take it.

'I only eat plant food from the land,' he explained aloud to Elethea. 'You don't take the fruit from my garden. I don't take the fish from your sea.'

Elethea ate the fish herself. Melody did not understand the man's words, but she understood the thoughts behind them. They contradicted everything she knew about humans. Their ships took more fish than any being that ever lived in the sea. And this human would not eat even one?

Melody touched the hull to test its stability and then gave it a gentle whack. Rōreka laughed.

'I've seen this man before,' said Libran. 'He's often out on the water in his little boat, singing to himself.'

'I like his voice,' said Melody. 'If only he had better tunes.'

Ātārangi carried Tangles alongside the boat. The octopus was bold in the presence of her big strong friends. Bold and curious. Ātārangi let her touch the hard yellow hull. Rōreka froze. He rested one hand on his cockpit coaming, watching her. She tasted his boat with roving suckers and turned yellow to match its colour. One minion sneaked up over the gunwale and touched the weird human hand. Rōreka did not flinch. The minion changed colour again to match his hand. He stared into the see-forever eyes of the octopus, while roving suckers explored and tasted his skin.

Questions arose in him.

'How sentient are you?' he whispered to Tangles. 'Are these dolphins friends of yours? Are you their pet? I have a pet too.'

A picture of his cat, Te Patiki, came into his mind. The sea-beings saw it clearly there.

'Te Patiki trusts me, like you trust your dolphins. But aren't you worried they might eat you?'

'Yes, she's my pet,' replied Ātārangi, 'and she's very clever. You should see her juggling. I like your cat.'

'Shut up, Ātārangi,' scolded the octopus. 'He's talking to me – not you.'

She turned to Rōreka and said, 'If you can hear me, hold up three of your minions.' She pointed upwards with three of her own.'

But Rōreka heard nothing from either of them.

'Hold up two then,' she said.

He scratched his head with five.

'He doesn't understand anything!' she announced. 'Humans must be stupid.'

'Not stupid,' said Melody, 'They just don't do thoughtstreaming.'

'Why not?' asked Ātārangi, but no-one answered.

Rōreka moved his hand at sea-snail speed and took the end of one minion gently between his fingers. He shook hands with her in slow-mo. The octopus allowed this. She counted his fingers and thumb and copied him by contributing an equal number of limbs to this weird dance. This left her three to retain hold on Ātārangi. They shook again and this time she delivered a confident handshake and held his gaze. He lost all doubt of her sentience.

'Are you thinking of coming aboard?' he asked.

But the octopus slithered back to Ātārangi and let him carry her away.

If I told anyone what just happened, thought Rōreka, who'd believe me?


Weeks passed. Melody taught Ātārangi strategies for encounters with predators, or venomous creatures like rays. He learnt quickly, so she began to let him venture off alone or with Elethea or other friends his age. He always returned to her side within an hour or two, to describe the wonders he'd seen.

How empty life was, before he came! thought Melody.

His independence grew. He was adventurous too, and curious, but he still most loved to be beside his mother.

## 9 – PROMISES AND PRAYERS

And then one day a shark attacked him.

Ātārangi hunted with Melody, Zeta, and others near the Black Rocks. A young shark cruised in, attracted by the dolphins' prey. Ātārangi darted towards the shark, hoping it might play with him. But like most sharks, it was timid, and the suddenness startled it. It turned and bit Ātārangi, raking his side with its teeth.

Ātārangi turned away, blood trailing from his wounds. A flash of adrenalin ignited in Melody's veins.

A silent howl rang in her head through the eternal second it took her to charge at this enemy of the moment that had attacked her firstborn son. She knocked it sideways with a blow between the stomach and kidneys, then spun on the spot, charged again, and delivered one more to the liver, sending her victim spiralling into the deep. Zeta dived and followed it down.

Melody thoughtscreamed at the sinking creature: 'I don't care if you're dead or alive!'

She and Elethea turned to check Ātārangi's wounds. They were superficial. He was in no pain and seemed disappointed by the disappearance of a possible new playmate. Five minutes later, Zeta returned to the group at the surface.

'Did I kill it?' asked Melody.

'It's recovering,' said Zeta. 'I gave it healing sounds.'

'I'm glad,' said Melody. 'I was too angry. I didn't mean what I said.'

'Wow! Mum gave healing sounds to the shark?' said Elethea. 'That was a good idea. I gave some to Ātārangi, but he didn't really need them.' She seemed almost disappointed.

'You wanted me to be hurt,' said Ātārangi, 'just so you could have fun healing me?'

Later Melody allowed Ātārangi to spend time playing with the same shark, but she taught him to play without alarming it, and the shark, having learnt its lesson early, never dared bite another dolphin as long as it lived.


One morning, when their pod was far out to sea, Melody and Ātārangi heard the whispers flying. The weather adepts were predicting great surf on the eastern beaches of Te Tai Tokerau in about three days' time. The school began swimming south-west.

'Why are we going to the surf, Mother?' he asked.

She streamed a moving picture to him: smooth ocean swells changing shape as the sea floor pushed them upwards on their approach to land, the forward faces of the waves curving inwards as they towered towards collapse. She added dolphins to the picture, riding the waves towards the beach, exploiting the energy of the ocean, and leaping out at the last moment to race seawards for their next ride.

Melody also showed him the dangers – the surf smashing onto jagged rocks or washing all the way up onto the sand where a dolphin might strand and die. But Ātārangi saw only the thrills.

'Mother, I can't wait to go surfing. What does it feel like?'

So, she described the sensation of being swept along, pressing fin and fluke against the muscle of the water, the thunder, the speed, the dazzle of white exploding on blue, the exhilarating chaos of the wave's final collapse.

Ātārangi played those thoughtstreams over and over, more interested in re-runs of surfing scenes than hunting for breakfast.

'Do you like surfing mother?' he asked.

'Every dolphin loves surfing,' she told him. 'It celebrates the energies of Azure.'

'Where does the energy come from?'

'The sun's energy creates the wind-song that drives the waves. The moon adds tidal energy to the harmony. Dolphins love to sing and dance along, especially you young ones.'

She shared songs of the surf with him, including some of her own creations. He loved surf-songs more than all others. He dreamed of the great waves charging towards destruction taking dozens of rejoicing dolphins along for the ride.

'But you must remember the dangers,' she warned for the tenth time.

'Mother, I'll be fine with you beside me.'

She laughed, buried her anxieties, and looked forward to surfing with him soon.

By this time, Ātārangi was spending several hours at a time away from Melody's side, sometimes exploring alone or with groups of friends. Later that same day, Melody picked up his excited thoughtstream from ten minutes swim away.

'Mother, there are so many fish here. I've never seen them so dense.'

At first, she thought nothing of it. Then he called again.

'They're getting thicker. They don't swim away when I chase them.'

That didn't sound natural.

'Take care, dear. Perhaps you should come back now.'

She began to swim towards him.

'Mother! Mother!' Then there was a pause and another call.

'Mother, I can't get away from the fish. They're all around me and there's something holding us in. I can't see it, but it's hard – it cuts my skin.'

Adrenaline pulsed, sending Melody to top speed in an instant. She charged across the sea and soon saw the fish-ball trapping him. There was a death-ship nearby. It told her all she needed to know.

Then began the worst hour of Melody's life.

'Mother! I can't get to the surface to breathe! The fish are pressing down on me. Help me please.'

'Fight Ātārangi! Get up to the surface or you'll suffocate in there!' But when she scanned the mass of solidly packed fish, she knew it was already too late. She located her child pressed near the bottom, trapped.

'Mother, it hurts! Will I die in here? I don't want to miss the surfing.'

How could he swim up for air through a solid mass like that? She swam at the fish-ball and bit at it, feeling the harsh strands of the net in her teeth. It was like biting on rock. She was helpless.

She thoughtscreamed, 'Save my baby!'

Other dolphins heard. They rocketed towards her.

Melody swam alongside as the net, with her son inside it, grew ever tighter, and crawled towards the ship in a hideous lumbering motion. What animal could want to eat so many fish? Her brain spun through a thousand possible ways of splitting the mesh and freeing him but found nothing that could work.

She heard his panicked and repetitive thoughtstreams.

'It hurts, it hurts. I want to get out. I can't breathe.'

For his sake she kept calm, stayed with him in mind, tried to drive the pain away with strong music and gentle images, promised him it would be over soon. Still, he begged her for help with cries that would haunt her forever. Vaguely she sensed the presence of other dolphins swimming around her.

'My baby, you must pray. Ask to be surfing, free as the wind. Your prayers will be answered, I promise. There are many of us out here, trying to help you. We're all trying to break the net and set you free.'

'Help him!' she cried to the universe and to the newly arrived dolphins. All heard.

The dolphins bit at the strands of the net, trying to break through. They might as well have tried to bite the hull of the ship. Melody felt his pain increase, his need for air grow as the net crushed him. But still he obeyed her and prayed to be surfing. She picked up one last message from him – a simple good-bye. Then Ātārangi gave a final voiceless cry, slid into a coma and nothing more was heard from him. He lived on for some time, unconscious.

Melody recognised the moment of death. She stayed swimming beside the net – swimming, but no longer breathing, as the spirit of Ātārangi departed. Time passed. A strange greyness appeared at the edges of her vision and began to spread inwards towards the centre, blocking the blueness. A thoughtstream came from a dolphin nearby. It arrived like a bullet in her brain.

'Melody! Breathe!'

The others were pushing her, shoving her towards the surface. She breathed. The colours returned, unwelcome now.

The advice of the octopus screamed up from her memory: 'Make sure he enjoys every moment of his life.' Now she understood.

A line from her own first song seared into the zenith, from her spirit to his.

'Live on, beloved one. Live on beyond the sun.'


The Powers of the universe were already busy, honouring all her promises and prayers, as they had when Aria died, but Melody didn't know that.

The spirit of Ātārangi soared away from Azure, a thread of dark energy trailing behind it, like an invisible filament across the galaxies. It was the supernatural link in the chain of pain, between Melody and the one who was departing.

Aue!

# 10 – BLUE AND RED MAKE PURPLE

In the days that passed after Natia and Manaia returned from Samoa, both hoped she was not pregnant. They hoped in vain. A test was positive. The doctor confirmed it. Then even Manaia agreed that Tawera had to know everything. She refused to be there when Natia told him.

For Natia it was a relief to share the horror with her husband. Secrets had never been part of their world.

'You haven't seen the skin on her back, Tawera. She has scars there too. That's what brought the shark. She'd already washed the other blood away by then.'

'Her back?'

'Shells and sharp stones on the ground where it happened.'

Tawera was a gentle man. Natia had never seen him show violence. But when he heard that final detail, he punched a hole in the plaster-board wall of their bedroom with his bare fist.

'We'll care for this baby,' he said later to Manaia. 'It's part of you. We always wanted another child. Might be a boy. A grandson would be a fine thing.'

'Dad, I'm not keeping it. It's only another monster.'

Wind breathed through the leaves of the tree outside the open window. But nothing else broke the long silence in the room.

'You're gonna kill it?'

'No Dad. I'm giving it up. I hate that man – don't want his baby. They never have enough babies for adoption now. Someone else will love it. I never could.'

'She's too young, Tawera,' said Natia. 'A baby will be a prison for her.'

'But couldn't we all care for it? It's part of our family.'

'NO! I don't want it anywhere near me. I hate it. If you don't let me give it away, I will kill it.'

Natia contacted the adoption services and helped Manaia to set the process in motion.

Tawera repaired and repainted the damaged wall.

To her surprise, Manaia felt better once her father knew. He was very angry, but not at her.

Dad would kill that guy if he ever met him, she thought. I'm glad he's far away. I don't want Dad to go to jail for murder.

She went out on the boat with Tawera once or twice and one hot day went with him to the surf at Elliot Bay. They took surfboards, but her body was already changing so she covered herself with a baggy shirt and waited on the sand. Her niggling new sea-fear provided a second reason for staying on the beach. She watched Tawera in action on the waves, envying him the coolness of the watery world out there. There were several others out surfing that day. Sometimes their numbers made it hard to pick Tawera out from the others. Her attention wandered.

But this was an uneasy day on the ocean. Tāwhiri-mātea was arguing with his father Ranginui. Tāwhiri pushed hot air around, stirred up air pressures and twisted winds in the atmosphere above the sea. Their argument was short, but it disturbed the water. Rangi spread himself smooth again and Tāwhiri blew himself calm. But their brief conflict sent some very odd waves heading shoreward.

The surfers were enjoying waves that were both powerful and safe. But then came the first unusual currents. Tawera was furthest out and was sucked under by a weird surge. He went deep. He struggled underwater and in the confusion between froth, air, and solid water, he thought he was at the surface and breathed too soon. Water flowed into his lungs and stomach. He went down again. He fought for the surface, but the heavy water pressed upon him. Time passed as he struggled. One minute, two. Five minutes.

The other surfers felt the unusual energies in the water. The waves had become unpredictable. Most went ashore. A group formed, chatting on the beach.

'Those waves were nasty.'

'Is everyone safe?'

'Where's that guy, Tawera? He was out there, wasn't he?'

'Anyone seen him recently?'

'Yep! He was beside me on a wave.'

'Where is he now?'

They all scanned the sea but saw no-one out there.

'Must have come in before the rest of us. That's his daughter on the beach,' he said, pointing. 'Ask her where he went.'

They moved towards Manaia.

'Are you Tawera's daughter?'

'Yes.'

'Where is he?'

'He's surfing.'

'You're sure he hasn't come ashore?'

'Yes, I'm sure! What's happened to him?'

Manaia scanned the sea. Nobody was out there. Then she saw his board tossing in the shallows. She ran to it, screaming.

'This is his board! We have to find him.'

Elliot Bay had no surf patrols, no rescue boats. It was up to the other surfers to help.

A short fair-haired man took charge, speaking first to his wife standing nearby. 'Lisa! Call 111.'

Lisa ran for her phone.

The short man sent the surfers back out into the water in pairs, with one board between each pair.

'One at the surface with the board while the other dives. When you find him, get the board under him. Bring him in.'

The surfers rushed into the water, running and jumping through the surf, searching all around for a human form – in the shallows, on the sand or even floating somewhere, perhaps further out. They saw only empty water.

Two men and a woman remained standing nearby.

'You three stay here and keep everyone else out of the water,' the short man ordered. Then he headed out to sea to help the rescuers.

Manaia started to wade out but the two men on beach-watch ran in to grab her. Manaia screamed, struggling to escape from their well-meaning clutches, wanting only to find Tawera for herself. It took all their strength to hold her back.

'They're all doing their best. Stay here. It's not safe for you.'

The searchers did not find him. Manaia stood on the beach, wild-eyed and staring, knowing too much time had passed, blaming the murderous ocean.

An hour later, the police arrived with kitted-up divers and an inflatable rescue boat. They did not rush. There was no point by this time. They were searching for a body, and everyone knew it, including Manaia.

She sat on the grass, his board beside her.

'It's not even scratched,' she whimpered.

She stared dry-eyed at the surfboard, expecting to see him materialise beside it.

'What happened to you, Dad?'

She asked the same question many times in the next hour and a half. She stared out to sea to watch the rescuers. She stared at the board because it was his board. People offered her cups of tea and food. It would have choked her to swallow anything.

In the end they found him, lying on the sand in deep water. It was hard for them to heave him onto the boat. He was heavy, bloated with water. They turned him on his side and water poured from his dead mouth. The medic found no pulse, no point in attempting resuscitation. They returned ashore.

Manaia ran to the boat, saw the covered-up shape of him.

'Revive him!' she screamed at the medic. 'Why aren't you reviving him?'

The medic asked the bystanders, 'Who's this?'

'His daughter, Manaia.'

'Manaia,' he said, 'It's too late. He's long gone.'

A policeman drove Manaia home in Tawera's car, and another followed in a police car. Natia heard the car arrive and went out expecting to meet Tawera and Manaia coming home, full of stories of surf, sand, and sunshine. Instead, she saw the uniformed stranger at the wheel of their car. Then she saw Manaia's face.

When the police car pulled up behind them, she knew.

'What's happened to Tawera?'

'Dad drowned,' said Manaia. 'We don't know why.'


Manaia wanted to run into the forests and up into the hills, anywhere she could pretend that everything was as it was before. Swimming away was out of the question. But her changing body made running impossible, slowing her to a jog and then a walk. She dragged herself daily back and forth along Te Wahapu and its side-roads. At low-tide she would cross to Toretore Island and walk its track, always hiding inside tent-like clothes, turning her eyes away from the horror of the sea, forgetting how much she had once loved it.

But she painted as before. Hundreds of stones, populated with insects, dolphins, flowers, and stars, all hues now edged with black outlines, overlaid with charcoal cobwebs, or picked out in filigrees of ebony, dark purple and jet. The new dark colours from her after time intensified the lighter colours that came from before.

When she started to run out of storage space, she took some to the markets in Paihia, Kerikeri and Kororareka. Being small, locally inspired, and unique, the stones made perfect souvenirs for the many tourists who poured through all these towns in summer. People had to hold them. The stones caressed their palms, and the colours seduced them. Many paid the price. For some, one was not enough. The stones looked better in groups. Manaia sold dozens. Now she could afford the best paints and brushes. So began her life as an artist by vocation.

Natia continued arrangements for the adoption, wading through profiles of hopeful would-be parents.

'I don't care who has it, as long as it isn't me,' said Manaia.

It was Natia who arranged for doctor's appointments and for Manaia to give birth at Kawakawa hospital. It was Natia who made sure Manaia avoided alcohol and ate carefully, and it was Natia who answered the very few questions Manaia asked about the approaching ordeal. It had to be Natia because Manaia didn't care if the baby died. She refused to attend ante-natal sessions, could hardly bring herself to go to the doctor. She only dreamed of being free and light again, to run and leap as she had before, to escape this jail sentence. She packed her bag for the hospital, weeks before she needed to.

But the baby was late, and every day seemed like a year, every sleepless night an eternity of leg-cramps, heartburn, and self-hatred.

At last, the waters broke, and the contractions began. Good. The nightmare would soon be over, the parasite gone.

Natia phoned the hospital.

'It's her first, so probably no rush, but bring her over before the car ferry stops running,' they advised. 'Better to save them an after-hours call-out.'

The pain increased. The contractions were more frequent now. Natia drove her to the ferry, well before the last one sailed.

Then on to the hospital in Kawakawa. Natia admitted her, stayed with her, communicated for her.

It was a long labour, and in the end the pain went beyond all Manaia had imagined, and when it stopped, the effort started. She'd never guessed she was capable of such a feat of strength. There was torn flesh requiring stitches. Manaia blamed every moment of this torment on the monster and this thing – his son. And when it was over, Manaia closed her eyes and refused to look at it, would not hold it. As she had previously insisted, the nurses took it away from her as soon as it was born.

They had hesitated at first, but she screamed at them.

'Stick to the plan! Keep it away from me.'

The plan was to care for it elsewhere in the hospital to await collection by the adoptive parents who were so impatient to take it home. The nurses explained how important the mother's milk from the first few days was for the health of the child, so Manaia allowed them to take milk from her using a pump. But she would not touch or see the child herself.

Straight after the birth they took Manaia to the maternity ward. There were women around her in the other beds, some feeding their new babies and staring at them moronically as though the ugly little things were anything worth looking at. She did not envy them these leeches hanging off their bodies. She detested this cold sterile place with its squalling babies everywhere. A maternity ward was nothing to do with her. She even hated the word itself.

Maternity maternity – a burden for eternity, she thought. Just get me out of here please.

'Don't you want to know how your baby is?' said the nurse.

'I don't care if it's dead.' said Manaia. 'It's NOT my baby.'

'Let us know if you change your mind, dear.'

'I won't change my mind. Don't mention that thing to me.'

She was fiercely glad for the first twenty-four hours after the birth, glad to be able to bend in the middle again, to sleep on her stomach, to have her own body back, to be free at last of the shackle that had stolen her freedom. Now she was excited and ready to reclaim her old life.

But on the second day she fell into a black hole of horrors filled with truths she could never escape. She would die. Her mother would die. Everything would die. Even that monster's child would die and the sooner the better. All this was true. No-one could deny it. So why did they all even bother to live? Why didn't they all just lie down right now and let the worms start their work straight away? Outside the sun shone but Manaia didn't notice that and didn't want to.

Natia arrived at her bedside with papers.

'You have to do some paperwork.'

'Why?'

'The adoption can't go ahead without a birth certificate, so we have to register the birth.'

Manaia looked at the papers, a mass of details and dotted lines and fields to fill in. None of it interested her. Nothing interested her. She turned her head away and covered her face with her hands.

'Send the papers to the monster in Samoa. Let him do it. It's his kid.'

'I'll do it for you.' Natia sat and wrote, filling in every field. She worked in silence for a few minutes and then suddenly stopped, looking thoughtful. 'You have to name the baby.'

There was a long silence. Natia waited.

'Baby. Just call it Baby.'

Natia sighed. 'I'll choose a name then.'

She continued working on the papers.

'You have to sign it. Do you want to read it first?'

'No. Give me the pen. Where do I sign?' Manaia reached across, scribbled a rough signature, dropped the pen and turned away, hating the feel of her lank hair and her slack and damaged body. It hurt to sit, and it hurt to think. She wished she could hide forever.

Natia took the completed papers and registered the unwanted birth.


Three days after the birth, Natia collected Manaia from the hospital. By this time Manaia was aware of the sunshine but was not yet ready to enjoy it.

'Want a coffee before we head home?' suggested Natia.

'Whatever,' replied Manaia.

They drove to the pink coffee caravan in the carpark of Kawakawa's small war memorial park, bought coffees and sat in the car with the fragrant cups. Natia began sipping but Manaia just stared at her cup until Natia broke the long silence.

'The baby stays at the hospital until ten days are up. If the birth certificate has come by then, you can sign the adoption papers and they can take her away. That gives you until she's ten days old to change your mind.'

Manaia's mouth gaped slightly. Then she turned to stare at her mother.

She? Had she heard correctly?

Natia continued sipping. Manaia had not started hers. She spoke at last, a strangled question. 'Did you say she?'

'Yes I did.'

Manaia stared around at the trees and lawns of the little park, as though she was noticing them for the first time. When she next spoke, it was a flood, a panic.

'Mum! I didn't know she was a girl. I thought it was a boy like its father. I thought it would grow up to be a monster like him. I would hate to be reminded of that beast. That's why I didn't want the baby. But if she's a girl she can't be like him. Why didn't you tell me?'

'I thought you did know. You didn't ask,' said Natia.

Manaia sat in the car and stared at the shadows of the trees playing on the grass in the park, where tiny daisies lay scattered like stars. She pictured a little girl playing in the daisies. Her girl. Her baby. Perhaps with a daisy chain around her neck. So pretty.

Natia sat beside her, as patient as the trees around them. Manaia became very still and for a long time she and Natia sat together in absolute silence, hardly breathing. A middle-aged couple walked on the grass, their big yellow dog bounding beside them, full of life and freedom. The woman threw a stick and the dog dashed to fetch it. Did the dog have a name?

'What name did you give my baby, Mum?'

'You love the scent of frangipani, so I called her Fran.'

'Fran,' whispered Manaia. 'Fran for frangipani. A beautiful flower.'

'She was a sweet flower, Manaia, just like her mother.'

'Was? Why do you say was? She's still alive, isn't she?'

'Of course, she's still alive. I only said it because she was your baby.'

Manaia gaped at the daisies for another moment, and they blazed in her face – so sharp and bright with their white and gold against the green of the grass and she saw the shadows of the leaves dancing over them like laughter in the sunshine.

'She's still mine. I want to go back. I want to see her.'

Natia turned the key, backed up, drove out of the carpark, waited for the traffic to clear. and drove back to the hospital.

*

Manaia put Fran's little plastic bathtub into the big adult bathtub and filled it with warm tap-water. She placed a towel within reach for use afterwards and then undressed Fran and slid her into the water facing up and lying back. She looked for the soap, but it was on the hand basin, just out of reach.

Fran had recently learned to sit unsupported, so Manaia raised her to a sitting position, keeping her eyes on Fran to make sure she stayed upright while she stepped away for the soap.

Fran sat transfixed by the shifting light on the water's surface. She patted it and watched the ripples and splashes. She gurgled in pleasure, mesmerised by the bathwater. For several minutes, Manaia did not touch her, not wanting to break the spell. She passed her a bath toy, but Fran ignored it, interested only in the water itself.

From that day on, Fran loved bath time more than anything else. If Manaia poured water from a cup or tap, Fran would stare at the glistening light on the moving surface, reaching her hand into the stream as though she was grasping for an elusive treasure. By the time summer came, her favourite game was splashing in her tub in the sunlight or playing with a trickling hose.

A hundred times Manaia thought: Is it my duty to show her the sea?

Manaia had not gone swimming since Samoa, but the sea had not bitten Fran, never stolen anyone she loved. The calm waters of their home beach called to her through the needs of her baby.

So, when Fran was about a year old, Manaia carried her into the sea for the first time with Natia nearby to ease Manaia's fear. Manaia fought against her dread of the sea, holding her naked baby close as she waded out to thigh depth. No deeper could she make herself go, but she crouched to let the water envelop them. Fran gasped a little at the cold but soon she was squealing with delight as the ripples slapped her skin. Natia stayed close by, while mother and baby played, until finally they knew Fran's little body must have had enough of the cold. As they walked away, Fran protested loudly, wriggling to get back, her arms outstretched to the sea, as they left the beach.

*

Another year passed. By this time Manaia found it hard to believe she'd ever wanted to reject the child she now loved so much.

One morning the three generations set off early, heading for the coast road. They planned to meet up with Tawera's niece, Sarah, while she was holidaying in Bland Bay. Sarah had a toddler the same age as Fran. Manaia looked forward to watching the two children playing together.

She buckled Fran into the child-seat in the rear of the car, behind the driver. She put the stroller into the boot, then threw a sand-bucket and spade beside it. Then she settled in the rear next to Fran. As usual, Natia was driving, and the front passenger seat stayed empty. Manaia opened her carry-all to do a final contents check. Sunscreen, sunhat, tissues, two bibs, towels, spare clothes, blue teddy. It was all there.

Glancing at Fran now, she saw the sunlight shining on her dark hair. It brought out the red tinge they shared, Tawera's legacy to both. She opened the carry-all, took out the beloved blue teddy and passed it to Fran. The toddler snuggled into her seat, hugging the teddy as the car began to move.

They took the coastal route towards Bland Bay, passing Elliot Bay for the first time since Tawera died there. The car became very silent at that point. The route by the beach allowed only a glimpse of the Elliot surf before winding on uphill.

'Doesn't seem like two years does it,' said Natia.

'No,' agreed Manaia. The silence continued.

A few minutes later, Fran squawked and started to cry. She'd dropped her blue teddy. Manaia stretched across and just managed to pick it up and pass it over. Fran gurgled with pleasure, clutching the teddy in her tiny brown hand, beaming through her tears. Manaia was filled with love as she looked at her child. She only turned to look forwards at the last second or she would have seen nothing.

The truck appeared on a bend; its driver slumped motionless over the wheel. Natia had too little room, nowhere to go. She managed to veer slightly before the impact. That evasive action was all she had time for, and it saved Manaia's life. The unguided mountain of steel ploughed into the driver's side. There was a smash into screeching blackness, and Manaia plunged into unconsciousness. She woke to find that she was trapped by her legs in a twisted position in the car, facing left out the side window. Turning slowly, she first saw the steering wheel with Natia's motionless hand still on it. The blood on the hand came from everywhere. Like red paint, still wet. There was no sound from Fran.

Nothing.

Manaia twisted her neck still further to look at her child in the seat beside her. She needed no-one to tell her that Fran had gone. Like her grandmother, the part of the body least changed by the collision was one little hand, holding a purple teddy, which only moments before had been blue.

Blue and red make purple, she thought.

A car pulled up behind. Two people emerged from it. One of them was on his phone. The other walked towards the wreck. There was little he could do to release Manaia from the wreckage. He tried to comfort her with words. She couldn't hear him because of her screaming, which wasn't because of the pain.

It was thirty minutes before the fire-truck and the ambulance arrived. She stayed trapped there with her mother and her crushed baby until the medics and firemen managed to cut her free at last from the blood-drenched prison. When they finally dragged her away from the wreck, the car-boot was cracked open, and she saw the bucket and spade lying unharmed inside.

Natia never awoke and died before reaching hospital.

Three generations diminished to one.

The truck driver failed drug tests.

Manaia spent a few days in hospital, and in time the injuries healed over, adding a few more to the old Samoan scars. Manaia found things to say that kept the psychiatrist happy, so he did not detect the spirit wounds that would not heal.

'There's freedom in my life now,' she told him. 'My time is my own to spend as I like. I can paint and walk as much as I want.'

'Good,' said the shrink, 'you're finding the positive angle.'

Manaia lived on, alone in the old house at Te Wahapu. Painting, painting, painting. She spoke to people at the markets where she sold her stones. Those were easy conversations, and they broke the solitude. Just chat about the stones, the art. It was all she needed for now.

I watched her walking alone along the beaches for hours, always in search of the perfect stones. She allowed me to tickle her feet sometimes but never to embrace her. I longed to hold her, but she gave me no chance.

'It wasn't my fault,' I whispered as I splashed along beside her.

'Remember how I sheltered you when the bad man stole your childhood?

It wasn't me who bit your leg.

It wasn't me who stole your Tawera.

It wasn't me who slaughtered Natia and Fran.

It wasn't me.

I'm innocent.

Let me soothe you.

Let me soothe you.'

On and on I swished and soothed as she wandered there beside me and I fancy my whisperings consoled her, sometimes.

At the end of every stone-hunting expedition, she returned to the house at Te Wahapu. Aue! It was empty, cold, and full of echoes. I tried to comfort her with lullabies on the long, lonely nights. She thought I was a growling enemy biding my time to strike again.

## 11 – THE WAKE

Melody watched the net being winched aboard. Ātārangi's body was inside that net. She heard voices of the men sorting the fish, the smacks of fish on fish or fish on metal, the weird cacophony of human music.

She heard water gushing on deck and then saw the same water, now red and lumpy with remains, pouring down from the ship. Gulls and small sharks squabbled over the carrion.

Melody floated in the bloody water and focused on the minds of the humans on the ship, hoping to spot Ātārangi through their thoughts. A man was pulling out unwanted creatures and debris from among the river of flesh arriving from the sea. He grunted with effort and concentrated on disentangling dead fish from a long strip of meshed plastic and tough cords.

Bits and pieces of discarded flesh floated around Melody. All had been living beings before the net trapped them. Now everything was dead – the cataclysm of a death-ship.

She hoped a shark would take her, but they had easier options.

An idea struck.

Might she still find her baby, here amongst the carrion?

It gave her sudden purpose. She took a breath – the first in too long. She began to search for any remnant of him. A shark nosed at her, but now she was too busy to die. She turned and drove it off. She scoured the gory sea but found no trace of Ātārangi.

The sun began to sink. Then a final great slew of blood, entrails, and unwanted fish arrived in the sea, swept from the deck of the ship. His body was there among it, and he was still whole. They had chosen not to use him for food.

The body sank and she followed it down. She saw the deep cuts in his beautiful flesh, made by the net. There were other injuries caused by the crushing weight he had endured, and the tools of the men. She looked into his eyes and saw only death staring back at her. She positioned him in front of her dorsal fin and pushed him to the surface – perhaps he might need to breathe one more time. She listened and hoped in vain for one last heartbeat and when the current caused his fin to brush against her, she pretended he was caressing her.

Melody carried the body as the school moved west. Libran, Zeta, Elethea, Antares and other dolphins she knew well, stayed close in their wake.

It was over for him now, but Melody's own skin felt the cuts of the net, her muscles bore the pressure of the packed fish, and her lungs, like his, could find no air. And so she would not breathe. Throughout that first night and day, the members of her pod worked around her, using sound and penetrating thought to force her to breathe.

By the second night, she was breathing for herself. She spent the hours streaming messages into Ātārangi's dead brain. She told him of the dreams she'd held for his future, suggested vocations he might have chosen. She described to him the hunter he would have become, the physical strength and endurance he would have gained as he grew to swim all day in the open sea with no barriers to limit his journeys, and she sent the vision he would most have loved, - his future self, surfing the waves of the great gales.

As darkness and daylight came and went, she imagined every detail of the physical appearance and personalities of the children he might have fathered, the love he would have known from the mothers of those children. She sent him all these visions, hoping that somewhere his spirit was listening. It was not. It had gone.

Libran saw that Melody's flesh was dehydrating from lack of food. He brought fish to her and encouraged other dolphins to do the same. They all tried to make her eat but Melody could not. Zeta brought a special high-fluid jellyfish. But before she offered it, young Elethea streamed a healing song to reduce her auntie's pain. The song allowed Melody to swallow the near-liquid food. But she kept her decomposing baby draped across her body, until three days and nights had passed since the net.

When her last imaginings of life in his body were over, it was time to let him go. She noticed a hungry shark following her, drawn by the smell of carrion. She recognised his need and considered giving him the remains of Ātārangi as food. It would be cleaner than letting the hagfish and bottom dwellers have the body. The other dolphins saw the time of surrender approaching. They withdrew, leaving only Libran by her side.

But a wild idea germinated in Melody's brain.

'Don't give him to the shark. Give him to the ones who killed him. Show them. Teach them.'

The impulse was strong. Perhaps the humans were unaware of the destruction they spread around them. She would show them.

By this time, they were seaward of Waewaetorea and Okahu Islands. A yacht sailed by, heeling in the wind, the weight of its keel biting into the sea, holding it upright against the pressure of wind in the sails. There was poetry in the bird-like harnessing of the wind by human sailing vessels, but Melody ignored this one and continued west. She turned into the Okahu Passage.

A small motorboat lay at anchor beside the pale sand of the beach on the western end of Waewaetorea. Melody struggled closer, under her dreadful burden. The boat had a platform suspended from the stern, hanging so low it touched the ripples. Two humans stood on the platform, one male and one female.

Libran stayed in the area but not close enough to disturb her privacy. The two humans slid into the water and swam about clumsily as humans do. Melody scanned their bodies and saw the hearts beating inside them, and an unborn baby turning and twisting inside the female. The male human scrambled back onto the stern platform, then turned to help the female aboard. Melody approached, still supporting her dead baby.

The woman pointed and called.

'Look at that! What is it?'

Another two humans emerged from the boat's interior. As Melody swam slowly towards them, all four tried to decipher what they were seeing. All had seen dolphins before but this one's burden distorted its shape beyond recognition. One of them spotted Libran in the distance as he surfaced to breathe.

'It must be a dolphin. Look, there's another one over there.'

Melody scanned the vessel and crew with eyesight and soundsight – the wooden skin of the hull, the propeller underneath with blades now motionless. The modified weeds the humans wore failed to disguise the strangeness of their tuberous bodies.

By now she was within a few body lengths of the boat. The pregnant female stood on the stern platform. The other three all watched from the cockpit and the sound of their voices flittered around Melody as she inched closer.

They have intelligence to create ships and flying machines, yet they can only communicate with noises? It can't be true, she thought. These are sentient beings surely? They must understand me.

She began sending her message to them.

'This is my baby. Your net killed him. Do you see the cuts on his skin? Why did you do this? Look at him. Look at him!'

Melody sent them pure ideas, sharper than any words. The people on the boat were lucky not to receive them. The images would have scorched their thoughtscapes like a fiery wind, teaching them that the rotting corpse she carried was her beloved child. They'd experience his suffering and death as though it was their own child.

But despite the messages arriving unheard, the pregnant woman sensed the dolphin's pain.

'Oh no,' she cried, 'that's her dead baby. But why would she carry it? Can dolphins feel grief?'

'No. They're only animals. She doesn't know it's dead. It's just an instinct to keep it at the surface.'

'Oh, I don't think so … look, it's so sad.'

'Don't be silly. You're anthropomorphising.'

'I wonder how it died?'

Melody thoughtscreamed, 'You stupid weedmonkeys! You killed him! I carry him in case he needs to take one more breath! Even though I know he'll never breathe the air of this world again.'

But it was like talking to jellyfish or oysters. They understood nothing.

She pushed Ātārangi's remains towards them.

'Take him. Take him! See for yourselves.' She guided his head onto the platform near the female. She pushed him twice more with her rostrum until the platform was fully supporting him, and he lay close beside the ludicrous human feet. All four land-beings stood with their mouths hanging open, watching Melody's every move.

She sent one more thoughtscream over the body of her child.

'May you all die in agony as my baby died!'

Suddenly all the humans spoke at once.

'Why's it doing this?'

'Quick! Get the camera.'

'God, it smells.'

'It's bycatch – you can see the marks of the net.'

Melody touched his still-beautiful flukes one last time and swam away.

One of them used a clumsy tool to take pictures of Ātārangi, being unable to mentally record and share images as dolphins do.

He did his best to capture details like the gashes made by the net on the body.

Once he'd finished, they eased Ātārangi's grisly remains back into the sea. The corpse spiralled slowly down. It never reached the bottom. In the end, as Melody would have wished, the hungry shark, still following, scavenged the meal he needed.

The humans used plenty of seawater to wash themselves and their boat. Then they up-anchored and started their engine. As they puttered home towards Kororareka, they were quieter than usual and their photographer wondered who to send the pictures to, where they might do some good.


Libran returned to Melody's side, but he stared at her with a look she did not recognise.

'What are you staring at?'

'Your aura is changing.'

'How?'

'It's contracting as though you're sick.'

'Was it only my musician's aura you loved?'

'I love all of you, then and now, but I hate to see this happen to you. There's a wraith in it – just behind you, where you can't see it.'

'I don't need to see it. It sits before my brain every minute.'

'It's him Melody. Our son.'

'Not Ātārangi. It's an evil spectre.'

'Let him go. Make music to heal yourself.'

'I can't let go of it. It won't let go of me.'

'Use your vocation. Bring back your old aura. Save yourself from this nightmare!'

She shot into the air and splashed down.

'Aue! What touched me? Did you touch me?'

'I did not.'

'The spectre touched me. It's freezing.'

Then came the spectral sound. A whistling screech that shrieked across the sea to slash the spirits of all who heard. It came from the spectre and from Melody, one or the other or both. The sound was the opposite of music, the antithesis of Melody and her son. Libran himself quailed and wished to flee.

She departed at top speed, trying to outswim the presence. But it followed, spectral tentacles clawing after her. Icy tendrils reached in through her flesh, squeezing her muscles. Libran stayed beside her but had no comfort to give. Melody could not outswim the spectre.

She bolted east, seeking refuge in the unreachable horizon.

'Don't follow,' she cried to Libran.

He obeyed but leapt skywards to glimpse her flight. Never had she swum so fast.

The speed helped. Her physical heat disguised the spirit chill. She swam in huge circles, taking prey as she went. Sometimes she allowed Libran or Zeta to swim alongside her but mostly she battled alone.

Conditions on many east coast beaches of Te Tai Tokerau were now perfect for surfing. Melody sought out the wildest surf but there was a group of dolphins already riding it. She swam with Libran to join them.

'Look look!' cried one who saw her approach.

They were shocked at the sight of the spectre but when its shriek sounded, they darted away, leaving Melody alone with Libran.

The spectre's pursuit blinded her to the beauty of the blue dazzle and the white thunder. She rode a huge wave, then out to sea and back to the sand, over and over, with never a moment of rest. Libran could hardly believe how she worked those waves. She couldn't stop, though she longed to. The spectre cracked his icy whip, drove her body to its limits and forced her dangerously close to shore.

On the inward trips, when the waves provided most of the energy, she was like a block of ice sweeping along while the spectre celebrated, enjoying the ride and her chill. Each outward trip, the opposing ocean gave her something to fight against, letting her recover some warmth.

In the end, the tide turned, the wind died, the waves calmed, and nothing had changed. Night fell. Another pod approached. Libran guessed what would happen and stayed close to her. As he expected, the newcomers all turned away as soon as they saw her. She called to him across the wind.

'All are avoiding me. Is it the spectre?'

'All dolphins can see him rotting there,' he replied. 'It's not just me. Only the brightest stars can shine through the loom of it. Think of other things. He cannot come back. I want your old aura back. We all do.'

Thus, Melody's mind and aura both carried the picture of her son, as he was when she last saw him, dead, crushed, damaged and torn, his flesh beginning to decay. It obscured all her older memories of him. And from time to time, it produced the whistling screech.

Only Libran and Antares stayed close. Zeta too sometimes, but she dared not bring Elethea with her. The spectre interfered with their appetites. It took courage to face the apparition. They could feel it when they swam close to Melody. They took turns to hunt elsewhere but made sure she was rarely alone.

Melody could see that they were suffering as well. She should leave them in peace.

The young dolphins who'd been Ātārangi's playmates in the school were the most terrified of his new spectral image. They avoided coming within an hour's swim of it.

That could be us, they thought.

She did not blame them, for choosing to remember him when he was alive and free.

She even urged her own pod to leave her alone.

'You'll feed easier without me,' she said.

Two days after the big surf died, the spectre chased her south, alone, down the eastern side of Rākaumangamanga towards Whangamumu.

Whangamumu. Aue!

Beautiful cove of terrible memories. So many beautiful whales had died here in agony. Why would Melody choose such a place? But her endurance had almost run out. At Whangamumu, she swam towards the beach, glancing right to where the forest was gradually strangling the ruins of the old death factory and the waves were reclaiming the torture ramp where once men hauled whales ashore to be boiled for oil. She swam by that place of death, torment, and waste.

Then on to where the water lapped on quiet sands, shaded by massive pohutukawa trees. Behind them a steep grassy slope led up into the forested hills. No human lived or worked here now. There was no profit here anymore. No roads. And the wild hills kept people back, protecting the sheltered beauty and loneliness.

She swam towards the beach until the sand brushed her belly. The tide was coming in and as she lifted above the water, the sun's heat struck her body.

This will banish the chill, she told herself. Let it burn me!

She jammed herself into the sand, at the shallowest spot she could reach. The sun beat down and yes, the rising heat soothed her. Sharp shells scratched her belly, and that pain also masked the cold, so she welcomed it. She wriggled further up the beach as the tide rose higher and higher.

A vibration! A presence? Who was with Melody now? There were entities in the universe who loved the music this dolphin created. Their presence honoured her. But she had not called them. What use were they? They would respect her decision. How would events play out now, in these beautiful waters of terrible memories?

Libran's searching thoughtstream arrived in her brain.

'Melody! Where are you?'

She closed her thoughts so no trace could escape to him.

'Don't find me, Libran,' she whispered. 'Don't find me!'

The tide rose a little more. Up, up she went with it and its rate of rise slowed as it approached its turn . . . and her moment of no-return.

There was a flurry of foam at the entrance to the cove. It was Libran, with Zeta and Antares.

'Melody! Come back! It's too shallow.'

She thoughtscreamed at them: 'Go away all of you!'

'You'll be stranded.'

'As I intend.'

They sent healing songs. She rejected them. They swam close, calling to her. She ignored them and waited for the tide to finalise her decision.

Then Libran pushed himself up into the shallows behind her. Melody, Zeta, and Antares, all heard the stones grinding under his body. He came close enough to pull at her flukes with his teeth.

The tide turned – all felt the shift in the water.

'Go back!' she screamed, but he came closer.

'If you stay here, I die with you,' he said.

'Go back! Go back!'

He ignored her words. Antares and Zeta followed him into the shallows, defying the danger. A spectral shriek ripped them like claws, but they'd heard it before and did not turn back.

The divine light froze as death approached.

The highest swell of the tide reached Melody at that moment. If she stayed, they would all die there, stranded by the receding tide.

She wished death for herself – not for her loved ones.

The immortal presences would have crossed every finger they had, if they'd had any fingers to cross.


Melody lifted her pectoral fins releasing their grip on the sand and let the backwash of the wave take her a few millimetres seawards.

A faint resonance of harmonising chords drew out into a vast sigh, as though the unseen ones breathed air instead of divine ether.

The water drained away, leaving the dolphins stranded, but another wave soon came and the small retreat she'd made before was enough that the next wave allowed Melody to edge further towards safety. And now she carried with her a dry-land-heat build-up to give temporary relief from the chill of the spectre.

The breath of the unseen morphed into song as the four dolphins wriggled their way free of the shallows. The easterly freshened. The waters danced.

Libran orbited Melody's body, caressing her with beak and fins as they rode the swells to deeper water. Antares and Zeta sang to her, soothing her. She managed to rest a little. First one side of her brain and then the other.

The sea soon washed the sand and blood away from the cuts and scratches, left by sharp shells on the skin of their bellies.

In the Divine Dimension beyond reach or knowledge of the dolphins, music swelled into harmony.

The little pod swam away to the open sea, having cheated Whangamumu of one more terrible memory.

The spectral chill returned as soon as Melody's body temperature fell to normal. She hid her torment to reassure her companions and she veiled her disappointment at failing to die. But death was only postponed.

The spectre hung over her, more luminous than ever, forcing the others to look away. She wanted solitude for their sake, but now they were reluctant to allow it.

Melody made a show of hunting, but they all watched her too closely. She'd need to be more careful next time. Ideas circulated in her mind until she had a plan in place.

While she was waiting for the chance to put it into action something happened that Melody long remembered. She was swimming with the others in the mouth of Manawaora Bay when they spotted the same yellow kayak they'd seen before, the one with the human musician aboard. Rōreka was not paddling now, nor was he singing. His kayak sat motionless on the water; his paddle fixed in place across his deck. He was leaning over the side, his hands busy and desperate. The dolphins swam underneath and looked up. He was too absorbed in his task to see them.

Alongside the little boat, a leatherback turtle struggled in terrible pain, ensnared in fishing gear, a bird's nest of tangled line and weights. He was too exhausted to care that some land creature was interfering with him. The dolphins wondered if the man was killing him. He held a sharp tool and was making hacking and sawing movements around the body of the turtle.

Then they saw the rope lines through the turtle's jaw, around his neck and flippers and across his ridged leathery carapace and tail. In places it was cutting into his skin. There was a hook hanging from the corner of his jaw. One of his flippers was so deeply cut, they could see into the open flesh – a wonder he hadn't bled out. Elethea and Zeta sent soothing sounds to the turtle to reduce his pain. Rōreka was cutting the hard strands.

It took a brutal action to remove the hook. The turtle resisted at first, but once the hook was out, he calmed, pacified by continuing sounds from Zeta and Elethea. Rōreka worked on around the turtle's body, gathering in the tough synthetic fibres as he worked, jamming them under the stretchy cords on the deck of his boat, where they could not snare another marine being. The turtle no longer struggled. His pain was diminishing.

Rōreka sawed away, cutting strand after strand, while the water slapped against the hull and gulls cried above and around.

He spoke aloud.

'Don't worry mate,' he said. 'We'll soon have you out of this snarl-up.'

He placed one paddle blade under the turtle's body to keep it from sinking before the job was done. He made the last cut or two. Now the turtle was free but made no move to swim away and waited beside the boat, supported by the paddle blade.

The turtle rested there while wavelets massaged his horrific cuts and abrasions. Elethea's flow of sounds continued to soothe and heal. Then he struggled slightly as though he wished to escape, so Rōreka lowered the paddle, and the turtle slid off and vanished into the deep. Only then did Rōreka notice the great shapes of the dolphins around him.

Melody suddenly remembered the comment made by Tangles last time they'd seen this man.

'He's the one for you,' she'd said.

Tangles had given her forewarning of Ātārangi's death. So had she also predicted that this man might help her in some way?

I don't get it, she thought. Humans use nets to kill, but this human stopped a net from killing.

A few days later a baby dolphin in a nearby pod snared a piece of plastic in her breathing passages and began to slowly suffocate. Melody's pod raced to assist.

'We have to pass Maunganui Bay to reach her,' said Antares as they swam. 'Let's pick up Tangles on the way!'

'Great idea,' said Libran. 'Tangles could save her.'

This was not the same Tangles befriended by Ātārangi. That prescient being had died after the usual short life of her kind. But her hole was always occupied by one of her descendants, and in the minds of the dolphins, Tangles bequeathed her name as well as her home to the current occupant. To them it was a kind of memorial to the lost Ātārangi,

The current Tangles was male. They found him hiding in his inherited cranny and persuaded him aboard Antares. Melody had no wish to make things worse by carrying her spectre too near the suffocating baby. She took advantage of her pod's distraction to slip away. This was her chance to carry out her plan.

# 12 – DIVINE DEAL

Dolphin astronomers learn the specialised skill of breathing during astral travel, but Melody was not an astronomer. She departed anyway, leaving her body to wallow, unbreathing, behind her. Her consciousness soared into outer space, an elliptical flash of spirit light.

So alone.

'Good-bye Libran,' she thought, 'and all the others I love.'

The spectre could not bring her back. He tormented her empty shell, but she felt nothing. Frustrated, he shrank to a red hook-shaped gleam, hardly visible in the water beside her, gripping her like a parasite.

She travelled between the stars, at the varying speed of her own thought. The Powers of the universe recognised this wrongness. Their thoughts drifted in like smoke, resonant with silent chords.

'Why are you here with us?' they asked.

'Who are you?' she asked.

'We are entities of the universe.'

It took her a few moments to digest this, but she answered their question at last.

'I seek my son.'

'He's not here. We sentenced him to new life.'

'Show me.'

They took her to him in a heartbeat, on a planet in a galaxy so distant, even dolphin astronomers had hardly heard of it. Here, Ātārangi was a liquid being, physically supported by a thick atmosphere. He shone magenta, in hues from an Azuran sunrise, and stretched his wings to catch the wind-waves beating between silver mountains. Dozens of others like him, coloured all shades of flame, rode the same currents, exploiting the waves of aerial energy tossing them from mountainside to mountainside.

'He's surfing as he always wished!' said Melody.

'Surfing was his dying prayer,' replied The Powers, 'so we fulfilled it. Life is lived this way by the windriders of Aerdluth. Here, his name is Aerthonn, of the family Maygen.'

'I promised him he'd soon be free as the wind and surfing. You've prevented my promise from being a lie,' she said.

'It was never a lie,' they replied. 'It was your intention.'

'Can you let him be re-born to me? I would return to Azure if he might one day swim in my slipstream again.'

'It is possible, but he could live here for a time equal to hundreds of Azuran years. His most recent life was unnaturally shortened, as you well know. Would you have this life shortened for him too? Just so he can return to Azure?'

She turned to watch Aerthonn, holder of the spirit of her son. He leapt to catch a wind-wave and let it hurl him over lakes, flower-forests, rivers, and cascading nectar-falls, through shifting clouds of perfumed air before sweeping all the way back to them. The windriders soared together, united in harmony with their world. He belonged here now. He deserved this life. Melody hoped he would live long on Aerdluth.

'My only prayer is to be beside him again, but I see now, it cannot be.'

'Anything is possible, Melody,' whispered The Powers.

But she was too distracted to notice that whisper.

She sent Aerthonn her love and his wings tripled their reach across the wind. His colour intensified. Tiny stars shimmered over him.

The wave of love from Melody swept aside the shrouds that covered the scars on his spirit. A stab of pain almost overwhelmed him, but it passed and left him lighter than before.

'He has forgotten Melody of Azure,' said The Powers. 'He no longer needs you, but he feels the love you send, and his spirit remembers . . . even the pain.'

'How does he feel it?'

'After the pain-memory passed, all of Aerdluth grew more beautiful to him.'

'How does he feed here?'

'Watch him interact with the mountainsides.'

She saw vast flowers supported in moss thickets on the silver precipices of the mountains. Rivers of nectar flowed from each flower, some of it cascading down into nectar lakes. Aerthonn and his companions either drank it from the wind or took it directly from the flowers.

The dense air blew among weirdly shaped rock formations creating sounds she'd never heard on Azure. And the sounds made by plants and animals were sometimes so strange they must surely be unique to Aerdluth.

The windriders wove the sounds into chords which they released among the audible rhythms of the airwaves.

Melody strove to commit every sound, every chord, every rhythm, to memory. Why was she doing this if she intended death?

Aerthonn favoured the nectar of a vivid blue flower shaped like an Azuran sea-anemone. Did its colour remind him of home?

The Powers merged Melody into Aerthonn's body, so she could experience his life. Windriders needed no sensory organs to know the sights, sounds and flavours of Aerdluth.

The atmosphere surged, hurling them at blinding speed towards the silver cliffs. They swept safely by, cushioned by wind. It was like surfing on Azure but with limits removed and thrills magnified. Aerthonn carried her lower, to rounded mountains where they rode gentler wind-currents and the sounds and smells were soft and sweet, then back to the heights where again they rocketed from cliff to cliff.

And everywhere the atmosphere throbbed with a thousand thoughtstreams. Every living thing shared consciousness.

Aerthonn slid across the wind to the opposite slopes, using a wingtip to stroke a swirl of blue nectar from a willing flower. The wingtip blushed briefly blue in contrast with his transparent magenta, before blending into the fluids of his body.

'Delicious,' he said. 'Thank-you.'

The flower puffed out its petals as though flattered.

Even the winds and mists were sentient enough to exchange thoughtstreams.

'Blow harder,' said Aerthonn to the gentle wind he rode. 'Take me over the high pass.'

The wind breathed a reply. 'I sing only softer songs. I brush the easy hills.'

'But I want to go higher and faster.'

'You haven't changed, my little thrill-seeker,' thought Melody, and soon enough the older Maygens guided him back to the wilder gales he loved, who carried him higher and faster.

Melody wanted to stay with him forever, but while she floated bodiless on Aerdluth, merged in the being who had once been her son, she felt a jolt from across the abyss of space.

'Libran!' she thought. 'Has he found me?'

She chose to ignore it and let her so-distant body suffer what it must, without her.

Another jolt.

'Is something attacking me at home? I don't care. Let it do its worst.'

It happened a third time and still she chose to soar with Aerthonn, like an albatross sailing the Roaring Forties of Azure.

But The Powers took her away. They would not compel her though, to return to a body and planet she'd left of her own will. And as they withdrew her from Aerdluth, a fourth jolt struck Melody.

On Azure, time had passed. Tangles had used his skills to grip and dislodge the tough plastic from the baby's blowhole, saving her life. The baby's pod rejoiced. They fed and fêted Tangles in their gratitude. He had never eaten so well.

Further off, Libran, Zeta, Antares, Elethea and two more specialist healer dolphins all surrounded Melody's corpse-like body. They saw her heart still beating faintly, but without air the body could not survive.

The six worked together, under the guidance of the three healers. They used penetrative sound on the muscles around the blowhole, all the way down into the lung. They stimulated the efficient flash of action that was a dolphin breath. It caused the jolt that had reached across space. It sent fresh oxygen flowing from the lungs to the bloodstream inside her empty body. The five had almost forgotten their own need for oxygen. Now they all breathed before working again.

Jolt!

Why should Melody return to a planet where the memory of her son's death stayed with her day and night? Even out here so far from it all, his last cries echoed to her from deep inside the hideous net. Death would take the memories away and heal her of the horror, as it had healed him.

'Tell me why those weedmonkeys killed my child when they did not need his flesh for food?'

'They didn't mean to kill him,' replied The Powers. 'They're not all evil. Their hands make them greedy, to have, to snatch, to own. But those same hands can create great beauty. Look at these human works.'

The Powers sent Melody images of The Starry Night by Van Gogh and The Great Wave off Kanagawa, by Hokusai.

Melody gaped in awe. 'How do they do that?' she said.

'They have hands,' said The Powers. 'But those hands distract them and prevent intellectual progress. They'd listen if they could, but their brains are not ready. You may be the one to teach them. Go back Melody and try! But you need to reach the entire species to be effective. You cannot force all humanity to understand Ocean Mind - we only ask you to give them the opportunity. Your skills may help you succeed where others of your species have failed. But it must go both ways. You need to get your thoughts into their heads and receive theirs back in return.'

'I hate weedmonkeys. I don't want to go back.'

'If you succeed in the task, we'll send you to Aerdluth at the end of it all, to spend your next life with he who was your son, but understand that neither of you will remember Azure, nor your time together there.'

She could be with him again! What else mattered?

'But how shall I communicate with a species so deaf as weedmonkeys? Sorry . . . humans.'

'The sounds you gathered on Aerdluth might help. It wouldn't be the first time you've put alien sounds into your songs.'

'I'd do that without your urging, if I could make a new song. And I'll do anything to be with him again – even endure continued life and memories on Azure.'

'But be careful Melody,' they warned. 'Have compassion for humans. They are among the most isolated of all the sentient species in the galaxy. Don't let hate and anger overwhelm you. It will make your task impossible. Love may be the key.'

The spirit of Melody gazed into their infinite eyes, considering their warning.

'It's true. Hate and anger do exist within me now. But I can't turn from even the chance of such a reward. I accept the task. As for love, how could I ever feel love for any human?'

The Powers spoke one last time to her.

'Melody, we have more advice for you. Beings in many galaxies are aware that the dolphins of Azure are dwindling in number. They understand the worth of your kind and do not wish to lose them forever. You and Libran have the genetics to create new life of great value. We urge you to this, some day when you're ready.'

*

The home oceans fizzed against her skin. She looked into the eyes of dolphins who had scarcely breathed themselves, during their ordeal. She thanked them for saving her. The healers swam away, free to hunt now. Zeta and Antares brought food for her. She accepted it, and her siblings departed, leaving her alone with Libran.

The spectre was weak in the aftermath of her absence. It remained pale for the next few days, allowing Melody and Libran a time of peace.

While night fell, she told him all she'd experienced on Aerdluth.

He was quiet for a while before responding.

'I'm sorry now for wanting to prevent your journey. This mission was worth every risk you took. But you should have told me before you went.'

'If I had, would you have let me go?'

'You had no intention to return.'

'True. It's a miracle I'm back,' she said. 'Libran, our son lives now in a world more beautiful than Azure but still I miss having him right here beside me.'

He had no reply, but for the first time since the death of their son, they danced together, flinging starlit spray sky-high, and sending their love all the way to Aerdluth. She imagined Aerthonn expanding to receive it as she'd seen him do before.

'Perhaps,' said Libran, 'we'll soon see traces of your true aura returning.'

Already, though, he'd glimpsed tiny gleams of the red poison.

When the dance was over, the truth remained that she would never see her son again in this life and so the ocean felt as empty to her as ever.

'I'm called to communicate with humans,' she explained, 'to tell them our stories, give them our songs, reveal Ocean Mind. Once they know us, humans could work to reverse the decline in our numbers. The Powers of the universe do not wish our species extinct.'

'I wish you luck,' he said, 'but many have failed before you.'

'The Powers have promised me rebirth on Aerdluth with Aerthonn if I succeed so you needn't fear I'd try another early departure.'

'I thank them for that,' he muttered.


Melody was now ready to work at her music. The Powers had suggested that sounds from Aerdluth might help her to reach humans. But though she felt the music billowing inside her, she heard no hint of it. Normally by now, she'd have chords, melodies and harmonies feeding her subconscious; working at composing even while she thought of other things. The sounds of Aerdluth inspired her, but here nothing was happening.

The coldness returned to her bones as the spectre gathered its forces, strangling every attempt at creativity.

She played the Aerdluthan sounds over and over, sometimes in the huge waves of the open sea and sometimes in the calm of sheltered waters, in starlight and sunlight, in mist, rain, and through the roaring gales – but no new song arrived. Only a silence that slowly gathered an echoing nightmare of whispers:

'It hurts! It hurts! I want to get out. Mother will I die in here?' And then that icy scream again, piercing the void.


She chose old songs she'd created herself. She chose songs by every other dolphin musician she valued. They were all as beautiful as ever, but they failed to revive her gift. 'Time will restore your skills,' Libran reassured her.

Time became her only hope.

'Losing my craft is a catastrophe,' she said to him. 'The spectre is another. But they are small calamities, compared to losing Ātārangi.'


The Powers and their divine choirs, so skilled at creating their own music, still eagerly anticipated each new song from Melody. Humanity may grieve at the early death of their Mozart, but there is no sorrow like that of celestial spirits, when the flow of music from a great dolphin composer ends before it should.

Perhaps it's just as well I have a new calling to fill my days, thought Melody, now that my old vocation is lost.

She swam away alone, seeking the company of the one Azuran species she most detested.

## 13 – TWENTY QUESTIONS

Rōreka lived in Jacks Bay in the greater Manawaora Bay. It was less than half an hour's drive east of Manaia's home on the Te Wahapu peninsula.

Jacks Bay contained two sheltered beaches separated by a reef that was submerged at high tide. The easternmost of the two beaches kept the name Jacks while the western one was called Jills. Rōreka could launch his kayak at Jills at any time of the tide.

His house was only three hundred metres from Jacks Bay. However, Jacks had no easy public access, while he could reach Jills on foot in under ten minutes, via a short gravel road and a bush-track. He either towed the kayak on its wheeled trolley or left it on the beach tied to a pohutukawa tree.

The land surrounding Manawaora Bay had once been densely populated by Rōreka's ancestors, but now this part of the coast, all the way out to Rawhiti further east, was a rural backwater. No shops. No school. Just native or regenerating bush surrounding a few coastal farms and a sprinkling of houses. The steep hills inland were mostly bush-covered wilderness. He often ran there.

His long strides relished the miles as they carried him towards the sun now rising in the east behind a cover of morning cloud. The road was sealed but hilly and winding, often overhung with vegetation. Where the trees thinned, the sea glimmered to his left. At this time of day, no cars were about, so he ran dead-centre of the road.

As he ran, he remembered the ragged breathing of his smoking days and felt gratitude for the cleaner breath now passing in and out of his lungs.

He was also grateful that last night's gig had been local, so at least he'd been able to sleep at home and run in the morning on familiar roads.

He ran as far as Parekura Bay before turning for home, a total of 10 kilometres.

Te Patiki, the Coalsack cat, was waiting at the door and entered with him. He put on some music, old songs from a previous decade, anything that he hadn't created himself. He needed a rest from his own tunes.

He longed for a smoke. Would it ever get easier? But he'd tossed every packet – even dumped all his ashtrays. There were none in the house and nowhere nearby to buy them.

He showered, dressed, and returned to the lounge where the windows looked north-west over the waters of Manawaora Bay. The cloud cover was now burning off in the morning sun and the sea glowed silver-blue in the expanding patches between the cloud shadows.

He cooked "super-porridge", savouring the grainy texture and nutty flavours produced by his invented recipe. He turned on the coffee machine he'd recently bought for too-many thousand dollars. He enjoyed grinding the beans, making the coffee, and drinking it, all while lecturing himself about the cost of the machine.

'How can you pay off a mortgage like yours if you keep buying stuff like this?'

But his inner rebel argued: 'Think how much I save by not smoking.'

The coffee didn't banish his craving for death-sticks, but it helped a little.

Rōreka had purchased his big old house when his music was in a brief lucrative phase. The house, despite its dodgy condition, suited his musical needs because its basement provided him an ideal music studio. He'd worked on its soundproofing and acoustics until it was close to perfect. The room faced away from the road and out to sea, so the occasional traffic noise was not a problem down there.

The lounge was directly above Rōreka's studio and above that was a big unused attic room. It was his shabbiest room, but he rarely went up there, though it had the best sea-view in the house, through its big glass sliders. The condition of the middle floor was reasonable. It contained all the living facilities, and its view was almost as good as the attic.

Needing to go food-shopping, he shut Te Patiki in the basement laundry where she could choose between her own little bed or the cat-door to outside. She huffed off outside in search of a good sulking spot.

'Greengroceries only today,' he resolved. 'Gotta get the mortgage down.'

It took around twenty minutes to drive from home to Kororareka village. He parked and shopped at the Four Square on York Street, manfully resisting the cigarettes he yearned for. He loaded the heavy bags of fruit and vegetables into the van.

Then he noticed the craft market in full swing on the green across the road. He couldn't resist a quick wander. He left his wallet in the van thinking he'd be safe from impulse buying with no cash on him.

He hummed his latest tune and soaked up the energy of the crowd of locals, weekend visitors and tourists.

There were stalls selling stitchery, paintings, woodcraft, jewellery, pottery, and every kind of hand-crafted cleverness, one little village might rustle up to tempt the tourists.

He passed a crowded stall where a flash of colour bedazzled him. Stones – smooth, flat, some rounded, most palm-sized to fit hands of many sizes. He waited until the crowd thinned a little and made his way closer.

Each stone glowed and seemed to vibrate with energy, painted with brilliant mandala patterns, glittering pointillist designs, or tiny realistic scenes from nature. There were abstract explorations of line, shape and colour and ethnic designs from multiple cultures. These were ordinary stones converted into precious jewels. He itched to touch them.

Some were clearly intended for children, showing animals, flowers and fantasy creatures. There was one bigger stone – a life-sized sleeping ginger cat – he expected it to yawn and stretch at any moment.

He watched the other customers. Some purchased stones. Of those who didn't, most at least took a card from the box on the table. Some fingered the merchandise while making their choices. Those who handled a stone, usually bought it. The girl selling them didn't seem to mind people touching the goods in her care. He wondered if she was the creator of the work. She was a part-Asian girl, hardly out of her teens, surely too young to be capable of producing such radiance.

Probably selling on behalf of some skilled city artist, he thought, and she's local. I've seen her around, I think. God! She's beautiful!

A middle-aged man stopped to examine the stall. He dragged on his cigarette and blew a cloud of smoke over the young seller. She waved it away, a fleeting expression of disgust on her face.

He worked his way through the crowd for a closer look. He needed to hold one of those stones. One leapt out at him. It carried the same visual symbols as the tattoo on his own back. It was a condensed version, but unlike his tattoo, the stone rang with colour. Seashell, spiral wave, fern frond, and feather, all intertwining with mysterious traceries of black.

He picked up the stone. It nestled into his hand as though it had always lived there. Lyrics of a song he'd written two years ago floated to mind as he stared at it. The words had inspired his tattoo.

Fern unfurl, seashell curl, feather floating free,
Unify,
land sea and sky,
In spiral galaxy.
Ripples grow, from embryo,
to waves across the sea.
Burst on sand,
Retreat from land,
Reborn as energy.

He could hardly believe the parallels between the design on the stone and the one on his own back. He'd no idea what it would cost but he had to have it. He turned it over to the plain side, saw a price sticker and winced. He felt for his wallet. It was in the car of course. He swore silently.

'Why that one?' The voice of the young seller held no trace of the Asian accent he'd half-expected. Now he saw that, like himself, she was a mix of races.

'Most people dither before making a choice,' she said. 'Not you.'

He hesitated before responding, mesmerised by her golden eyes, eyes so young and beautiful, yet older than the universe. He needed no further convincing that she was the artist selling her own work.

Laughter played round the corners of her mouth, encouraging him.

'This is why,' he replied at last.

He put the stone down, turned his back and pulled up his sweatshirt. Because his back was turned, he did not see the shock on her face. She recovered quickly. He twisted a little to show her the parts that wrapped around his side and over his shoulder.

'Yours has more detail,' she said, 'but my stone has all the colour.'

'I want to buy it, but I don't have enough cash on me. Can you hold it while I go and get my wallet from the car across the road?'

'No problem. I'll be here another hour or so.'

He returned, but now he found that one of the jewel-bright rocks was not enough, so he chose two more. She wrapped all three in tissue and placed them in a dainty paper bag which she handed him.

'Do you use a rock tumbler to make them smooth?' he asked.

'Two kinds. Oceans and rivers.'

The noise and clutter of the market vanished. He saw her wandering beside the ocean with stones in her hand and wind in her hair.

'Do you sell here often?'

'About once a month, summer months mainly.'

Her business cards were almost as irresistible as the stones themselves. He reached for one slowly, read it carefully, flicked her a glance and saw her eyes fill with terror. He froze. Should he put the card back?

'Is it okay to keep this?'

'Yes . . . yes. It's fine. In case anyone needs to contact me about *my work*.'

'Nice to meet you . . . Manaia. I'm Rōreka.' He pocketed the card and went home, shaken.


The music was still playing when he arrived home. He'd forgotten to turn it off again. Great for the power bill.

He placed the stones on a shelf in his lounge.

'Now you can look out to sea,' he told them.

He took a long time to arrange them, spellbound. He stood holding the 'tattoo' stone, as he called it, and imagined her on a beach, stooping for this very stone and holding it in her hand as he now held it in his. He remembered the amazing neatness of her stall at the fair, so organised and spotless. He looked around and noticed dust on floorboards and furniture.

'I should keep this place cleaner,' he thought.

He placed the business card under one of the stones and left the room, to spend a humdrum hour or two on dusting, vacuuming, kitchen-cleaning, and laundry. By then he was desperate for a smoke. He reached for the packet he'd always kept on the hutch dresser. It wasn't there now of course. The expression on Manaia's face when the man blew smoke at her floated to his mind. He turned and picked up the tattoo stone. As if by magic, it soothed his craving.

He looked at the sea. It was mirror smooth with no puff of breeze to ruffle it. So blue. So calm.

'I'm ravenous,' he thought.

He put the kettle on, crushed garlic, chopped veges, squeezed a lime and added condiments to create fragrant vegetable soup. Meanwhile Te Patiki was on the scrounge underfoot, so he let the soup simmer while he fed her.

He made toast and was about to sit down to his meal, but instead he took the two steps down to the lounge, returning moments later with the painted stones. He placed them on a plate nearby, so he could look at them while he ate. He took a sip or two of the too-hot soup, one eye on the stones, but the pattern on the plate was insulting the artwork. He exchanged the patterned plate for a plain one.

Afterwards, he returned the stones to their shelf, but they drew him back often. He held the tattoo stone and played the Fern Unfurl song through his sound system. The music, the image on the stone, and the marine world he saw through the window, all blended together into a brand-new universe, lit by golden eyes.


But he could not forget the fear he'd seen in those eyes. Had his lust been so obvious? He cringed to remember how he'd pulled up his shirt and shown her, a stranger, the tattoo. No wonder he'd terrified her.

His embarrassment at the memory helped Rōreka to resist phoning her, but he kept the card handy. For the next two months he worked hard at songwriting and recording, inspired to produce some of his best songs. He crossed to the "mainland" for some profitable gigs, taking all his gear in the van on the Opua car-ferry. He lost all interest in the girls who threw themselves at him during his work breaks. He'd never been keen on exploiting those airheads anyway – however pretty they were, their shallowness bored him.

As usual, he did a lot of running on the hilly roads and trails of the Kororareka peninsula and ate a lot to fuel it. In good weather, he spent time in his kayak, exploring the glittering waters between the islands and along the coastlines, of the bay.

When he needed to smoke, he held the smooth stone, remembering the beauty of its creator. He took it to gigs, kept it in his pocket as a remedy for nicotine cravings. The congestion continued to clear from his lungs. His voice smoothed out. He sang better, breathed easier, ran faster, kayaked further, and grew stronger.


Sooner or later, he was bound to run into her again in the small island-like community of Kororareka. It happened on the ferry. Rōreka was first on board at the Paihia wharf and spotted her in the queue coming aboard behind him. She sat towards the stern on the opposite side and appeared not to notice him. He looked over his shoulder at her several times, but she was always looking out at the passing seascape, her face half hidden by a shining curtain of dark hair, its red fire ignited by sunlight shafting through the cabin windows.

The boat docked at Kororareka wharf. Disembarking, he looked her way again and finally caught her eye. She showed no sign of recognition and turned away. Was she choosing to ignore him or simply not recognising him? He'd been one among dozens she spoke to that day. And she'd speak to hundreds more on other days. You couldn't expect her to remember. But then, how could she forget the shirt-raising incident? He cringed, just thinking of it.

A few weeks later, late at night, he'd just finished a gig at the boat club in Matauwhi Bay. He packed his music gear into the van, drove the half kilometre to Kororareka village, parked near the tennis court, and walked to the waterfront. The wharf stretched out into the darkness before him, but a hundred metres or so along the beach a fire burned. He stepped down onto the beach and crunched across the pebbles towards it. A small crowd of revellers sat round the flames, drinking, and singing raucously. They badly needed a guitarist. After playing two hours in the boat club, he wasn't about to volunteer. The fire lit up the frilly white edges of the wavelets combing the pebbles.

His eyes scanned the people sitting within reach of the firelight. And there she was, Manaia, chatting with a group of female friends. He stared at her for a moment and then dropped to the sand, fairly sure she hadn't noticed his arrival in the darkness.

The flamboyance of their clothing suggested her group were members of Kororareka's active art community. He recognised a couple of well-known local artists. She seemed comfortable among them, and he suspected she might exhibit her work with theirs at South Sea Art. He made a mental note to visit the little gallery behind the flowering bougainvillea on York Street.

After a few minutes of listening to the cacophony, he stood up again and walked back to his vehicle to collect the old guitar that lay among the more professional music equipment he'd used for the gig. He returned to the fire and began to strum and sing along, much to the delight of the revellers. The drunken singing roared louder and cheerier than before.

Rōreka hoped she would notice him, that she would like his singing as much as he liked her art. To keep them all happy, he mostly sang old party songs that everyone knew the words to, but also one or two of his own. Some of the locals knew even those well enough to sing along.

He did not look at Manaia, but he focused his singing on her.

Human music hardly compares to marine music. But this moment in the lives of two lonely people revealed the intent behind the song. He sang softly, but sweeter than ever, because she was there on the far side of the fire. On this night, even a dolphin might have heard the thin strain of true beauty in his songs.

He stopped singing at last, letting the old guitar rest across his knees. Wavelets rattled the pebbles and the fire sputtered. Many moored boats lay at rest in the bay, their hulls aglow in reflected light from the wharf. Far away across the bay, the lights of Paihia glittered.

Rōreka caught a movement from someone standing beyond the flames. The dying firelight revealed a face. Manaia was coming his way.

Would she walk straight past?

She sat beside him.

'The man with the tattoo,' she said.

Ouch, he thought, but he smiled at her.

'I like your songs,' she said.

'I love your art,' he said.

She asked if he still had the stones he'd bought.

'Of course,' he said, and she seemed pleased.

He almost pulled out the tattoo stone from his pocket as proof, but stopped himself in time, not wanting to smother her from the start. Start? Start of what?

'I wish,' he thought.

She asked him about his music. He asked her about her art. It made for easy conversation. Friendship flowered, right there on the fire-lit beach within sight of Kororareka wharf.

When she stood to leave at last, he walked her back with her friends to their car. Halfway there, he reached out to take her hand, but she pretended not to see and turned away. Clearly, the physical space between them must not be breached.

At home he checked in his mirror to see what had repulsed her, but his reflection was the same as always, nothing startling but nothing hideous either. He was twenty-six, average height, lean from all his running and kayaking, his dark hair and colouring reflecting his part-Māori ancestry. He found no newly developed vileness that could explain her response to him. Most girls were far more interested.

He kept her card but did not contact her, apart from a rare text to find out if she was coming to the market or to let her know he was going there himself. They met up casually a few times, and he bought more stones, but the no-touching rule stayed firm.

It stung. She was so friendly, as long as he never approached the line he wanted so much to cross.

He visited South Sea Art on York Street and found a collection of her work there. Larger stones than the ones she sold at the market. These were high-impact paintings, too big to hold in the hand, but perfect for wall or table-top display. They were not cheap, and he couldn't afford it but there was one he longed to own. A fantasy of dolphins, rays, orcas, seabirds, clouds, stars, and moonbeams. The subjects might have been nothing more than cute, but for the blackness haunting the design, twisting throughout like centuries of history.

He calculated how much he'd saved, not buying smokes. More than the cost of this beautiful object? Sure. The perfect reward for abstinence.

He took it home and placed it in the middle of the huge wooden coffee table he'd made himself from demo kauri. He placed the smaller stones around it like chicks around a mother bird. He sat on the couch, staring alternately out the window over the bay and down at the big stone before him. He reached out, caressed it. Then he picked up one of the smaller ones. It nestled in his palm, smooth and glowing, like her skin.

They were again sitting on Kororareka beach, a hundred metres or so from the Duke of Marlborough hotel, famous as the first public house in Aotearoa, and known to locals simply as The Duke. No firelight this time but there was light from the wharf and the stars. They were alone and sitting as usual with the gap between them, the gap she required for comfort, the gap he longed to close.

'Why don't you like me to touch you?' he said.

'It's not just you. It's all men. I fear all that.'

'Why?'

'It might trigger The Mávro.'

'Mávro?'

'Black shadow. Depression. My old struggle. Ever since I was sixteen, five years ago.'

So, she's twenty-one he thought, surprised she was that old and surprised she was that young.

'What causes The Mávro?'

'I can't be sure of the real reason, but I had a baby at that age, and it started after that.'

'You have a child?'

'Not anymore. She was killed.'

'Oh my God, that would give anyone depression.'

She looked away from him.

There was a very long silence. Rōreka saw that she'd begun to shake, was fighting for control. He so wanted to hold her, to comfort her, but he waited. She continued to face away, and gradually the shaking slowed, and she turned, not to look at him, but to stare out to sea.

And then she started to talk. She told him everything, from the rape in Samoa to the deaths of her closest family.

Another long silence. Only now did he recognise the knife-edge he'd been balancing on. He looked into her face. Was she even breathing?

'Breathe,' he whispered.

She breathed. He breathed.

'I knew there was something,' he said at last. 'It haunts all your work.'

His hand lay open on the sand. She laid her hand in his. His fingers closed around hers.

A light westerly blew in their faces raising wavelets that rattled the beach pebbles. Laughter floated their way – drinkers on the terrace at The Duke. He spoke again.

'Thanks for telling me this,' he said. 'I understand now.'

'I rarely speak of it,' she admitted.

They shared a long stillness.

She's been smashed to pieces, he thought, and stuck back together with too-thin glue.

'It's late,' she said at last.

'I'm going for a swim' he said. 'Want to come?'

'Now? In the dark?'

'I love swimming in the dark.'

'But there could be anything out there.'

'I swim at night all the time. It's safe as houses.'

'You go. I never swim.'

He stripped off his shirt and ran into the waves wearing nothing but his shorts. He dived under and disappeared into the black sea.


Manaia sat on the beach, a memory playing in her mind. She was a child again, sneaking to the beach at night, swimming in the velvet darkness. How had she done it? Why? She remembered the reason at last.

Because the tide was in. As simple as that.

Her hand crept down her leg and rubbed the spot where the shark-scars traced threads on her skin – so faint now that no-one but Manaia knew they were there.


A few days later she bought and downloaded an album of his songs and listened until she knew every word by heart. She collected all his music. Just as the tattoo/song had matched her painted stone, his other songs became soundtracks for some of her new stones.

Soon she allowed him to hold her hand as they walked, and one day as they strolled on the beach at Oneroa Bay, Manaia spoke again of her mother.

'She told me that not all men were monsters and one day I'd meet one who was kind and gentle. I tried to believe her.'

'She was right!' said Rōreka. 'And I'm him!'

He beat his chest like a rampant gorilla. Manaia laughed and he kissed her on the cheek, just once, so briefly, light as the touch of a butterfly. She accepted it unflinchingly.

Before they parted that day, he said, 'There's something I want to show you.'

'Something big or something small?' she asked.

'Small.'

'Worthless or valuable?'

'Very very valuable,' he said, 'at least it is to me.'

'Animal? Mineral? Or vegetable?' she asked.

He thought a moment.

'It's not animal or vegetable so I guess its mineral. Yes! Mineral.'

'Do you own it?'

'I do. And I'm not about to give it to you. Is this Twenty Questions?'

'Hmmm. Maybe. Meanie. What if I really want it?'

'You can't have it. Okay? Next question.'

'How old is this thing?'

'Ummm. As old as the hills. But probably less than a year old.'

'That doesn't make sense. But now I'm curious. Can I ask one last question?'

'Go for it.'

'Where is this thing?'

'In my pocket.'

'How long has it been there?'

'You said one last question.'

'I haven't had twenty yet. How long has it been in your pocket?' she said again.

'Since I met you. I keep it there always.'

'Did I make it?'

'Yes, you did.'

'Which stone is it?'

'This one – the tattoo stone.'

He pulled it out of his pocket and showed her. She stared down at it in silence for an eternal thirty seconds. He saw tears escaping. Then she kissed him.

Later he told her how many of her painted stones he already owned.

'That would have cost a bit – spendthrift,' she laughed.

'You're right,' he admitted, 'always in financial strife.'

'You don't fear the future then?' she asked.

'I fear all sorts of things about the future,' he replied. 'But I try to act on logic – not on fear.'

'That could have advantages and disadvantages,' she mused, 'Give me some examples.'

'OK. I fear poverty but that won't stop me from buying your beautiful art. And . . . I fear the effects of climate change but it's logic that keeps me vegan - not fear.'

'You're vegan because of climate change?'

'That's only one of three reasons. The other two are animal ethics and my own health.'

'Me too for the same reasons. It's a no-brainer in today's world,' she said.

'I'm also healthier if I don't smoke.'

'You look pretty healthy.'

'But I smoked too much before. There's another example. I stopped, not because I feared a future of ill-health but because logic told me the drawbacks outweigh the rewards. Stopping wasn't easy and really, I'm still addicted.'


As time passed Manaia found that Natia had spoken the truth. Rōreka was that kind man she'd spoken of so long ago. Little by little the two grew closer until, in the end, she couldn't imagine life without him. Within a year or two she was ready to move in with him.

Rōreka wanted to share everything he owned with her, so she returned the favour, sold her house at Te Wahapu and cleared Rōreka's mortgage, leaving them with equal shares in the Jacks Bay house, easing the financial pressure he'd been under for so long.

During the weeks that Manaia went through the procedure of selling up, Rōreka renovated the big attic room for her use as a studio. He remembered how beautiful the stones had looked on the white plate and decided that white was the colour for her workspace. The varnish on the sloping timber ceiling had aged well and only needed a good clean, but the walls and floor were a mess. He used the threadbare carpet as a drip-catcher while he repainted. Then he ripped it away, revealing the same original matai floorboards that lay throughout the house. He sanded and oiled the timber to celebrate its dark-honey colour.

The room had all the light an artist would need, from side windows and large sliders leading to the wooden deck facing the sea. He left the windows bare.

'She'll want to choose curtains herself,' he thought. 'I bet she chooses blue ones to go with that view.'

The view looked out over the waters and islands of Manawaora bay and the Te Rawhiti Inlet. Dazzling plumes of spray flew up where the ocean swells burst against the Black Rocks off the eastern end of Moturoa. Further off, the distant hills, faint on the northern side of the bay. The several headlands jutting seawards on the nearer left were all bush covered. No houses or buildings visible. He loved seeing nothing but nature, but he hoped she didn't find it too lonely. A handful of sailing boats swung on permanent moorings close below in Jills Bay, and you could nearly always spot a sail in the distance or some sign of life out on the water. That might help. And for two or three weeks around the Christmas "silly season" there would be whole floating villages of family cruising boats, temporarily occupying the most sheltered anchorages.

That view! No doubt the sea dominated it, glowing in from the north-west under sun and moon, swept by gentle breezes and raging storms. The neighbours' homes were so unobtrusive, he was well secluded from all on the land, but his hillside house was wide open to the sea.

Manaia was delighted with the room. She placed her own familiar big table in the middle as a work surface. She used skills she'd learnt from Tawera to build shelves and workbenches along the two side walls. She placed favourite chairs, lights, cabinets, and pictures, she'd brought from her once-loved childhood home. She pretended to admire the view, but the sea was wilder here, bluer too and far more alive. Surely it was trying to reach in and grab her.

Her choice of drapes amazed Rōreka. She hung two layers – a close white mesh, dense enough to almost block the view without shutting out the light, and over this a heavy jet-black fabric. She kept the mesh layer closed all day while she worked.

'It diffuses the light,' she explained. 'I can always open them to look at the view.'

But she rarely did.

Sometimes when she was alone, she closed the black ones too, even in the daytime. Then she sat in near darkness doing nothing. The dark curtains helped to keep the ocean at bay, but still she heard it out there, breathing at her, scratching on the sand.

The protective blackness spread from the curtains into her work in an ever-increasing line of defence against too much blue.

Manaia hoped her new life would banish The Mávro. She hoped in vain.


But a new hope sprung alive in her mind. If she could just give birth again, the baby might be Fran, come back to her. One day she found a stone the size and shape of a human womb and she painted a new-born baby onto the stone, into that womb. The little body, the little face was engraved so deep in her heart, she painted without reference to any photo. It was an image worthy of sharing with the universe if only humans knew how. But this was more than art. This was a visual prayer for Fran to be reborn to her – a prayer so powerful, The Powers of the universe must surely heed. But it was too late. Manaia was already pregnant.

Manaia did not sell the Fran stone. She displayed it in her studio. Its power did not wane with the passing of time.

# 14 – TAKING THE MOON PATH

Melody sped north alone, the spectre in tireless pursuit. She arrived at Takau Bay north of Ipipiri. Many humans were surfing there.

'They like surfing,' she thought, 'so they must have something in common with dolphins.'

The humans rode the surf on stiff boards.

She chose one female from a group of four humans and swam, submerged, behind her.

The woman drove her board out through the surf, trying to keep up with the others.

Melody listened to her thoughts. It was easier than reading most dolphins. Humans had no idea that others might be listening in.

They cover their bodies for physical privacy, she thought, but they think publicly.

Melody searched the woman's mind and saw its isolation. Her first impulse was to send comfort.

'You're not alone in the galaxy. You're not even alone on this planet. Let us teach you.'

She waited in vain for a response.

'Am I in the lead yet?' the woman thought, 'No, dammit.'

Melody tried again, 'You're not alone . . .'

'Oh, here's a good wave! But I've missed it. Has anyone else caught it? Yes, Mick, bugger him.'

'LET ME HELP YOU!'

But the woman thought only of herself in relation to the rest of the group. Melody tried with other members of the same group. The results were no better.

It seemed these humans were too focused on their companions. She decided to seek out solitary ones.

Solitary humans were harder to find. Most seemed pleased to see her, and though she swam near many, none noticed the spectre.

She surfaced and breathed, close to a lone man and his board. He jumped at the sudden sound but relaxed when he saw her.

He's not afraid of me! Don't humans see my spectre? She swam with the man for several minutes but detected no fear, no awareness of the dread presence. Perhaps humans can't see auras, she thought. Were they all as blind as oysters?

It was a change to be near warm-blooded beings who didn't fear her, even if they were only human. The humans did not see the evil presence, even though Melody could feel her bones, freezing harder and deeper by the hour.

She remembered the advice of The Powers to use music and tried streaming songs to them. Nothing worked. As futile as singing to a rock or a cloud.

She sped north and tried in vain to ignore the spirit freeze, unable to focus on her task. The spectre was recovering from all it had lost during her astral voyage and now it forced her to swim furiously back and forth along the coast, anywhere to keep moving. Physical exhaustion was better than supernatural chill. Would she swim herself to death?

She prayed to sea and sky, 'Help me!'

As though in answer to her prayer, the upper rim of the full moon appeared over the eastern horizon at that moment. Melody thought the moon had called her to swim that way and who knows? Perhaps it had. She accelerated away from all humans along the silver pathway leading to the open sea. She avoided rest, fed as she went, mainly on high-fluid jellies that kept her tissues hydrated. She ate a few denser fish, hoping their energy would help to warm her.

The spectre was unaware who waited in the east. He goaded her to swim but cared not which direction.

By the time she approached the waters of the Great Deep, she was floundering, colours and sounds beginning to fade. Breathing was too hard. She wallowed, approaching coma – certain death for dolphins.

She managed one last breath and stopped. Stopped breathing. Stopped swimming.

The spectre celebrated.

But he celebrated too soon. As consciousness faded, Melody became aware of a slight warming of her near-frozen Spirit. What had caused it? She made a last effort and breathed one more time. Oxygen to the blood. A faint revival.

Clicks and coda resounded through the water. Sperm whales! She summoned some last reserves of energy and struggled towards them. Six young bulls and one old one, socialising together at the surface. She hesitated, intimidated, almost turning aside. She breathed again. But they were aware of her now, scanning her. The spectre! Would it upset them? She allowed her thoughts to escape unveiled. The whales heard. They swam her way.

'Sick spirit, you may approach,' called the old one. 'Your phantom does not bother us.'

Her flukes fluttered, hesitated, pushed her closer.

'We invite you to swim within our auras. It will bring relief.'

As Melody entered the waters lit by their auras, her chill blew away like mist in the wind. Every muscle in her body released its tension, soaking in the spiritual radiance of the whales. She was like a human sliding into a warm bath after shivering too long through wind and snow. She floated, warm at last.

Melody cruised the bow-wave of Wairua Nui – the huge oldest whale. She dozed beside his massive blunt head, adrift in his healing slipstream. He carried her there until she'd rested her whole body and both sides of her brain. Then the whales took her to find sweet prey at suitable sizes and depths for her needs. The food hydrated and energised her. The spectral chill revived when she left the whales to hunt but faded when she returned to the glow of their auras.

Then it was the whales' turn to hunt. Their tails curved skywards, their heads plunged, their flukes powered them downwards to unimaginable depths. Their hunting coda echoed back from the abyss. But Wairua Nui, stayed with Melody, keeping her warm.

Melody had no need to tell him her story. He saw it all in the writhing coils of her spectre.

'Can you banish this thing?' she asked him.

'Only you can banish it forever,' he replied, 'but you'll need to build strength for the task.'

'How may I gain the strength?'

'We are mind, body, and spirit. This is a malady of spirit. Strength in body and mind will help to heal spirit. But there are other ways. This began when humans killed your son. How do you feel about humans?'

'I hate them with all my heart!'

'Why?'

'They killed my mother and my son. They kill so many things. Of course, I hate them.'

'What is the opposite of hate?'

'Love, I suppose.'

'What is love?'

'Love is what I feel for dolphins, the ocean itself, the singing wind and all the beautiful beings who live in the sea or fly across it.'

There was a long silence from Wairua Nui. Above them, a wandering albatross tilted to the breeze, rarely moving a feather of his wind-loving wings. Cloud shadows scurried over the ocean.

A question from Wairua Nui floated into Melody's consciousness.

'If you hate humans so much, why are you trying to communicate with them?'

'The Powers of the Universe asked me to.'

'Who are they, Melody?'

'I don't have a clue. I met them in outer space. Do you know?'

'I do. They are you.'

She did not reply. The albatross swooped low, his wingtips almost touching the water. The whale and the dolphin watched the great bird, admiring his grace.

'Give me some of your renowned music, Melody.'

'If I could make new music, I would make a song for that bird, but I can create no new songs. My vocation is lost to me. I can only give you my old ones.'

'Let's share your old songs then.'

No human would have heard a sound, but the whale, immersed himself in Melody's music. It rang in the thoughtstreams that poured from mind to mind. Even the albatross caught echoes.

'Your music is full of love,' said the whale.

One of the hunting whales arrived to release Wairua Nui to his own banquet in the deep. Thus, while the whales hunted, Melody was never alone and stayed always warm in the halo of at least one of them. She shared music with them all.

A young bull called Thunderflukes spoke to her on her third day among them.

'You are one of Libran's females, are you not?' he asked. 'He's given us great pleasure through his curation of the visual arts of the galaxies.'

'I met him just after he received the Raiman artworks,' she told him. 'I'll always treasure the first picture he showed me of that world.'

'Which one was it?'

'The triple-mooned landscape named Moondance. I loved it for the music in its vision.'

'Oh Moondance! I've stood beside that painting. It's over three hundred thousand years old.'

'Impossible!' whispered Melody.

'What's impossible? It's age? My being beside it? A legless whale standing? Or perhaps my remembering it?'

'All of those.'

'We whales bear Past Life Memory. Only one thousand, nine hundred and eighty-seven lives ago I lived on Raima as a multi-limbed species. That painting was already old then, but Raiman technology preserved it. When your Libran displayed it to us, I recognised it.'

Melody's mind turned somersaults. If Ātārangi had Past Life Memory, he'd remember the net. Why die, if memory must continue?

'Past Life Memory! How do you endure it?' she asked.

'Of all species on Azure, only whales have the spiritual maturity for such a burden. Some of our babies need careful nurture if their most recent death was painful or sad.'

'Have you ever lived here on Azure before?'

'No. Not me. And of course, the chances are slight, considering all the millions of inhabited planets in the universe. It did happen once though; a blue whale lived and died on Azure, thousands of years ago, then lived 378 alien lives before rebirth here as a fin whale just 600 years ago. She was delighted to be back, though I doubt she'd be so happy to return for a third time.'

'Tell me more about Raima,' said Melody.

Thunderflukes told stories of his life there. She enriched the stories with music, and they used Libran's visual treasures as illustrations. Before long Raima seemed almost as familiar as Azure itself. Then they talked of planets in other galaxies while music, art, and story from those planets, poured like rivers through their minds.

Meanwhile, as she basked in the warmth of the whales, with the spectre ever-present at her shoulder, his freezing spirit-chill receded until it seemed unlikely ever to return. When Melody left the whales to hunt, she felt it again, but less and less as time passed. Still, the only time it disappeared altogether was when she was close beside them.

She tried to create a song, hoping that the presence of the whales might allow the return of her gift. New music seemed closer than ever here in their protective zone, but as before it faded into a silence that soon echoed with dreaded memories. She stopped trying, not wanting to bring horrors into this sanctuary.

Fibre by fibre, all her muscles, blood vessels and bodily organs healed from the strain they had endured during her flight east. The training effect of recovery after effort left her stronger and fitter than before. She began looking forward to long fast swims in the future, now that she knew where to find rest again when she needed it.

Thunderflukes suffered from an ache in his caudal muscles. Melody scanned him and found a knot of tension there. She used penetrative sound to relax and re-align the tissues, happy to give this small reward for the relief the whole pod had brought her.

'I wish a dolphin would stay with us always,' he said.

'I can't stay for always,' she replied, 'but I promise to return often.'

She stayed six days. By then she could leave the protection of the whales and feel no chill from the spectre, though he was as visible as ever. Wairua Nui warned her that the chill would slowly rebuild.

'When it becomes too much to bear, return and we will warm you.'

'How can I repay you?'

'We'll save up our aches and pains for healing by your dolphin sounds, next time you visit us.'

'Done,' she said, and they laughed together.

'But seriously Melody, if you succeed in your task, the whole planet may have reason to thank you. It's our honour to help you in any way we can.'

Wairua Nui swam with her for the first hour or so, as she began her journey home.

When he turned back at last towards his pod, he whacked his mighty flukes on the surface in farewell. She replied with a corkscrew leap, sending a dazzle of spray sky-high as she hit the water on re-entry. Then she swam away to the west, in search of her own pod.

Remembering his advice to strengthen body and mind, she swam at great speed for long intervals and now she could rest at slower speeds when she needed to.

'So much for body, but what about mind?' she thought. 'How do I strengthen mind?'

The obvious was to create new music. If only.

Days later as she approached Ipipiri, she contacted Libran. He came to meet her bringing Zeta, Elethea and Antares. They swam together for an hour or two until twinges from the spectre reminded her that time was limited. She swam away north, alone, to continue her work with humans.

<h1 style="text-align:center">15 – BASHING THE WALL</h1>

Melody arrived at Coopers Beach – a curving stretch of pale sand on the southern reaches of Doubtless Bay. Low buildings sat between the beach and the hills beyond. A man walked by the water. He wore extra layers of body-coverings, perhaps for protection from the windy evening.

'Good,' she thought. 'He's alone.'

But he was not alone in mind.

He carried a rectangular object in his hands, about the size of a mussel shell. He was using it to send and receive long-distance messages. Why didn't he just use his own brain? Melody tried to show him how by demonstrating.

'You don't need that thing. Use your brain to do it. Can you hear me?'

'The stock price is sharply down in the after-hours market.'

'What are you talking about?' said Melody.

'We think they screwed up their earnings estimates,' he replied to his far-away contact.

'I have a message for you from the sea,' she said, 'Listen to me!'

'I'm probably going to talk to JK tonight about buying more shares.'

*'Answer me!'* she thoughtscreamed, but she was wasting her time again. No matter how intensely she beamed thoughts into his brain, there was not the slightest response. As before, she was thankful that no other dolphins were watching. And the chill of the spectre was already returning. She swam harder against it.

Marine music flowed towards her over the ocean.

Orcas. Four of them. Some orca pods were dangerous, but this was Vrinda's pod of eunivores - those who did not prey on warm blood. They were sharing music and conversation like any pod of dolphins.

'I need not fear them,' she thought. 'I just hope they don't fear me.'

'A being passes west of us at speed,' said Michio, the biggest male in the pod. His dorsal fin towered two metres tall.

'Is it food?' said Haru, his smallest brother.

'No. It's warm-blooded. A lone dolphin, I think,' said Vrinda, the matriarch. 'But take care. I see an unnatural aural loom. Something's wrong here.'

'It's red. Could this be Melody, the musician? They say she carries a red horror in her aura and travels alone on her futile mission,' said Michio.

'Yes, I'm Melody. I may alarm you.'

'Approach us. You're safe here.'

She swam into their view. They recoiled only slightly at the sight of her.

'My pod harms no dolphins and loves your music,' said Vrinda, 'But I doubt even the rogue orca pods would trouble you, my dear. Your visible affliction takes away the appetite.'

'You respond less fearfully than my own kind,' said Melody.

'Can we help you?'

'No, I must work alone. The spectre grows in power and when it becomes too much to bear, I seek relief from Wairua Nui.'

'Wairua Nui hunts far from here.'

'Yes, I must allow time for the journey to him. The horror limits my time, so I must work now while I can.'

'Good luck then, Melody. We wish you triumph. May your gift return quickly to our seas.'

Melody swam away, alone again, but her interaction with the mighty eunivores had warmed her.

She hunted as she travelled. To build body-heat, she swam triple the shortest distance to Cable Bay, arriving as the wind was dying and the sea calming.

A woman sat alone high on the beach, waves hushing towards her as she gazed out to sea. Melody hoped the woman's solitude and mellow surroundings might help her to receive a voice from the ocean. She sent her a thoughtstream so intense it would have hurt the sensitive reception of any dolphin.

'I have messages *from the sea*.'

'Our house is way too small. It's crazy to go on living like this.'

'Humanity is not alone. *Listen, listen!*'

'We have to get a bigger one.'

'Can you see me jumping? Can you hear me?'

'We only have one bathroom! Everyone else has two. I knew I should have married a richer guy.'

'Turn your mind this way. *I'm out here.*'

'Even my silly sister has two. It's so humiliating. I hate her.'

Melody kept trying but the woman only thought of complicated pipes, hard objects, coloured surfaces and running water arranged inside containing walls, a lot of material stuff, almost beyond a dolphin's power to comprehend. And this woman was wanting to have these objects, to own them and keep them near her. Why? Why not just forget it all and wander away in freedom?

Melody remembered what The Powers had told her: 'Not all humans are evil. They would listen if they could.'

The woman sat staring. She noticed neither the ocean nor the sweet scent of the breeze. She heard none of the thousand voices singing in the waters. Nor did she see the dolphin leaping in the distance, tiny but clear. She stood at last and walked away unconsoled. Melody pitied her.

By this time, she was very cold. She swam hard for two hours, returning to the same bay. The effort warmed her just enough to try again.

The bay was full of fish, so she hunted first.

As evening approached, a man rowed his light wooden dinghy out from the shore. The boat was beautifully crafted – leaf-shaped, with delicate ribs flaring from the keel.

This boat proves, she thought, that the human hand is capable, as well as dangerous.

She admired the physics of the rowlocks making a fulcrum for the oars.

Mankind, lacking useful fins, makes wooden ones, she mused, and there's no danger in wooden fins, unlike the spinning metal ones that killed my mother.

The man shipped his oars now and lowered his little anchor, paying out the warp until it reached the seabed. But a loop of the warp wrapped around the anchor flukes preventing them from gripping the mud. The tide and slight breeze slowly pushed the boat seawards. The man was too busy with his fishing gear to notice his drift.

Even without hands, I can help him with this, Melody thought.

Unseen by the human, she swam down, tucked her rostrum under the loop of warp and nosed it away, freeing the anchor flukes to grip the mud. The boat stopped drifting. Success!

She'd teamed with the man for that moment, not that he knew it, but it gave her a sense of kinship.

Now he was working on his fishing line, probably baiting the hook as humans do. She read the thoughts behind his muttered words.

'Good-oh Jimmy-me-boy,' he muttered, 'looks just like the real thing.'

He lowered the end of the fishing line into the water, and she saw that Jimmy had not baited the hook – instead he'd removed it. There was nothing on the end of the line but a small lead weight holding it down in the water. How could it possibly work?

As though in reply, Jimmy said, 'Wouldn't want to hurt a fish.'

How could this man, who didn't want to hurt a fish, belong to the same species that dragged fish to their doom by millions of tons? And Jimmy had some reason for pretending to fish. Her curiosity grew.

Jimmy sat with his back to the land. She watched him from behind and, staying tuned to his thoughts, she detected great loneliness.

The words of The Powers flashed to mind: 'the most isolated species in the galaxy.'

I could console this human, she thought, if only I could reach him.

Jimmy began searching through his bag of gear.

'Where did I put that bottle?'

He found the bottle, uncapped it, and sipped. A warm glow spread over his thoughts.

Aue! she thought. I believe he has his own solace on hand. A human version of our puffer-fish fumes.

She continued to read his thoughts: This is the life! The she-wolf can't get to me now. I can relax and have a drink after a hard day's work. Shame I don't have a few mates with me, or better still, any female except the she-wolf.


He ignored his non-functional fishing gear, settled into his seat, and gazed around at the fading light of day, enjoying his bottle. Unlike the unlucky woman at Cable Bay, this human was at least enjoying the beauty of his surroundings. Melody began streaming.

'Can you hear me? You're not as alone as you think.'

'Look at those clouds,' he thought, 'all golden and puffy. Hey, there's a cloud with big ears like Mickey Mouse.'

'Can you hear me? I have a message for you.'

'Now they're going pink. That one looks like a pink pig.'

She looked up, wondering what a pig looked like, but there were too many pink clouds. She sent him a song, so lively it would have woken any dolphin and inspired them to dance. Jimmy yawned and gave no sign he'd heard a note of it. She sent it again, louder this time, trying to pierce his brain. Still no response.

She tried the ancient technique invented by Ripple over twenty million years ago, to send songs by mathematical thoughtstreams, into minds that had never heard music.

Jimmy heard as much of her song as his anchor did. While he studied the clouds, she raised her head very slowly from the water and examined his face with her eye-vision. He did not notice her. He was too busy smiling at the sky, relaxing and sipping regularly.

'Pig. Pink. One little piggy went to market. One little piggy stayed home.'

What was the matter with him? She submerged again.

*'You are not alone.'*

Again and again, she tried to reach him with her thoughts and her music, but Jimmy just crooned a tuneless song and rocked gently in the boat, nursing his bottle. It was more than half empty now.

Would it help if she revealed herself? She surfaced suddenly in a rush of foam and looked straight into his face. He lurched and yelled, and the boat wobbled, almost tipping. He managed to steady it. Her fins worked, holding her in position. Might this direct stare help Jimmy to hear her thoughts?

'Well, whaddaya know,' said Jimmy. 'Good boyth. You'll be a good story to tell at work tomorrow.'

'There's only one of me and I'm female.'

Jimmy seemed happy to think and even talk aloud to her but remained as deaf as ever to the thoughts she sent him.

'Hey, you dolphins, porpishes, whaddever, what'll I do now? Rum's nearly gone.' His brain swirled. 'Can ya bring me up a bottle from Davey Jones? Haw haw! Hic!'

Melody lost her patience. The spectre was cold at her shoulder. She vanished underwater and continued her efforts from there.

'Listen to me, you screwball human!'

Anger simmered, almost erupted. She sensed the spectre goading her. But just in time she remembered the warnings of The Powers.

She breathed, calmed herself, aware of her narrow escape.

But how could disordered intellects like Jimmy's, create the great ships that killed her son? How could minds like these, build bridges and flying machines?

Jimmy checked his line for fish, knowing he could not have caught any. The boat rocked dangerously.

'Woops, easy does it Jimmy-me-boy. Well, waddaya know? No fish. Ha ha haw, and I tried sho hard to catch one. Nothing for the she-wolf's dinner. Never mind, dear – have ta have spuds instead.'

His eyes were as bleary as his brain. His head and shoulders drooped. He sat up, drained the bottle, and slumped back on the thwart.

'Home now. Work tomorrow.' He picked up an oar and tried to fit its rowlock into the chock. The oar fell overboard, and he almost capsized the boat trying to reach it. She nosed it towards him.

'Thought the dolphin passed me th'oar. Must be pissed. Thanks boys. Good boys.'

He saluted, then after much effort he fitted the two oars in place and tried to row, but the warp ran out and jerked the boat to a stop, and for the second time he almost tipped out. He dropped the oars half inboard and half out, then sat trying to work out what had made the boat stop. He remembered the anchor at last and laughed aloud.

'Oooh, Jimmy-me-boy, you won't get far with the anchor down.'

He staggered forward. The boat rolled dangerously. He pulled in the warp until it was in a straight line down to the anchor on the sea floor. He pulled again trying to dislodge it from its secure grip. The boat rocked and bucked. The anchor held. He stood to get a better pull. He pulled once, twice, and then gave a third mighty heave. The anchor popped out of the mud and Jimmy fell over backwards into the water. The boat tipped and took water on board but bounced back upright quite lightly now that his weight was gone from it.

Jimmy sank deep in the bay. He flailed his arms and kicked but kept sinking.

Hopeless! Melody dived after him, and he grabbed her so hard it hurt. She dragged him to the surface. He drew in a huge lungful of air in the slow human way of breathing, kept his grip and spluttered words.

'Gawd. That was close. I owe ya one.'

She swam towards the beach until he could stand waist deep and there, to her relief, he released his grip. He floundered a few steps, fell and swallowed a mouthful of water. He righted himself, stumbled ashore, crawled up the beach and collapsed in the sand. He groaned, overcome by vertigo from the poisons in his bloodstream. It made Melody dizzy just to witness that spinning brain. His stomach heaved its contents up and out through his mouth.

A female human was screaming from further up the beach. She ran down to Jimmy and shouted at him – meaningless words of rage, a she-wolf indeed.

He tried to rouse himself, failed and mumbled at her, 'Thorry dear, fish weren't biting. Have spudth instead. Fell in . . . Dolphin . . .'

'Dolphin what?'

'Dolphin thaved me.'

'Jimmy Weston, you're drunk as a skunk.'

He passed out. Melody swam out to where the dinghy bobbed freely, one oar with its blade in the air and the other with its shaft trailing in the water. She took the warp in her mouth and dragged the boat close to the beach. She released the warp, swam behind the boat, and gave it a good shove shoreward. The woman, as she waded out towards the dinghy, did not see the dolphin in the gathering darkness and she was too angry to wonder how Jimmy's boat had come ashore despite an offshore breeze.

The she-wolf struggled with the warp, retrieved the anchor, beached the boat, and dragged it up the sand. She examined the hookless fishing line, then pulled the empty bottle out of the boat and threw it at Jimmy's head. It clunked. The blow deepened his coma.

No wonder he preferred his lonely boat and his bottle, thought Melody as she departed.


Spectral ice crawled through her veins and again she tried to out-swim it, smashing through wave after wave as she hurtled northeast through the darkness. She cleared the headland that stretched north from the southern end of Doubtless Bay.

Already I need the whales, she admitted.

But instead she just kept bashing the same wall.


A light gleamed from the blackness of the open sea. She fled east towards its clear sparkle, ignoring the freezing talons that clawed at her.

That light is human generated, she thought. I'll make one last attempt.

Familiar music drifted faintly on the breeze. Vrinda's pod!


The light swayed like a low-hanging star inspecting the watery surface of Azure. It shone from the masthead of a wooden boat. This boat was the length of five dolphins, and it carried a lone sailor south-east along the coast of Te Tai Tokerau.

She slowed to follow this one small spot of wood-wrapped warmth that floated through her freezing world. The sailor adjusted his ropes and tiller to exploit the pressures of wind and water on his sails, rudder, and keel.

He listened to the whisper of the wind in his rigging, the chuckle of the water at his bows and watched the circumpolar stars as they arced across the sky.

He thinks like a dolphin, she thought. Dare I hope?

She ignored the growing cold.


'I'm Melody. Can you hear me?'

'The stars are turning in the sky,' thought the sailor.

'No, what you see is Azure turning,' she explained.

'The Southern Cross is ablaze!' he continued.

'I have a message for you from the sea.'

'The Milky Way is a river of light.'

'That's the arm of the galaxy. It's true name is Koru Maelstrom.'

'It truly seems like a river of milk.'

'It's nothing at all like milk.'

'With a good breeze tomorrow, I'll reach the Barrier by nightfall.'

She could tell by the pictures in his mind which island he meant by "The Barrier".

'It is a kind of barrier, I suppose,' she admitted.

'On a night like this, who needs a compass?' he thought. 'Every star before my eyes celebrates true south.'

'What on Azure is a compass?'

He accidentally answered her question, by briefly focusing his eyes and mind on a hard object on his boat - a circular device with pretty markings that showed direction. He needed a tool for that? Even a silly quacking duck knows where north is.

She sighed and began again.

'I'm Melody. Can you hear me? Stupid human! I'm going to show myself to you.'

She leapt alongside him, breathing loudly, then splashed down noisily. He missed seeing her but heard the sound. Then he saw a blue comet flying along just beneath the surface, bigger and brighter than any comet in the sky. He recognised that blue light as the living fire of bioluminescence, ignited by the passage of a dolphin.

He shouted aloud, 'Dolphins!' His spirits rose. He hoped they'd stay a while. Then he saw there was only one. He'd never seen a lone dolphin before.

'Hey dolphin!' he called, 'Talk to me. Tell me your stories, boy.'

'I've been talking to you for the last ten minutes!'

Why did these humans always think she was male? He was asking her to talk to him and if he wasn't so deaf to everything she said, she could almost believe he meant it.

She sent him music, using the Ripple techniques as she had with Jimmy, but like Jimmy he failed to receive it. She tried many songs as she swam beside the little vessel – happy songs, sad songs, vivid songs, and soft ones. She sent him her own songs and those of all her favourite dolphin composers. Nothing worked. He sat at his tiller, looking at the stars, glancing often at the flying comet beside him but thinking only his own thoughts, unheeding of hers. And all the time she grew colder and colder until the chill was too hard to ignore.

In desperation she thoughtstreamed a sound she'd never shared with anyone before – a single chord made by a tree-sized flower on the planet Aerdluth as part of a message to its ecosystem. It was literally unearthly - a high keening throb. But still it was only a thoughtstream – not a physical sound.

The man responded! He stood up suddenly, turned, and looked in her direction, supporting the tiller with the side of his leg.

He spoke aloud. 'What was that? Felt like my brain was ringing. That was no dolphin.'

Melody dived, hiding herself from his view. She sent the chord again. The man jumped and rubbed his head. He was hearing her! She was sure of it.

'Hope this isn't the start of a brain tumour,' he thought, 'or some ghost haunting me.'

He tied the tiller, entered the cabin, and somehow caused terrible human music to blare out from inside the boat. Then he re-emerged and focused on nothing but his compass and the hammering music.

'They would listen if they could,' The Powers had said.

But this man had heard it and he wouldn't listen. Her anger grew.

Melody was now too cold, too tired, too alone. Her resolve, her patience, and her courage all dissolved like salt in the rain. In that moment she forgot the warnings from The Powers.

'*Stupid human*! Why won't you listen? I hate you all! You killed my mother! You killed my baby!'

The spectre laughed and clawed at her with demon talons. His coldness engulfed her. Her spirit froze.

Her body became numb, her fins ignored the weakening commands sent to them by her fading consciousness. She made a huge effort and managed one weak cry for help before her mind closed down and she sank like a stone, comatose and paralysed.

Deeper.

Deeper.

The surface glimmered, distant, unreachable, then vanished altogether.

Inky darkness.

Deeper.

Into the abyss.

The spectre began to laugh: 'You're too deep now my beauty. There's no going back from here. I've won.'

But she was past hearing.

'What was that?' said Michio.

'I heard nothing,' said little Haru.

'You're deaf from chomping too many squid. It was a cry for help.'

'I heard it too,' said Vrinda, 'It came from the direction of that human vessel. Swim all of you. Swim!'

They charged towards it, scanning the ocean as they went until Michio picked up the sinking body of a dolphin far too deep in the black water beyond the little sailboat.

'It's Melody,' said Michio.

He dived, using all the power in his huge flukes to rocket his great body down through the blackness until far below him he saw a faint red glow that brightened as he neared it. The laughter of the fiend rang out.

'I win. She's dead. I win. I win.'

Michio thoughtscreamed, 'Don't count your kingfish before you catch, Horror.'

Yes, it was too deep for any dolphin, but not for the huge lungs of a healthy orca.

A last thrust of his flukes sent him all the way down to her. He took her in his massive jaws, ignored the screeching of the enraged spectre and began the return journey. Up, up – towards the glimmer of the starlit surface. He burst through in a blue explosion of bioluminescence.

'She may not be alive,' he warned.

'She's unconscious at least,' said one of the others. 'It's too long since she breathed.'

'If she's alive, I'll make her breathe,' said Vrinda. She sent a mighty pulse of sound into Melody's lungs. Such energy would have shocked a whale to breathe. This was not the subtle style of a team of healer dolphins, but it worked. Melody's lungs were bruised for days afterwards from the force of Vrinda's sound-hit. She breathed and half-woke. First one side of her brain and then the other, returned to life. By then the enraged spectre had slithered back into position just behind her line-of-sight.

But she was beyond helping herself. Even normal speeds were now too hard to maintain. A slight spirit-glow warmed the auras of the orcas surrounding her – just enough to keep her from sliding back into coma and death. It was a diluted version of the great glow given off by the whales of Wairua Nui's pod, but she needed more.

'What happened?' asked Vrinda.

'My own fault. The hate. They warned me.'

'It's over now. Be warm little one.'

'Wairua Nui and his pod are my only hope. But it's too far for me.'

'We'll help you,' said Vrinda.

Melody never forgot those three beautiful words.

For days she swam east in the auras of the orcas, so weak she often dropped out of their slipstream. When that happened, one would carry her back to the easy spot in their massive wake. They hunted for her, bringing jellies, squid, and high-fluid prey. The spectre clung like a leech, burying his ghostly talons to an agonising depth. Oh, how he loved to see her suffer. But whenever she was too beaten to swim, the orcas carried her on their warm backs or gently in their jaws.

On the night of the third day of the journey east, they came to an oxygen-rich current. It provided perfect sleep conditions for a huge white-tip shark they found resting there. Spinal signals kept its muscles operating while its brain slept. It swam slowly into the current with unseeing eyes. It had not expected orcas to pass this way.

Vrinda scanned its body. She saw no fertilised eggs or unborn pups. It was male! A gift to the hungry pod. Michio approached, belly up. He took the shark in his jaws. It woke and thrashed briefly but Michio quickly turned right side up. This flipped the shark upside down, sending it into a trance. In its trance the shark felt neither panic nor pain. Michio held it until it suffocated from the lack of oxygen. Then while he held it firm, the others tore it open to extract the huge liver. The liver floated, making it easy for each orca to take a share.

Michio gave a generous chunk to Melody. Its richness amazed her. Vrinda's eunivores had a no-waste ethic. Once the liver was eaten, they shared the work of carrying the carcass until most of its flesh was consumed. It wasn't easy to rip away the tough outer skin to reach the flesh inside, but they persevered. When the long feast was over, the great hard jaw, still holding tight to rows of massive teeth, and the tough cartilage of the skeleton, escaped at last. The remains made a banquet for many smaller beings of the sea.

Wairua Nui had expected Melody to return by now. He was worried. After all this time, she must surely have succumbed to the spectre. He moved the pod westward hoping to meet her. As he swam, he scanned the ocean for Melody's vibrations and there she was . . . in the jaws of an orca!

Were they rogue orcas? No. This was sweet Vrinda and her pod carrying Melody towards him. The great whales hurried to meet them.

Vrinda released her burden into the warm cloud of whale auras. The spectre gave a final twist to his talons as they arrived, Melody screamed one last time, but his grip weakened, his ice melted and he withdrew to the outer edges of her aura, defeated for now, but biding his time.

Vrinda stayed close for the first hour because Melody's sleep stayed dangerously close to coma. By now Vrinda had learned to moderate her breath-stimulation to suit a dolphin's smaller lungs. Twice during that hour, she helped Melody breathe without bruising her. Only when the coma-danger was over, did Vrinda's pod swim away to their home waters.

Soon Melody was well enough to enjoy her second respite.

The whales kept her warm and safe, ignoring the foulness seething near her as only whales could do.

'How close have you come to succeeding?' Wairua Nui asked Melody.

'I've had only one response from one human when I sent a single sound from the planet Aerdluth.'

'Aerdluth! A world so advanced in compassion.'

'My son lives there with no memory of Azure.'

'The perfect haven for him. How did your human react to the Aerdluthan sound.'

'It terrified him.'

'Was it the sound itself that frightened him?'

'I don't think so. It was the shock. This was not just the first thoughtstream of his life, it was also the first human taste of any kind of life from an alien world.'

'Then,' said the whale, 'perhaps, his terror was understandable despite the chord's origins among the harmonies of Aerdluth.'

'If I could compose again, I could blend the Aerdluthan sounds into Azuran chords to make them less alien to the human mind.'

'Now I understand why The Powers chose you. Only you could do that.'

'Not anymore.'

'There's always hope.'

'I made a mistake with that human,' said Melody.

'Tell me,' said Wairua Nui.

'I'd been warned against it too. I worked so hard with him because at first, he seemed so dolphin-like, in his love of stars and the forces of nature. But still nothing worked. The Aerdluthan chord was my last hope and he heard! I'm sure of it. But in his terror, he refused to accept that beautiful thoughtstreamed sound. By then I was so weakened by the spectre, I forgot the warning and gave in to hate and anger. If not for Vrinda's pod I would have died alone right there.'

'But this is progress of a kind,' he said. 'Though it failed, it's still a hopeful sign that humans are reachable.'

'Yes,' she agreed. 'I've learned much from this failure.'

Once home in Ipipiri, she returned to her task. But now she worked harder at controlling all those fiery emotions. The spectre fed on them, so she starved him. It left her hollow but eventually she could last months without needing rejuvenation by the whales. Years slipped by. She slogged away. The few humans who received the Aerdluthan chord blocked it in terror, just as the lone sailor had done.

Her musical creativity did not return, though she sought for it in every passing ripple, every breath of wind, and every living heart, beating in the sea.

The Powers had encouraged her to have another child. Was giving birth again, now the only worthwhile achievement she could hope for?

So, from time to time she holidayed with her home pod near Ipipiri and spent time whenever possible with Libran.

# 16 - STAR-CHILD AND WATER-BABY

Manaia lumbered up the stairs to her studio, no easy task with the baby due any day. This pregnancy felt so different. Could it be a boy? But the scans said girl.

So, it must be Fran, she thought.

She ran her hand over the cool surface of the Fran stone.

'You're coming back to me. I'm sure of it,' she whispered.

Sure enough, a girl arrived on schedule. This birth was much easier. Manaia wished she looked more like Fran.

You'll be her on the inside though, she thought. You'll be Fran in spirit, and that's the important thing.

She thought of naming her Fran but Rōreka suggested Takurua, for Sirius – the brightest star. Manaia liked the idea that she would have a star-name like her grandfather Tawera. So Takurua it was.

When Takurua cried, Manaia listened for echoes of Fran in her voice, but heard none. She sought Fran in Takurua's eyes but saw no trace.

There were moments of hope.

'She reached out her hand just like Fran used to.'

Or . . .

'She rolled over like Fran did.'

But when Manaia showed Takurua pictures in the bright colours Fran loved, Takurua ignored them. The baby smiled and gurgled at a quilt lying over the back of a chair, lost in its delicate pastel colours and intricate pattern. When Manaia moved the quilt, Takurua's eyes followed it. When she could not see it, she stopped smiling. When Manaia brought it back, Takurua smiled again and reached out to it.

'Are you abnormal or something?' said Manaia. 'Your sister would have ignored this wishy-washy thing. Babies are supposed to like bright colours.'

Takurua played in the bath with her duck and the other floating toys. Manaia let water run before her eyes. Takurua chewed the plastic duck and ignored the flowing water. Manaia tried again, but Takurua was not Fran and she preferred the toys. Manaia took them away and poured water again. Takurua cried because the toys had gone.

'What's the matter with you?' snapped Manaia. She wanted to shake some sense into the child.

Manaia's Mávro stayed for three days after that. It was hard to drag herself through each hour and continue caring for her baby. Dirt threatened from every corner and shadow. She fought back by cleaning until the house sparkled.

'Not the kid's fault,' she told herself, but the gloom and imaginary dirt were heavy burdens when the sun was shining and nothing was wrong.

Takurua grew, healthy and beautiful. Rōreka carried her around in their baby-carrier backpack. He talked to her and sang to her. When summer came, she and Rōreka took Takurua down to Jills Bay. Manaia sat on the sand with the brim of her floppy hat turned down to hide all my blueness. Rōreka made sand sculptures and sand drawings to entertain his precious cargo. Takurua peeped over his shoulder at the works-in-progress. Manaia closed her eyes and rebuked herself.

I'm an ungrateful sulk, she thought. I have a healthy baby, a loving husband, a seaside home, an interesting vocation, everything I need and enough to eat. But I can hardly smile at my own baby.

'I'll take Takurua into the water,' said Rōreka. 'It's so hot - it'll cool her and wash the sand off.'

'Are you sure it's safe?'

'There's nothing dangerous.'

'You see sharks from your kayak.'

'The sharks are timid – even the big ones. Nicky swims with whole schools of them and they never hurt her.'

'Who's Nicky?'

'A kayaker I know. She's a marine biologist.'

'Okay, but don't go too deep.'

'I'll stay close to shore and hold her tight.'

Manaia did not watch. Rōreka carried the baby slowly into the waves. Takurua cried aloud.

Manaia heard. She looked up. Rōreka seemed untroubled. It can't be a shark she thought. Was it a sea louse biting, or a jellyfish? There were so many dangers in the sea.

Takurua only cried because of the sudden cold and the new

experience of slapping waves, but her father took heed and brought her back to the sand.

Takurua soon learned to enjoy the water, just like any other child but unlike her lost older sister, she failed to worship every sunlit ripple. Manaia saw no trace of Fran in Takurua. This baby was someone else.

Manaia called silently to sea and sky: 'Where is my beautiful girl? Why can't she come back to me?'

The Mávro visited more often now – choking her with its brain-fog. Her doctor labelled it post-natal depression and promised it would pass.

With a baby to look after, Manaia had little time to paint. But she cooked and cleaned as usual. When Rōreka cooked, as he loved to do, she cleaned up afterwards to make sure no spot was left in the kitchen. During visits from The Mávro, she swept, dusted, vacuumed, wiped, and polished. Every task was an enemy she must kill to save herself.

The unnatural cleanness of the house alerted Rōreka to the return of The Mávro. Sometimes he longed for a comfortable mess.

'Take your shoes off,' she snapped as he entered the house. 'There might be dogshit on them.'

He could have told her he'd checked them, and they were clean, but it was neither himself nor his shoes she was fighting. He could not take this warrior-at-work into his arms and comfort her. She was unreachable. All he could do was remove the shoes and wait for The Mávro to pass.

Manaia found it hard to paint. She tried, and it helped if she succeeded, but sometimes when she tried, The Mávro overwhelmed her and left her helpless in its grip.

Takurua was usually a good sleeper. But one night when Rōreka was away performing, she was fractious and wouldn't settle. Manaia carried her from room to room, but she only fretted more. It was a fine cold night, so Manaia wrapped her warmly, and carried her out onto the deck to feel the night air on her face. Takurua whimpered and writhed. The sky was clear, and the stars blazed. Manaia turned the baby to face upwards. The child stared at the sky, then stilled. A smile warmed her face. She gurgled and reached up, trying to touch the sky. Takurua looked at the stars the same way her dead sister had once looked at water.

The glow of Takurua's aura expanded skywards, silvery-white and glittering. One tiny hand reached up into its own light. Manaia, being human, saw nothing, but the aura pulsed, out and back, out and back; exactly what happens to young dolphins at the moment they discover their true vocation.

Had Takurua found her calling?

It would have been funny if it hadn't been so sad to watch Manaia answering what seemed to her to be a call of duty. Something made this not-Fran baby respond to the stars, so Manaia felt obliged to point out her namesake star. It wouldn't matter what words she used. Babies this age didn't understand words. She just hoped to soothe the child, so she'd sleep and leave her mother in peace.

'That's your name-star – Takurua. Some call it Sirius. It's the brightest star in the sky. Some planets look brighter, but they're not stars.'

This was extraordinary. Takurua had employed a dolphin-like ability to pick up her mother's thought-meanings. This was her own special star, the brightest in the sky and she shared its name! Nobody ever needed to explain it to her again – she just grew up knowing. In later years, Manaia forgot that whole stressful night and thought Rōreka must have told her.

Takurua's delighted response on that night brought Fran back so vividly, that a wall of black cloud rolled over Manaia's internal sky, obscuring all stars for her there.

'Is this baby safe with me?' she thought. 'So, she's a star baby. Fine. At least she suits her name, but I want my water baby back!'

She looked down at her tiny jailer and her mind collapsed inwards like a black hole in space. But not even a real black hole can trap spiritual energy. Her spirit escaped and shot outwards with a not-so-simple request.

'God-in-Heaven please bring my parents back to life, so they can take this thing away for a few days and give me a break from it.'

Manaia put Takurua to bed, covering her carefully despite the brain-fog stopping her from caring if the child was warm enough or not. She hurried out of the room, needing to get away.

The next day Rōreka returned on an early car ferry. He was not her parents coming back to life but he fulfilled her current reason for needing them. Always keen to spend time with Takurua, now he focussed on her to the exclusion of all else. For three days the two of them held long conversations in gobble-de-gook. He fed her, dressed her, changed her, He lay on the floor, letting her crawl and dribble all over him. He cuddled her. He read to her. He played his guitar and sang songs to her. He put her in the backpack and walked with her for miles, across the hills, through the forests and along the local beaches.

'She's lucky to have him, anyway,' thought Manaia.

She climbed to her studio and sat cradling the Fran stone in her lap.

Tapeka beach was one of Manaia's favourite stone-collecting beaches. They parked the van and Rōreka placed his daughter into the backpack and hoisted her up. Takurua laughed, waved her pudgy hands, and reached forward to grab at him, bouncing with excitement. She loved this high-up view of the world, and the closeness of her father.

Manaia collected her treasure bag from the back seat. It was as strong and functional as ever, though the colours had mellowed with age. She ran her hand over the embroidered letters and remembered Natia's flying fingers stitching them so long ago. Fingers. Another image came – those same fingers. Red. She shook her head, looked up, saw a gull fly over, focussed on the whiteness of its wings, blocked the other image from her mind.

She slung the bag over her shoulder and the family set off in search of "precious" stones. All three went barefoot. Takurua's tiny toes swung loose in the sea-breeze while her parents' feet trod the pebbles and sand of Tapeka.

Manaia looked for dense hard stones with a pleasing shape, stones that wanted to become her canvases. Mostly she chose silk-smooth textures but sometimes a rough-texture would call her. She picked up a multi-coloured egg-sized stone, washed it in the sea to remove the sand and passed it to Takurua. Takurua sucked it, tasted salt, and felt the hardness on her tongue and lips. The family wandered on at Manaia's treasure-hunting speed. She found a few good stones and dropped them into her bag.

Something white caught her eye. A smooth bone about twelve centimetres in length, well bleached and sterilised by the sea. It was dense – an animal bone – a perfect canvas. She wondered how the animal had died, whether it had drowned in the sea. Would it like to be immortalised this way? She would choose a design carefully. She dropped it into one of the padded pockets at the rim of the bag. As they approached the rocky headland at the far end of the beach, Takurua tired of her well-sucked stone and tossed it. It hit Manaia on the arm.

'Ouch! That hurt.'

'What hurt?'

'Your daughter chucked her stone at me, from behind your back.'

'Bad girl! Sticks and stones can break your mother's bones,' he said.

'Throw it at Daddy next time,' said Manaia.

Manaia rubbed the sore spot and looked towards the headland. A big rock lay partly buried in the last stretch of beach, before the sand gave way to the rocks at the end. She pointed.

'Look at that!'

'That's not a stone. It's a bloody great boulder.'

They approached and stopped beside it. Manaia crouched to run both hands across its surface. Takurua gurgled.

'It's beautiful. Feel it.'

Rōreka crouched too, put his hand to the rock. It was dense, like marble, mid-grey in colour.

'We'll never get it home. Won't the colour be too dark?'

'I'd prime it white. It's a great shape – look at the even curve. I could paint the whole universe.'

'It's way bigger than your other stones.' He kicked it. It didn't budge. 'Might be the tip of an iceberg.'

'I want it, Rōreka.'

'It'll weigh a ton.'

'Can't we just try?'

Rōreka squatted, put his hands around the rock, twisted and heaved. It moved.

'I might manage it – just.' He groaned. 'Christ Manaia! Why can't you fall in love with a little seashell?'

'There's rope and a sack in the van. I'll bring them.'

She left her treasure bag in the van and returned with rope and sack. Rōreka unclipped the backpack and transferred Takurua to Manaia. He placed the sack on the sand, then manoeuvred the rock into it, his lean brown arm muscles bulging with the effort. He bunched the end of the sack, tied the rope around it, took a good grip and began dragging. The work became easier once he reached the drier sand, but the stony parts of the beach were harder to negotiate and in places he had to clear a pathway through the stones. It was a slow job and the sweat poured. The hardest part was lifting it into the van. They found a thick old flotsam plank on the beach and managed to drag-slide the boulder up the plank and heave it in through the rear door.

They drove home. Manaia hosed and scrubbed the rock with fresh water, dried it with a rag and they put it on the furniture trundler and wheeled it bump bump bump upstairs to her studio.

It lay grey and unassuming in the warm patch on the floor until the day she white-primed it. Still, it waited, biding its time, glowing like the moon through her phases of darkness. Sometimes she sat on the floor beside it, sipping from a cup, one hand resting on her future universe.

*

Manaia by this time was expecting her third baby, her second to Rōreka.

One mid-winter night, two years after the birth of Takurua, Manaia woke in the early hours. The baby was due and it was hard to stay comfortable in bed. It was still pitch dark. She threw off the covers.

She wrapped herself in a thick quilt and dragged her heavy body from room to room. She stopped at the window, pulled back the curtain, and saw the night was fine. She opened the slider and walked onto the deck.

Something moved. A bird? No, just a breath of wind in the leaves. She looked out to sea. Something glittered there, low in the sky. Matariki! What had Rōreka told her about those stars? They were the teardrops of Tāwhiri-mātea. Long ago, he had shed tears of lightning and blasted them into the sky, where their annual midwinter reappearance signalled the rebirth of new life in a new year. Rebirth?

Lately, her memories of Fran had revived, brighter than ever. She had no doubt this was another girl. But she would not be fooled again. New babies did not replace lost ones.

So Hinewai was born and of course she looked nothing like Fran, nor even like Manaia herself. She was a little female edition of Rōreka, showing his Māori heritage in her face and skin colour. But, as she grew, that red tint was there in the dark hair again, a powerful link to her dead sister, Fran.

But Manaia stared into the child's eyes and felt a twang of recognition. She stared and stared, and the child stared back, loving the attention, as babies do. Manaia hardly dared to hope. She ordered herself to ignore it.

Hinewai's birth diminished the Fran-pain in a way that Takurua's had failed to do. Then came a day when Manaia heard Hinewai gurgling at the bathwater, ignoring the bath toys, and splashing and patting at the water. The baby was mesmerised by its light patterns, the feel of it on her skin, her fingertips. Manaia crouched there beside the bath; an arm ready to support her if needed. But Hinewai was supporting herself.

Takurua toddled in and stood beside her mother, watching her baby sister. Manaia's right arm went out around her, as she reached for Hinewai with the left. Manaia knelt there with one arm around each child and in that moment, she felt complete.

'You're my perfect daughters, all three of you,' she whispered.

Fran and Hinewai worshipped water and Takurua ignored it. At night Takurua's feet tried to leave the ground and carry her to the stars. Manaia had to watch carefully in case she tripped over something on the forgotten earth. But now that she had a water-baby again, it felt lovely to have a star-child too.

But still The Mávro persisted. Visiting her like an unwanted guest trapping her inside on a sunny day. Haunting her on dark nights that never seemed to end. Why? Again, she listed her blessings to fight The Mávro. The list was longer now that Hinewai was here, and she had two living daughters. Other people lost close ones and got over it. So should she, she thought.

'I'm an ungrateful witch,' she whispered to herself from deep in the pit. Even when The Mávro lifted, she lived with the fear of its return. She tried to hide it but although Rōreka pretended otherwise, he always knew when it was upon her.

*

Manaia watched the girls cross the road to catch their school bus. Her face was pale, her body thin and tense. Rōreka was already working, the music pulsing faintly through the soundproofing.

She cleaned the kitchen into submission then dragged herself upstairs to her own workspace. Hinewai must have been up here – the curtains were open. She stared at the calm sea outside her window. It could rise up any moment, a massive tsunami, clutching and killing. She pictured it smashing the window and crushing the house, her painted stones tossing, everyone drowning, the school inundated, its windows shattering on the children, cutting them as they struggled. She could do nothing, so she quailed, waiting for the flood to come. The imagined shrieking faded. Then everything was as quiet as death.

Wanting to put some sounds between herself and the deadly hush, she crept downstairs and cowered in the bedroom where Rōreka's music reached her faintly. She focused on the sounds, trying to shut out everything else. The music stopped. His footsteps came up the stairs and she forced herself to move to the kitchen and switch on the coffee machine. She wiped the spotless benchtop. He entered and recognised The Mávro. She could not speak, could not let him hold her. She watched him make coffee, while they both pretended that everything was alright.

# 17 – BIRTH OF ATARAU

Melody and Libran were expecting their second baby.

'Please stay tranquil,' Zeta advised, 'for the baby's sake.'

'Impossible,' laughed Melody. 'I work with humans, remember?'

Zeta did not laugh.

'Then don't!' she said. 'For now, stop working with humans.'

'But it's my only vocation.'

'No vocation is as important as new life. I forbid you to work until well after the birth. I mean it, Melody. Have a holiday.'

'I would love that,' replied Melody.

'And next time you go to the whales, you must not go alone. We all want to meet Wairua Nui and Thunderflukes.'

So, during the pregnancy, one or more of the others always escorted her. The whales' migrations made some journeys longer than others for the dolphins. The pod kept her safe and well-fed while travelling, and their company was reassuring. Libran enjoyed it most because he talked to the whales about visual art, and even curated some works they remembered from earlier lives on distant worlds.

Melody appreciated Zeta's protectiveness of her unborn one. They both wanted to cherish this child. Melody obeyed her sister and stayed far from mankind.

Away from humans she calmed down, and the red horror diminished. The dolphins of her home pod trained themselves to barely notice the spectre. Soon they could hunt and eat comfortably in its presence.

The now-grown Elethea, to the pride of her mother, had chosen healing as her vocation. Her songs helped Melody, and all agreed Elethea should take the major role in the birth of her new cousin.

Melody needed the whales less often now, but despite the closeness of her pod and all the magic of their healing songs, her gift to compose did not return.

When the time came, Libran and Antares joined the fighters patrolling to protect the birth pod. Zeta and Elethea stayed close to Melody, and under Elethea's care all went smoothly for the birth – a whole new dolphin to join the pod! They all wondered who and what she might become.

The name came easily for a baby born under the light of the full moon. Atarau – moonlight. Nothing happened to change Melody's decision this time. She felt sure that this spirit had journeyed through many lives, only to forget them all, once she was reborn on the seas of Azure.

The birth blood dispersed. The danger was over. Libran joined the females.

Atarau was as physically perfect as her long-lost older brother. Her virgin brain awaited enrichment by the culture of her kind.

Melody prayed: 'May this one stay close to me, all the days of my life.'

Atarau's aura was a silver cloud spangled with starry pinpricks of light that floated around her as though she belonged to the night skies. Perhaps she'll become an astronomer, like her uncle Antares, thought Melody, or even an adept of the moon and its tides.

Atarau adjusted quickly to her new world. She saw the eastern sky, striped magenta and gold, slowly brightening in advance of the sun, the waves becoming transparent, side-lit from the east. She heard the cries of hunting gulls, the songs of dolphinkind reaching her through the water, and the heartbeats of the beings in the deep. She smelled the tang of salt on the wind and felt the pull of the tides on her skin.

A single too-bright star appeared on the eastern horizon. It was the centre spot of the uppermost edge of Atarau's new sun, which then rose before her. Melody and Libran saw these wonders afresh through her eyes, and in that moment, they too felt new-born.

## 18 – SHADOWS IN BODY AND MIND

Rōreka found strength to climb the stairs from the basement studio and walk to the bedroom. He rested for half an hour, recovering. Then he phoned the doctor and made an appointment for the next day. The doctor looked serious, put him through a series of tests, and over the next week or two, Rōreka had to visit Whangarei hospital for more tests and procedures. He combined these trips with music gigs and other errands and did not tell Manaia the real reason.

His GP in Kororareka gave him the final diagnosis.

'I'm going to tell you straight,' he said. 'It's cancer and terminal. You may not have much time.'

Rōreka had somehow known it was serious. What was there to say? The doctor began explaining specifics of the disease and speaking of treatments that might or might not help. Rōreka would need to decide quickly if he wished to submit to them.

'What caused this?' asked Rōreka.

'Sometimes nobody knows,' replied the doctor, 'why cancer strikes one person and not another.'

'Is it because I used to smoke?'

'Hmm, you gave up a while ago, but this began in your lungs and there are many carcinogens in tobacco. This could have been with you a long time before it became aggressive.'

Rōreka exited the doctor's rooms and moved stiffly towards the van. He watched as a runner passed him. He tried to remember that freedom.

I don't believe that doctor, he thought. They don't know why I'm dying and if I survive, they won't understand that either.

At home he sat in his studio, thinking of Manaia's fragility. How would she and the girls manage without him? He'd earned enough in his life but why hadn't he hadn't saved more.

He did not want to bring on The Mávro, so he kept the news to himself.

Rōreka had once run fluidly over all the hills of the peninsula. Now, even walking exhausted him. Manaia loved her husband, but she hardly noticed his decline. He hid it well and her own shadows blinded her to his failing health.

One morning Manaia woke up unaware of the pretty sunny day and the fresh summer breezes that shifted the air around the house. She only knew that the ocean was sick, the climate was changing, animals were dying, and her own species was a virus on the face of the earth. Her children would inherit a diseased world. This was all real. Most people ignored it. Not Manaia. Not when The Mávro was around.

She ate no breakfast, saw the girls onto the school bus, cleaned her spotless oven, and then battled upstairs to her studio. She found paper and began to draw – animal bones, dead trees, human corpses lying on dried up farms. A skeleton grasped a wad of money in one hand and an empty plastic water bottle in the other. This was the known future. How could anyone be happy?

She stared at her work. The Mávro shrieked from all the drawings. She rejected them all.

'I'll beat this,' she vowed. 'Choose something cheerful.'

Nothing suggested itself. She moved to the window, opened the curtains, and forced herself to look at the sea. Two dolphins leapt in the bay, tiny at this distance. Surely, the world's most cheery subject. And they were real too. For now.

'You'll do,' she said to them. 'I'll draw you.'

She closed the white mesh curtains, shutting out the sea, but pulled the black ones aside to let the light through. Then she eyed the white-primed boulder sitting by the wall of the studio.

'This is your day,' she said to the boulder. 'You can be the dolphins' universe.'

She knelt beside it, ran her hand across the satin-smooth white surface, willing it to fight the darkness lurking behind her eyes. She forced The Mávro aside and dragged dolphin-inspired marine and universal themes into her brain. She arranged her paints and brushes around the rock on the floor.

She began to paint. Colour oozed from the tubes – pure and brilliant

– a weapon against her enemy. Brushstroke by brushstroke, two dolphins leapt to life, light blazing from their hearts, their bodies pulsing with currents of colour, rainbows trailing from their flukes. Around them, their universe expanded, from sunlit ocean to starlit sky. Many suns lit the image, and seabirds tossed in the breeze that blew over the painted ocean. Leviathans glided in the depths. Smaller sea-beings flickered through undersea gardens. Here, a filigree of black lines danced, intensifying the sparkle of the star-scape it reflected. There, a tracery of white ripples gleamed. Elsewhere a spiral galaxy blazed, scattering jewels to the void.

The Mávro menaced every brushstroke, but she fought back with all her colours. While she kept painting, The Mávro could not win, giving her a true and powerful respite. Soon every millimetre of the surface of the rock had its share of the dolphins' universe.

It was finished, but the moment she stopped painting, The Mávro returned.

She stared at the painted rock, seeing only a gaudy mess.

The dolphins will grow old and a shark will rip them to bits and eat them, she thought.

The Mávro rattled its hag-laugh and settled inside her.

Nearly four o'clock. Kids on the porch. Front door slam. Fridge door open/close. She could almost hear the munching from here. Stomp stomp stomp, on the stairs. Door opening. It was Hinewai.

Hinewai gaped at the rock. Her face alight.

'A dolphin rock! Wow! Can I have it please?'

'On one condition.'

'What?'

'You don't keep it inside. This is waterproof paint so it can go outside.'

'Why?'

'Your room's a mess – there's no room for any more junk in there.'

'Mum! This isn't junk. It's your best painting ever. What about in the lounge?'

'It's only yours if it's outside. I don't want it in the house.'

'Did you say it's waterproof?'

'You heard me.'

'Can I put it in the sea?'

Silence.

The idea jolted her, bringing temporary clarity despite The Mávro. Put it in the sea? She wasn't happy with the work, but she often felt that way about work that later sold well. No-one could buy it once it was underwater.

But she couldn't sell it, anyway – she'd just given it to Hinewai!

And there was something right about the idea of the colours of the painted rock glimmering through water, the currents caressing it.

'So … can I put it in the sea?'

'Whatever. But not now. It needs to dry first. Do your homework.'

Hinewai thumped down the stairs, with far fewer thumps than stairs.

After she'd gone, the image of the rock in underwater light persisted for Manaia. A childhood memory surfaced, the sensation of the living ocean enfolding her own skin, her hair washing round her like seaweed. The Mávro receded for a moment just slightly. Her mood lifted.

A sacrifice – is that what this would be? No, it was koha – a gift to the sea she had once so loved. Why had she never thought of it before? The sea! Look at it. Look at it!

She opened the curtains a crack, and peered out. She saw none of the ocean's beauty – only blue horror. The clarity faded into blackness. She told herself no-one with any taste was likely to want the bloody thing so she might as well let Rōreka take it out in the boat and chuck it overboard if that was what Hinewai wanted. She snapped the curtains shut and went to clean the kitchen. The girls would have left crumbs everywhere by now.

*

Rōreka agreed to help put the stone in the sea. As he studied it, a gentle breeze of music blew through his brain; suggestions of chords, melodies, and lyrics – a waiata for the rock. He sent Hinewai and Takurua to cut harakeke. They used the flax to make rope and a hammock-shaped kete to hold the stone, while he crafted the waiata.

When all was ready, they placed the painted stone inside the kete, with plenty of rope at each end. Manaia took the furniture trundler upstairs and carefully worked the boulder onto it, placing padding to protect the paint at points of contact. They tied it securely to the sidebars and wheeled it downstairs, outside, downhill, along the gravel road and through the bush track to Jills Bay.

The bay was calm, edged with lacy ripples. The usual handful of local boats rested on their moorings. Further out, Rōreka's beloved islands lay dreaming under the sun.

The dinghy lay upside down, tied to a root under a huge pohutukawa tree – its name, Kon-tiki, painted on the stern. It belonged to a friend, who'd encouraged them to use it. They rarely did, being kayak people, but it was perfect for this task. They carried it down the sand and hung the heavy kete over the stern.

The Mávro had retreated for now. Manaia waited on the beach, screening out the blue dazzle with the wide brim of her sun hat.

To keep the boat trimmed with the weight of the stone astern, the girls stayed well forward, and each paddled with one oar. Rōreka sat amidships, controlling the load as it hung suspended in the water. The boat moved seaward.

When it was deep enough, they stopped. Rōreka began lowering the stone while they all sang the waiata he'd created, first in Māori and then in English.

Bless this stone, thrice-gifted to the ocean:
From the body of Papatūānuku
From the hand of Manaia.
From the heart of Hinewai,
For Hinemoana, Tangaroa, Tāwhiri-mātea
And to all the children of the sea.
From our family to the sea.
This gift carries our spirit of love.
To spread through all the oceans.

He paid out the rope, while the girls sang. He let the weight of the stone carry it deeper. When it almost touched the seabed, he lashed the ropes around the thwart to secure it. He lowered himself into the water, paused, breathed deeply and dived. He followed the rope down, released a slip knot and pulled the kete away from the stone. It settled among sand, mud, and pebbles. The sunlight rippled through the water animating the painted image. Rōreka surfaced beside the boat but lacked the strength to climb aboard. This dive would once have been easy. Not anymore. He rested, one hand on the gunwale, the other still holding the rope. His lungs hurt. Everything hurt. Breathing was painful. He smiled at the girls as though all was well.

'I'll swim back,' he said.

Takurua dragged the kete aboard. Rōreka lay on his back and breathed for a full minute, recovering, then wallowed towards the beach.

The girls spent a few minutes looking down, trying to see the rock in the water, but the light glittering on the surface made it hard to see anything clearly down there. They sat together on the centre thwart, which gave them the best rowing trim now that Rōreka's weight was gone. They put the rowlocks in the chocks, took an oar each and rowed back to the beach. They dragged the boat part-way up the sand, then swam out again and dived to admire the rock in its new home.

Hinewai waved at her mother on the beach.

'It looks cool!' she shrieked, before diving for another look.

They dived again and again to admire the painted boulder, then swam back at last to shore. Rōreka had been watching them as he rested, exhausted, in the shallows, when he noticed a disturbance in the water over the spot where they'd sunk the rock. Was that a fin? Trick of light? He kept staring but saw nothing more.

The family worked together to haul the dinghy out and secure it under its tree. Rōreka headed for home with the furniture trundler. Manaia and the girls lingered on the beach. Manaia tried to picture the boulder sitting underwater. Her eyes were drawn to the spot where her family had created a new link with the ocean. She too saw movement there, as Rōreka had before. She stared harder and moments later saw a dolphin leap away, to seaward of the spot, unmistakable. She remembered her glimpse of the two who'd inspired the painting. Was this one of them?

'Dolphins!' she said.

'Yay!' said Hinewai, 'They're visiting the koha-rock already.'

'Hope they like it,' said Manaia. 'How did it look to you, Takurua?'

'It comes alive underwater,' she replied. 'All its stars are twinkling.

# 19 – KOHA TO THE SEA

When the rock-sinking ceremony began, Libran, Antares, Zeta, Elethea, Melody and baby Atarau, were hunting the waters of neighbouring Clendon Cove.

Zeta sensed unusual human activity coming from Jills Bay. She swam around the point towards them. She kept out of sight as Rōreka's family performed their ritual with the rock. Her thoughts flowed back to the other dolphins as she watched.

'They're intentionally placing a land boulder in the sea.'

'Why?' they asked her.

'There's no obvious reason.'

'What's in their minds?'

Zeta focused on the human family.

'The man is weary. The whole process is tiring him. The young ones on the boat are thinking of the ocean. They're giving. This rock is like a fish that one dolphin catches for another to eat. They did not create this object and yet the younger one feels ownership of it. It was given to her. Now she in her turn gives it to Hinemoana and all her children, including ourselves.'

'Do they value this thing?'

As though in answer to Libran's question the humans sang:

Bless this stone, thrice-gifted to the ocean:
From the body of Papatūānuku
From the hand of Manaia.
From the heart of Hinewai,
For Hinemoana, Tangaroa, Tāwhiri-mātea
And to all the children of the sea.

From our family to the sea.
This gift carries our spirit of love.
To spread through all the oceans.


The words themselves meant nothing to Zeta. Yet she understood. 'Yes,' she said, 'they value it greatly.'

She swam closer and glimpsed the colours. 'That's no ordinary boulder.'

The man moved between the dolphin and the rock as he worked at removing the kete and ropes. Zeta scanned his body, then swam out of view behind a moored boat to breathe. While hidden there, she called in the pod from Clendon Cove. They arrived quietly and met up with her behind the boat.

'The adult human is as sick as a poisoned oyster!' said Zeta. 'I've seen him before somewhere I think.'

'What kind of illness?' asked Elethea.

'Come and see for yourself,' said Zeta.

They all swam together, stealthily scanning the human. By this time Rōreka was struggling back towards the beach. Elethea swam close, examining his organs with her well-trained ultra-sound.

'Too sick for physical sounds alone to heal him, I think,' she told the others. 'But if he could just receive music by thoughtstream it might only take a few healing songs to banish it.'

'Why would they let one of their kind suffer from an illness so easy to cure?' asked Zeta.

'I know only too well,' said Melody, 'that humans don't do thoughtstreaming.'

'Not even for healing?' said Elethea.

'I suppose not. I don't think they're capable.'

'So will they just let him die?'

'It looks that way,' said Libran, 'and really, he's too young to die. His children are not yet grown. But Melody, we do know this man. We've seen him often. He's the musician who comes out alone in his waka.'

She studied the man again.

'You're right!' she replied. 'He's the one who saved that turtle. He was so strong and healthy before; I hardly recognise him now. He doesn't deserve to die this way.'

The pod watched from afar as the girls rowed the boat ashore. They saw them swim back out and dive to see the rock in its new home. Atarau wanted to go and play with them, but Melody kept her back.

'Beware of humans! They're not your playmates.'

'Oh, please Mother!' Atarau begged. 'How can they hurt me?'

'I forbid it!' snapped Melody. 'Never approach them.'

Atarau obeyed. But she was suddenly very curious. Who were these weird-shaped animals? Why were they forbidden?

A familiar charge of energy flashed through Atarau's aura. It was the charge that marks the moment when a baby dolphin discovers its true vocation. Might she become an adept of humanity?

As soon as the girls left the water, the pod took a closer look at the new object that had arrived in their world. They breathed rarely, trying to keep themselves out of sight of the humans on the beach. Sometimes they used the moored boats as screens to hide their breathing. Underwater, they swam around the koha-rock, looking at it from all directions.

They saw the starry river flowing across the centre, the great blazing suns, the colours flickering as the moving light danced across them.

'This,' said Libran, 'is a gift worth receiving. It's us with our ocean and our universe, all condensed to one image on one rock.'

'Humans made this?' breathed Atarau. Her aura flared again.

The dolphins needed to focus their eyes carefully to pick out the dolphin-shapes from the mass of coloured detail. It was a little like trying to spot an octopus who had camouflaged himself against the brilliant colours of his reef community, but trickier because the rock painting made no sounds to help them interpret.

'Music,' said Antares, 'would enrich this treasure and help us understand it.'

'If only you still had your gift,' said Zeta to Melody. 'You'd do it better than anyone.'

'If only. If only,' Melody replied. 'Don't think I haven't tried.'

'Music can come later,' said Libran, 'but I must curate this art at once. We don't know how long the image may survive in its full beauty, underwater.'

He studied the boulder. His long years of experience in visual art helped him to create a perfect three-dimensional mind-picture. He sent the picture and the story surrounding it, by long-distance thoughtstream, to contacts all over the sea. He went out into the middle of Manawaora Bay and spent two hours alone completing this work.

He returned and spoke to Antares privately.

'Your team is welcome to take it off-planet, but I recommend you wait in case we find a musician to enrich it first.' He glanced towards Melody. Antares understood that glance.

'Thank-you,' said Antares. 'I'll wait and hope for that to happen. No need to rush, now that the image is safely curated. It would surprise our friends in other worlds to have visual art arriving with our music.'

The image was soon criss-crossing the idea-sphere, but many came to see it with their physical eyes, wanting to be close to it. Some stayed for hours, returning often to watch its changing moods.

Atarau found a moment alone with her cousin Elethea.

'Why won't my mother let me near humans?'

'Humans killed her mother and her son, your own older brother.'

'But they didn't mean to.'

'Look at the spectre she carries, Atarau.'

'That silly red thing? It doesn't bother me. She's always had it. The whales defeat it every time, since even before I was born.'

'You're accustomed, little cousin. You didn't know your mother before that thing was there.'

Inevitably, mud began to build up on the surface of the koha- rock. Small weeds colonised the mud. It obscured parts of the image and would cause damage in time. How could they protect it?

Antares found a solution. He swam to Maunganui Bay and brought Tangles back with him. This Tangles was female like her well-remembered ancestor and had inherited those famous see-forever eyes. At Antares' request, she used her delicate suckers to remove every weed and every speck of mud where weeds might cling. He rewarded her with a small fish.

We should employ her permanently, he thought.

Tangles loved the koha-rock, even more than the dolphins did. Her magical vision found details most of them missed, including a tiny painted octopus low down on one side, almost where the rock curved under out of sight.

That's me! she thought. It's really me. I must be famous!

Antares took her back to her old home for now, but over the next few days he searched the seabed inspecting items discarded by humans – broken glass bottles, old pots and pans, drums, plastic, and rusting metal. He found what he was looking for, lying on the seabed near Motukauri – a heavy ceramic vase, half buried in mud.

No barnacles, he thought, so it couldn't have been there long. He brushed some of the mud away with his pectoral fin. The body of the vase was ellipsoid in shape, with a short neck that flared out to the opening. It had a few chips but was tough as a rock, soft grey in colour, patterned with brown and blue markings.

Perfect!

He and Zeta collected Tangles and brought her to the spot. Tangles used her suckers and clever minions to clean the mud and debris from the vase, inside and out. The opening was much narrower than her own body, but her magical flexibility let her disappear inside, in one quick squelch, then out again, just as smoothly.

'Climb aboard,' said Antares.

She settled on his back, gripping his dorsal fin. Antares took the neck of the vase in his teeth and moved it towards Jills Bay. He and Zeta took turns to carry the heavy vase and when they stopped to hunt or rest, Tangles took refuge inside it.

The task was tiring but they arrived at last. Antares dug with his rostrum to make a hole in the seabed near the koha-rock. Tangles helped by hauling out stubborn stones with her powerful minions. When it was deep enough, they pushed the vase into the hole and swept sand and stones around it until it was mostly buried, with only the top end of the neck now visible.

'Your new home,' said Antares. 'If you use your skills to look after the painting, we'll bring as much food as you need.'

Tangles wasn't sure if it was the new home or the new vocation that delighted her the most.

I have a calling now, she thought, just like the dolphins. And I have the best house in Manawaora.

She dashed in and out of her new doorway, swam around the koha-rock twenty times, just for the fun of returning home. Finally, she settled on the mud between it and the rock with one minion around the neck of the vase and another laid across the artwork.

She cleaned the koha-rock daily, allowing no shred of weed to live there. But she transplanted the prettier weeds nearby, not close enough to obscure the stone but close enough to become its perfect garden setting. She collected iridescent shells, pretty stones and pearls, to enhance the little paradise that began spreading around the taonga glowing at its heart.

The dolphins brought her all the food she could eat. She no longer needed to hunt, so she used the time to expand the garden. Vibrant fish moved in, to act as living flowers amongst the swaying plants, and with the flicker of light from the surface there was a kind of beauty no land garden could rival. Images of the garden and the artwork at its heart entered the idea-sphere and spread through the sea.

Tangles settled in to a whole new life, as keeper of the koha-rock and creator of The Octopus's Garden.

Libran circulated a ban on any predation of the octopus caretaker, in case visitors from afar might be tempted. Tangles took full advantage of this. She pranced under the noses of fierce fighter dolphins who could easily have eaten her.

She enjoyed pointing out interesting features with her minions, and spilling pompous thoughtstreams to her audience, specifically directing their attention to the painting of the tiny octopus:

'A being with good eyesight cannot fail to notice this marvellous detail. It was no doubt included by the artist in reverence to a species of great beauty, intelligence, and importance.'

She would then emphasise her point with a series of dazzling colour changes, which impressed them all.

Hinewai could not have chosen a better corner of Ipipiri to place the taonga. Humans had made new rules banning the noise and disruption of speeding boats throughout Manawaora Bay and all other bays between it and Tapeka. The dolphins felt safer here now, and there was a beautiful artwork to enjoy, as well as a loopy octopus and plenty of mullet.

## 20 – SIMPLE SOUNDS

The Mávro imprisoned Manaia in walls of illusory smoke. She worked on autopilot to feed the girls, make their lunches and send them off to school. She forced all the beds into stiff perfection, and dusted and wiped every surface of the house to spotlessness. Then she slumped in her studio with the black curtains closed.

Imagined voices of trying-to-help friends penetrated the gloom.

'Pull yourself together,' they'd say. 'Count your blessings. You have so much to be thankful for.'

They were right. She could be a blind beggar, living in a stinking city slum. She took their advice and once again, forced herself to count her blessings.

'I have the perfect family. I live in paradise. I love my work. I have a talent. The buttercups are incredibly yellow. The weather is great.' The list went on until she ran out of ideas.

It didn't help. The unreal smoke still billowed, and this time, nothing inspired her to paint.

The voice of her doctor whispered in her ears: 'Exercise is the best thing for depression.' She did a few yoga exercises, then walked to the beach hoping to meet no-one.

'Exercise! If only I could swim again – to be free like the girls.'

It was low tide. Manaia forced herself to look out to sea. It took courage but she walked to the rippled edge and dragged her eyes to the spot where lay the koha-rock.

The Mávro reminded her what a gaudy piece of work it was. But she remembered Takurua's words too.

'It comes alive underwater,' she'd said.

Suddenly Manaia was gripped by an urgency to see it again, in the ocean, where it lived.

She looked down at the sandy mud between her toes and pictured worms lurking below its surface, consuming one another, and being consumed by larger slugs and crabs. She shivered but battled on.

'I'll walk into the shallows. That couldn't hurt me.' She put one foot into the white lace edging of a wavelet and stopped. The water retreated, leaving her standing on empty sand. She took another step and waited until the next wave licked her feet. It withdrew as before. The next wave was bigger. It seized her calves, and legs. She froze. But again, it retreated, and she stood unharmed.

'It's only water. It can't hurt me,' she assured herself, but she knew it wasn't true. It could and it had. It had taken her father.

But today Tāwhiri-mātea and Ranginui were squabbling far out at sea. The islands were sheltering her from them. All was calm in Manawaora. All was calm in Ipipiri. Nothing there to harm her.


Manaia walked deeper.

I did it! she thought.

The sea glowed up into her eyes and she tried to remember how much she'd loved it once.

She took another step.

'Go back!' screamed The Mávro.

Come on! Come on! Come on! she urged herself.

The initial victory strengthened her for the next battle. Each step forward was an easier conquest. Her shorts were wet, then her T-shirt. She gasped with shock at the cold and pushed against The Mávro. She thought the sea was a predator swallowing her whole. But really, the waves were soothing her with love.

Such a battle was taking place between Manaia and her Mávro that the local pod, picked up the vibrations from out to sea. They began to move that way in curiosity.

What am I doing here? Manaia thought. I already carry the scars of sea monsters with razor teeth.

But she waded deeper, repeating all the old platitudes.

'Pull yourself together. Exercise is the best thing for depression. You used to love swimming when you were a kid.'

Her legs floated up off the sand. Manaia was afloat in the sea for the first time in years. She propelled herself through the water, with none of her old fluidity. The scars on her leg felt the teeth that had created them. She reminded herself she was more likely to be killed by one of the many local wild deer, than by any shark.

But The Mávro butted in.

'The shark that bites you, hasn't read the statistics,' it whispered. She pulled up her feet to escape imagined teeth. Then kicked to fend them off. She looked down through the water, and saw, instead of a shark, a fiery splash of colour a few metres away on the bottom.

'My rock! Hinewai's rock! Hinewai-Fran, lovers of the ocean. As I once was…'

And there was no shadow, no monster with sharp teeth, just the colours of the koha-rock vibrating through the water. She approached it, swimming with all the grace of an arthritic camel.

The young Manaia would have dived to examine closely the object down there. This Manaia just gazed down as she floated on the surface, her hair flaring from her head like the flames of a black sun. She watched the sea-light dancing over the painted dolphins on the rock.

'Yes, it's the dolphin rock, little though I loved it. May the new owners appreciate it more.'

Then she saw that although there was a space around the rock itself, beyond that space lay a fairyland of underwater plants, where bright fish glimmered like flowers in a garden. A pair of eyes peeped from behind the koha-rock. It looked like an octopus but it vanished so quickly into the mud; maybe she was seeing things.

Her eyes moved away from the rock, on over the sand, the shells, the fantasy gardens and on to the hazy limits of underwater visibility. Beyond those limits lurked millions of teeth, all as sharp as ever. And tentacles with venomous stings. Her muscles tensed and marred her swimming.

'Go back! Go back!' shouted The Mávro.

Despite this goading, Manaia did not return to the beach. She ignored the voice of the screaming Mávro and stayed where the water was over her depth. She struggled along, at the edge of panic, repeating her mantras:

'Exercise is the best thing for depression. You used to love swimming when you were a kid.'

Humans sometimes say, 'Heaven helps those who help themselves.'

In Manaia's case it held true this time.

Libran, Melody, and the family pod, all saw Manaia swimming over the rock, looking down at it and recognising the work of her own hands.

'This is the one who created the design,' said Libran. 'I'm grateful to her.'

'How can she create beauty while burdened with that darkness?' asked Zeta.

'Perhaps we can help her,' said Libran.

'Dolphins help a human?' asked Zeta.

'She created this treasure for us. She deserves our help,' he replied.

'What harm could it do to try?' said Elethea. 'She carries grief and fear, but no anger. No hatred. That's a good sign.'

'She's human,' said Libran. 'Your thoughtstreams can't reach her.'

'Libran,' said Elethea, 'I'm a healer. I know of simple sounds that may heal this kind of illness, with no need of thoughtpower.'

'Try them then!' said Libran. 'What harm can it do?'


Manaia swam parallel to the beach, her thoughts struggling in time with her limbs. The Mávro shadowed her, thicker than ever. It grabbed at her, choking her.

'It's way too deep. I have to go back.'

She turned towards the beach, but her swimming rhythm worsened. She flailed her arms, gasped for air, reached down with her feet but felt no sand - nothing but empty water with the talons of unreal sea monsters clutching up at her. She tried to kick them away, but instead sank towards them. They would rip her to pieces. Why had she ever left dry land? She thrashed her limbs to stay afloat, trying and failing to reach the air, to escape the imagined monsters, but now the surface was unreachable. Her throat clenched. Her lungs screamed.

Then an odd sound began ringing faintly between her ears

Her flailing slowed, her lungs stopped their screaming, and found more air than they needed. Bubbles escaped her lips, taking her panic with them. Time slowed. Was she dying? She came to the surface — breathed in again and now, when she tried to swim, some rhythm returned, just enough to keep her afloat.

Someone was here with her. Who was it? What was it?

Manaia didn't see Elethea, so close below, generating sounds that were simple to her, sounds carried down through the ancient marine science of sound. Most were beyond the range of human hearing.

Having eased Manaia's panic enough to save her from drowning, Elethea swam behind a moored boat to breathe before returning to continue her task from underwater, out of sight.

Manaia trod water, looked around, but saw no-one on the beach, no-one in the water. She struggled on. There it was again. Gentle in her head more of a vibration than a sound. It rose and fell inside her skull, focusing on tensions in mind and brain, releasing and untangling them.

To Manaia it felt as though tiny fingers worked with gentle strokes of the softest brush at smoothing textures, realigning fibres and soothing all garish colours into pastel rainbows. Vibrations purred from her brain to her body, calming every muscle. She turned on her back and floated, while the sensation enveloped her. Her hands relaxed, their motion morphing into harmony with the water that rocked her. Air flowed into her lungs and out again. In out, in out, fresh as a new-made song. On and on flowed the simple sounds from Elethea. Manaia could hardly hear them, but she wanted them to ring forever.

They faded at last. She was alone in her beloved ocean.

Beloved? Yes.

Alone? Perhaps. She drifted. A gannet dived.

Pouff! Only one thing made such a sound out here. She looked seaward and saw dorsal fins rolling up and over in the familiar dolphin action. One leapt clear of the water, trailing liquid diamonds from its flukes.

'Was it you?' she whispered. 'Did you do this for me?'

She lay back, relaxing in the water. Then her old family came to her, and floated bodiless and invisible, one parent either side and Fran in her arms, beloved like the sea. Her lost ones were all together, as they ought to have been in life. When they slid away at last, they took her pain with them. Then they were gone, and yet they were not. And they stayed with her for the rest of her life.

The sea supported her then, with hues as bright as her favourite paint. She drank in the colour and tasted the tang of salt on her lips and heard the rush of waves on the beach, the music of summer. Fears of teeth, tentacles and stings joined her anxieties around earthquakes and lightning strikes – real enough but banished to zones where they could no longer paralyse her.

I could swim here forever, she thought. I feel like a kid again.

Her body stretched in the water, her arms reaching out to the full length of her natural swim-stroke. She glided forward like an eel and then dived to swim open-eyed along the sand, her hair streaming, a cascade of darkness, behind her.

She surfaced and swam the length of the beach and back, then stopped and lowered her feet to the sand, which massaged them as a lover might.

When the girls come home from school, she thought, I'll swim again with them.

She sat on the beach in the sun, waiting for the breeze to dry her clothes.

Next time she'd wear a swimsuit.

Then she saw the dolphins again – tiny stars leaping in the distance.

'Thank-you,' she whispered.

'My pleasure,' said Elethea, picking up the message clearly, though Manaia would not have believed it.

Later, walking into her studio, she noticed the black curtains. What had she been thinking?

She removed them from the curtain rail and put them in the van.

'I'll ask if the school needs blackout curtains,' she thought.

In the afternoon Manaia returned to the beach with her daughters. They all stripped to their swimsuits.

'Mum's got her togs on. Are you swimming with us?'

'Why else would I wear my togs?'

'But you never swim.'

'Yay! We'll stay close in case you need us.'

The three entered the water together.

'Look at her swim!' said Takurua. 'You're good, Mum. Wow, I never knew that.'

'She can beat me!' Hinewai complained. 'I thought I was the fastest in the family.'

'Why should the smallest be the fastest?' Manaia put her hand on Hinewai's head and pushed her under the water.

Hinewai came up spluttering and splashed water into her mother's eyes.

Takurua laughed so hard she took a mouthful and gagged on it.

They recovered and swam out to view the painted rock.

'Mum's diving!'

'OMG, she stays under for ages!'

Underwater, the three joined hands facing inwards to form a circle around the boulder. They moved clockwise until Takurua got the giggles and had to swim up to avoid drowning.

Out at sea, Libran watched.

'The humans have linked their split fins. They're circling the art!'

'It was those split fins that held the tools to make the image on the rock.'

'Why do they link them?'

'It amuses them – we should try it.

'Yes let's!' said Atarau. 'I'll be boulder-in-the-middle and you all go round me.'

The adult dolphins swam in a circle around Atarau, each gently biting the fluke of the one in front. Their circle stayed perfect, until Atarau's laughter infected them all, and ruined the dance.

# 21 – HUMAN SLEEPERS

That winter, Melody received a long-distance thoughtstream from Wairua Nui.

'Local pelagic dolphins have told me a story that may help you, Melody.'

Melody stopped hunting to listen. Wairua Nui continued.

'They found a human dying of thirst on a raft in the open sea. They tossed high-fluid jellies to him, but the man thought they were poisonous. He only trusted the jellies after the dolphins messaged him in his sleep. Then he ate some and survived three more days until a ship came by and rescued him. It made me wonder, Melody, if you've ever worked with sleeping humans?'

'I have not.'

'Have you ever worked with humans in need?'

She remembered the drunken Jimmy. He'd certainly needed her.

'Yes. Once,' she said.

'The man on the raft needed the help of the dolphins. Perhaps his need opened the channels.'

'It didn't work with my drunken oarsman.'

'Sleep? Need? Perhaps both?' said Wairua Nui.

'Interesting idea,' she replied. 'I'll look for needy sleeping humans,' though privately she wondered where in the ocean she would find one.

With Atarau beside her, Melody watched human vessels, looking for sleeping people. The humans fascinated Atarau, though Melody would never allow her to approach them.

But it was winter so only a few boats were overnighting around Ipipiri.

A few might be all I need, thought Melody.

She entered sheltered coves at night where the few lay at anchor. She never found any needy humans but she found a few sleeping ones.

Some were hallucinating. Aue! Their minds swooped and danced, zooming away on astral travels and cosmic flights. Colours swirled and logic vanished.

It was as if sleep liberated them. She almost envied them their special kind of sleeping.

Atarau longed to learn more of these strange knobbly land-beings with their crazy dreams and impossible skills.

They're so clever, she thought, but when Mother tries to talk to them, she never gets anywhere.

Melody left Atarau with the pod and cruised Otehei Bay on the western side of Urupukapuka Island. Five boats lay at anchor there. She glided through the darkness between them. When she needed air, she swam away before breathing, to avoid detection.

On the deck of a double-hulled boat a woman spread soft material on the open mesh of ropes between the two hulls near the bows, then settled herself between its thick layers. She lay still and warm as the chill of night deepened around her. One hand lay outside the coverings, resting on the mesh. To Melody it looked like a stranded starfish. The woman's mind quietened, her consciousness faded.

Melody stayed with her in mind. She swam between the hulls of the boat, directly underneath the sleeper, so close she could easily have stretched up and touched the uncovered hand with her rostrum. She hovered there, her pectoral fins gently working to hold her in place.

The woman's mind stayed blank at first, then soared suddenly to the highest point on the island. Though it was night, the sun beat down as bright as mid-day in her dream. A fantail alighted on her shoulder and twittered in her ear. Then it gripped her and flew away carrying her. The woman did not question that the tiny bird could do such a thing. She enjoyed flying over the island, looking down on other birds as she passed above them. The bird began to feel the weight at last and they flew lower and lower over the sea until the woman dropped into the water and the bird stood on her head to keep dry.

'Stay with me. I'll keep you safe,' said the woman to the bird. The two dream-beings floated together soothed by the motion of the waves. The bird faded and disappeared. The sea vanished also as the woman's sleep deepened.

Melody marvelled. How could a being keep breathing in such a state? The woman's heartbeats slowed. It was time to try to reach her. Melody swam away to breathe and returned to her position under the boat.

First some reassurance, 'I'm a friend. You're safe with me.'

Then she streamed the same Aerdluthan chord that had so badly frightened the lone sailor.

Melody waited, watching, and listening, but all she heard was the woman's heart beating . . . beating . . . beating. No reaction.

The chord drifted across the woman's mind, but her sleep protected her from fear. The chord wafted about like audible smoke and tried to grip the spindle neurons it found there but they did not grasp the offering, instead letting the chord slip over them and fade. The woman's sleeping spirit did not stir.

Melody tried again. One direction only this time – short range, straight to the brain. She paused, watching for a response. Nothing. She tried from various distances and directions, from underwater and above it, sometimes in wide swathes of thought energy, then in arrows so intense, the moonbeams shivered, but the human did not respond. Nothing. Nothing. Nothing.

Melody breathed. Pouff! Right there beneath the sleeper, not caring who she disturbed. Nobody heard.

This woman talked to an imaginary bird in her sleep, thought Melody. How could she ignore me – a real dolphin so close to her?

She swam away to the mouth of the bay and raced in huge circles, jumping high and diving deep. It warmed her and released frustration.

The sun rose, the humans woke. Melody returned to Atarau and the pod who were hunting in the Te Rawhiti Inlet.

The pod swam north-west between Motukiekie and Moturua, then west towards the Black Rocks where they hunted again before swimming out into open water. Already the chill of the spectre was discernible. With Atarau to think of now, Melody could take no risks so she, Atarau, and Zeta crossed the open sea to find healing with the whales.

*

Spring had arrived by the time they returned. Atarau was old enough to spend more time without her mother. So Melody left her sometimes with Zeta and Elethea while she returned to her thankless task. To minimise the time spent away from her baby, she worked in short bursts only and always stayed close to her family pod, mainly within Ipipiri or not far beyond it.

But soon Atarau needed education, and more interaction with dolphins her own age. Melody let Zeta take her to the main school to choose teachers and playmates. She kept herself away to avoid distressing the young ones with her spectre.

139

Atarau loved her time with her teachers in the education pods. She learned quickly and made friends easily. She explored all the basic subjects – maths, astronomy, science, poetry, history, psychology, music and gymnastics, but her favourite was always the study of humans.

And all this important schooling gave Melody more time to work. She focused on working with sleeping humans but not once did she encounter a sleeping human in any kind of need.

## 22 - ENTANGLED

Melody raced back to the main school, top speed to defeat the chill. She'd been away from Atarau too long and could hardly wait to see her. She called her pod by long-distance thoughtstream. Zeta replied saying she and Atarau would head east towards her. The three met up near Red Head on Okahu Island, and it wasn't long before Libran joined them there. Antares was out at sea in body, his mind in space as he worked with the astronomy team. Elethea was busy at her healing work elsewhere in the bay. Libran and the three females hunted off Red Head for a while, finding good prey to replenish their fluids and energy. Their company soothed her, reduced the spectral chill.

Towers of rock jutted skyward off the north-western corner of the island and among them ran a labyrinth of narrow passages, fun for a baby dolphin to investigate. Atarau wanted to play there so the adults guided her into the maze.

She swam back and forth, in and out, exploring at every depth, poking her nose up to watch the swells hitting the rocks and cascading off again. She would have played there for hours.

'Time to head for sheltered water,' said Melody at last. 'We hate to spoil your game, but we need to find a cosier spot to spend the night.'

'But Mother, I like it here! Can we come back tomorrow?'

'We can, but I can show you lots more places like this in other parts of the bay. Why not explore some others?'

'Yes. Yes. I want to see all of them.'

They cruised south past Motukiekie and into the Te Rawhiti Inlet.

In the morning Atarau reminded her mother of her promise to show her other narrow passages like the Okahu labyrinth.

'There are some close by,' said Melody.

'Show me now!' said Atarau.

Melody, Zeta, and Libran took her to the seaward side of Moturua and its smaller surrounding islands, where they swam back and forth together through many narrow places. Then they crossed to Motuarohia where Atarau found the wide channel between tall rocks at the north-eastern end of the island. She dashed straight into it from the southern end. Melody felt no need to hurry after her. She'd swum there many times and never found danger. Near the end, the channel forked. Atarau took the left fork, diving as she entered to explore its deeper mysteries. Her busy flukes thrust her forward and down and she disappeared.

The three adults followed at a more leisurely pace and came upon Atarau near the end, a body-length below the surface. It surprised them. The speed she'd been going, they'd expected her to be through by now. But for some reason she'd stopped swimming and was struggling on the spot.

'Mother! Mother! I'm trapped!'

Melody shot closer. Atarau was caught beneath the surface, out of reach of air. She thrashed, trying to free herself, but her struggles only entangled her further.

'Keep still!' ordered Melody. The adults swam under Atarau and found a great birds-nest of fine strands, transparent green, invisible in the water. There were heavier ropes around the edges. She'd swum straight into the trap. The strands were also tangled around protrusions on the rocky sides of the channel. This held the whole mess underwater and made it impossible for Atarau to swim up for air. Blood was seeping into the water from cuts on her skin made by the nylon strands of the net. The loops around her fins and flukes cut deeper with every move she made. She cried in pain, but the priority was to stop her from suffocating under the water.

'Keep still!' ordered Melody again. 'You're making it worse.'

The adults tried to push her upwards.

Libran warned, 'Be careful where you put your fins. We can't help her, if we're entangled ourselves.'

Libran and Melody managed to grab the heavier ropes on the edges to free the strands that held the net to the rocks.

It took the combined strength of all of them to push Atarau to the surface. She breathed at last but it made her cry with pain. They examined the strands hoping to find a way to untangle them, but it was hopeless. Melody bit at the strands but nothing helped. Most attempts just hurt

Atarau, made the tangles worse and the cuts deeper.

'Mother! Mother! It hurts! Will I die?'

This was the second time in Melody's life that her child had cried those words to her from inside a net. The old nightmare was beginning again.

Just like last time she thoughtscreamed: 'Save my baby!' Like the other time, other dolphins heard and began racing their way.

At least this time the child could breathe. But there were lines cutting into the corners of her mouth. Another slicing across her blowhole; every breath made the strand there pierce her skin further. It hurt too much. So Atarau breathed as little as possible. A rescue team of about a dozen dolphins arrived on the scene. Elethea was among them. Melody sent calming songs to help Atarau keep still, but she couldn't stop the movement of the waves, which was just as agonising, or worse.

'We have to move her to calmer water,' said Elethea. 'It'll be sheltered all day in Manawaora. But to get her there we'll have to cross the inlet before the easterlies come up.'

Thor, the weather adept, was among the dolphins who'd arrived to help.

'We have until noon before that happens,' he said.

Elethea knew that if they didn't reach shelter in time, the thrashing waves of the easterlies funnelling down the inlet could cut this child to pieces. She kept that thought well screened from Melody and Atarau. Melody knew anyway but refused to face the possibility. Her brain was too busy circulating ideas of how to free her child but finding no answer.

The dolphins began working in teams to move the death-web and its prisoner. A body-length at a time they heaved her towards the Te Rawhiti Inlet and then slowly across it. The long heavy net and weighted ropes trailed behind them, slowing their progress and snatching at their fins and flukes.

Melody noticed Atarau losing consciousness.

'Breathe!' she screamed. But Atarau did not breathe and slid deeper towards coma.

'She's not breathing!' cried Melody to Elethea.

Elethea focused all her pain-relief songs on the baby's blowhole. When she was sure the area was numb, she and Melody used penetrative sound to stimulate a new breath. Atarau revived. Elethea worked without pause, streaming healing sounds, thoughts and specialised music to keep Atarau's pain in control until breathing was easier and coma was prevented. Melody helped Elethea while also helping the others to move the entanglement.

Time was running out, but they were halfway across. A human boat roared past and Elethea saw the huge wake-waves approaching. She sent a special thoughtstream that sent the baby's brain into a brief coma to protect her from the pain she was about to feel. The coma anaesthetised the pain but could not prevent the damage caused by such turbulence. The wake arrived and tossed the entanglement back and forth and up and down, while the strands cut deeper than ever.

Atarau's blood poured into the sea, attracting a large mako shark. He cruised towards them and began closing in. Two of the team were well-trained fighter dolphins. They hit the shark with firm blows to the liver, removing his appetite, and he slunk away. The fighters returned to the task, and all pushed onwards. Just as the easterlies began to strengthen, they reached the shelter of Manawaora Bay.

They rested in the millpond calm of the shallows between Whangaiwahine Point and Motukauri. The sea was shallow but would not dry out at low tide. There was good hunting nearby. They found a spot shallow enough for the sandy bottom to keep the mess high enough to let Atarau breathe. They took care to keep adjusting for the tide. The rescuers alternated between hunting and keeping the patient safe.

But Atarau could not feed and was already beginning to dehydrate. Melody felt imaginary strands cutting as deeply into the corners of her own mouth as the real ones that slashed the mouth and body of her baby. She could no more eat than Atarau could.

Elethea's soothing stream of healing songs and music continued.

'But how can we get her out of there?' wailed Melody.

No-one had any ideas of how to release the baby from the entanglement slowly killing her.

The spectre was still weak from the recent time with the whales, but he bided his time, waiting for the child to die. He would win then, and he knew it.

But now at last, something was wiggling its way to the surface of Melody's brain. Nets could not be bitten away by dolphin teeth, but she'd seen something once. Something to do with humans. It came to her in a rush. The turtle! The man, the musician. The one who was now so sick. He'd once saved an entangled turtle with his cutting tool. She'd watched him do it.

She swam out into the mouth of Manawaora Bay. If he was on the water today, dolphins could drag him here in their slipstream. Once on the spot, he'd know what to do. He'd help them. He came out so often in his little yellow boat.

But … not today.


Suddenly she was back to the same old problem she'd been facing for years. How to contact humans. But this time there was terrible need. Humans had caused this problem. Only a human could save her baby. She knew where he kept his boat. He must live somewhere near there. She knew his mind, had heard its music.

She searched the atmosphere over the land and found thoughtstreams from several humans. Just a few dozen body-lengths inland on the hillside, she picked up those of the woman who'd painted the rock. This woman was often with the musician. He might be nearby. Sure enough, Melody now detected his familiar thoughtstreams somewhere close to the art-woman, inside the house.

'Come here! We need you! Help my child. She's dying. Please save my baby.'

But he did not hear. Melody sent a group of ten dolphins to swim to the head of the bay where the man kept his waka under the tree.

'Wait there in case he comes out in his boat,' she urged. 'He's our only hope and he often comes out in weather like this. Bring him here. Ten of you should be enough to compel him.' They left her and swam towards Jills Bay. Other dolphins arrived quickly to replace them in helping with Atarau. Melody found a clear jelly, small enough to slide into Atarau's restricted mouth for hydration.

# 23 – SLEEP, NEED, COURAGE, AND LOVE

Rōreka had woken that morning convinced that today would be a good day. He'd had some bad ones recently, when it had taken all his efforts to disguise his true condition.

After the girls had left for school, he sat a minute or two at the breakfast table staring out to sea. The bay gleamed blue and calm. It called to him, as always. Then he and Manaia did the breakfast dishes together. She was letting him help with housework more these days. Her cleaning mania had diminished to almost normal levels. The house was not much cleaner than most other people's houses. He even occasionally spotted a friendly dust ball or two hiding under the bookshelf, as he came up the stairs. She was now expecting the girls to do their share of the washing up, no longer terrified that they might not do it properly. It was such a novelty for them, they happily complied, though he wondered how long that would last.

Manaia was so rational, so peaceful these days, he thought. Once he'd gone, this new absence of The Mávro would make life for her and the girls much easier, unless his own death revived the depression. But money would still be a problem, the cost of rates, power, food, house maintenance, children's expenses. Would she raise enough from her artwork to support them without input from his gigs and music sales?

Already he found live performances much more exhausting than usual He was now turning them down in favour of working on an album, which might bring in good money, even after he'd gone. For the hundredth time he regretted not saving more over his lifetime. But even now, he thought, just one song, if it went viral, could bring in enough to make up for his lifelong lack of thrift. He spent the next few hours at work in his studio.

A little after noon, he returned upstairs, just as Manaia came down from her studio. Again he looked out to sea. There was something out there. At first, he thought it was a mooring buoy but this one had a dorsal fin. He grabbed the binoculars.

'Dolphins in the bay again,' he said.

'They sure like the new rules,' she replied. 'They were there when we sank the dolphin boulder. Then I stupidly swam with The Mávro one day, and they came along and healed me.'

'What!' he said, amazed that she would swim at all, let alone while depressed.

'It was my first swim in years and I've had no depression since that day.'

'You think the dolphins helped you? Really?'

'I'm sure of it. They made some kind of vibration. I felt it in my head. I had a panic attack in the water, forgot how to swim. I was drowning.'

'Drowning!'

'Obviously I didn't. But Rorie, I believe I would have, if not for them.'

'Tell me more. How sure are you? What happened?'

'I have no proof. But I've thought about it ever since. I forced myself to swim out, to see the koha-rock. I was okay at first but then I panicked, turned to stone. I was sinking, but I felt this . . . sound-vibration . . . and suddenly my muscles relaxed, and I just swam up and floated and breathed. Then I felt more vibrations, like an alien was zapping me with a euphoria-ray. Since then, I've had no more depression. It's gone. I'm sure of it.'

She glowed with such health today, he found it easy to believe. He took her in his arms, told her he believed her and how happy it made him.

'I knew this would be a good day,' he said to her, 'the moment I woke up. And look, the dolphins are still there.'

He passed her the binoculars, and she watched them milling around in the bay.

'Let's go upstairs. We can see more from up there.'

They went upstairs. He took his turn to look through the glasses.

There were about ten of them, still swimming back and forth along the beach. Usually, they just swam by once and swam away. This behaviour was unusual.

'Might be here to check out the koha-rock,' she joked.

'That weather looks great for a paddle' he said. 'I think I'll head out.'

'I was wondering if you'd ever go out again. It's ages since you last kayaked.'

'Well today will be the day,' he said. 'But just for an hour or two – I need to work on the album.'

'How's that going?'

'Not bad, but I can always use inspiration from the sea.'

It was true, the sea often inspired him.

'You might have dolphin company,' she said, peering again through the binoculars. 'They're still out there.'

'They'll be gone by the time I get to the beach,' he said. 'They always are.'

He grabbed his paddle, threw all his usual gear on the trundler and towed it to the beach. He untied his boat from the tree, dragged it to the water's edge, loaded his gear into the bow and stern compartments, covered the hatches and secured the paddle in its groove. He donned spray skirt and flotation vest and placed the boat with bow in the sea and stern on the sand.

He climbed aboard and attached the neoprene spray-skirt around the cockpit coaming. When the next wave brought momentary extra depth, he pushed off and slid seaward. He paddled a few metres out before flicking his rudder down. The waka was long and slender, designed to skim effortlessly over the sea.

He'd been so focused on launching his boat, he'd forgotten the dolphins. But when he looked about at last, he was surprised to see them, still here in the bay, among the moored boats.

Rōreka reminded himself the new rules did not allow anyone to exceed a speed of five knots anywhere in Manawaora Bay. And to stop altogether if there were dolphins within a few hundred metres. He stopped paddling but the waka glided on, slowing as it approached the moored boats.

A dolphin swam towards him, circled the waka and then leapt clear of the water, right in front of him, pointing out to sea.

Now all ten of them surrounded him, all jumping and splashing. Were they hunting? The new rules required him not to paddle until they went away. He wasn't paddling, but the boat continued to glide forward, pulled in their slipstream. In all his years of kayaking he'd never had so many dolphins so close to him before. He could reach out and touch them. He did not. That was against the new rules too. Chasing dolphins was not allowed, not even in a boat that lacked the dangers of noise and spinning blades. He must sit and wait until they were gone.

These dolphins did not go away. They thrashed around him, and the boat rocked. A soft jolt shunted the waka. It wasn't a touch by the dolphin itself but a quick blast of air from a blowhole, as though it was testing the stability of the kayak. A few seconds later, he felt a stronger impact. This was the physical body of the dolphin hitting his boat, shoving it through the water. He swore, struggling to stay balanced.

This was weird. They were aggressive now, pushing him around. He felt them moving him north-west, out to sea, picking up speed. Faster still and the little waka was gathering momentum. Still, he did not use his paddle. Six of the ten clustered close around his bows. The other four crowded in behind.

He'd often seen dolphins taking a free ride on the bow-wave of fast yachts, but now it was the other way around. These dolphins were giving him *their* slipstream. It was this, not their occasional shoves, that kept him moving. His light waka glided among them effortlessly, exactly like migrating birds who rest at high speed while the slipstream of their flock carries them onwards, exactly as fish are carried in the wake of their school, exactly as human cyclists work together to keep the weakest going.

But now those same laws of physics were crossing the species divide.

Frequently he dropped back out of their wake but always the six in front would slow until the four swimming behind maneuvered him back among the leaders. He wanted to use his paddle to save them effort, but its hard edge might have hit a dolphin. Their skins were delicate. Besides, it was against the new rules. If he paddled, he was chasing and that was forbidden for reasons he respected.

'Leave me!' he called to them. 'Go and hunt! Feed your young – help them stay alive.'

If they take me beyond Manawaora, he thought, I might be too weak to get home.

The old ability to paddle tirelessly all day was long gone. He ought to escape for his own sake as well as for theirs. Taking care not to hit a dolphin, he back-paddled to slow himself. The dolphins in front were body-lengths ahead within seconds. The four followers slowed, confused, then began nudging him, but he persevered. He turned the kayak, intending to leave the dolphins and make his way home.

It didn't work. The dolphins who'd been out front came straight back. All blocked his homeward path. Then some pushed his stern to port while others pushed his bow to starboard, towards the open sea again. One even nudged the rudder, encouraging the turn. Together the dolphins maneuvered him back into their chosen path.

They were off again, and he made no more attempts to stop them. The sick Rōreka was no match for ten strong dolphins. He marvelled at their teamwork.

Something weird is going on, he thought. There had to be a reason for this. Would he ever get home again? He hoped they weren't kidnapping him to South America. Chile was nine thousand kilometres away!

Never had Rōreka imagined that one day wild free animals would come and spirit him away into their world. He knew he would never forget this as long as he lived. All his life, he'd heard mind-music at inspiring moments and now it was pouring through him. A tune pulsed to the beat of this sea, these waves. The melody began to dance and leap and race like the dolphins. It developed strange urgency.

Oh my god! he thought, I came out here for inspiration and I've found it. *Slipstream.* That's the name for this song. But … where are they taking me?

They skirted the reef protruding from Jack's Point and rolled on towards Motukauri. Something big was moving about in the calm water between the island and Whangaiwahine Point. More dolphins, milling at the surface. The water was streaked red. Was it blood?

His escorts slowed as they carried him closer to the new group, about six dolphins surrounding some object he couldn't understand, some kind of misshapen jumble. It was at the surface and the dolphins worked together to keep it in position.

He glided to a stop alongside the jumbled mass. A blood-drenched fishing net! There was something alive inside it. Was it a dolphin? Yes, a half-mashed baby dolphin!

He understood at last. None of this had been a game. This was crisis for the dolphins. And he'd tried to turn back, to escape their summons for help.

The two adults closest to the baby focused on the entangled one. They had this weird intensity. It reminded him of something. He'd seen this before somewhere, many times. Yes! Human musicians. Occasionally they entered a zone of musical focus so intense that nothing else existed for them. They became the vibrating strings of their own guitars or violins.

These two beings made no sound that he could hear and yet he was convinced they were musicians performing at the height of their power. Their vibrations streamed around the trapped baby. The silence was so charged with musical energy that it seemed some vast orchestra was playing its heart out inaudibly before him.

He knew what he must do. It was like the turtle so long ago, when he was fit and strong, but this would be a much harder job.

The baby dolphin was slashed all over with deep gashes, and her mouth and blowhole were cut and bleeding. The beautiful tail flukes were twisted into a lumpy mess, with blood oozing from the wounds. The left pectoral fin was partly sliced through at the crease where it joined the body. Where to start?

It would take strength and endurance to save this baby. And these days he had little of either.

He secured his paddle, undid his spray skirt, fumbled at the little shelf under the deck to pull out the dry-bag he always kept there. Inside was his knife, always sharp and wrapped in an oily rag to keep it free of rust. Thank God for that. A long cord was tied through a hole in the handle of the knife. He tied it to a deck-line on the waka. He couldn't help much if he dropped his knife.

The dolphins maneuvered him close alongside. He began sawing in from the edges of the tangle to get closer to the baby. He was soon within reach and able to sever the single strand cutting so deeply into the dainty left pectoral. It was cut nearly half off! Could that ever heal?

Then he severed the lines slicing into the corners of the mouth. This caused a few other strands to loosen, and he worked slowly on around the dolphin's little body, always sliding his knife under the strands, with the blunt side of the blade against the skin and the sharp side cutting away from it. He soon had the most damaging strands cleared away. In most places it took two hands, one to grip the net, the other to wield the knife. Little by little the mess came free. The tangle around the flukes was the most difficult. Dozens of strands created a massive birds-nest there and it took many cuts just to get through to where he could find the ones that tied the mess to the tail. By this time his arms were tiring, and his back ached from the unusual angle he was sitting to reach the baby. He sat upright and rested briefly. He stretched his arms and tried to massage the tension out of his aching muscles. Then he returned to the task – cutting, cutting. At last, the final strand came free of the bleeding flukes and the job was done. The baby was free. He dragged the mess of strands away from it. The pod homed in, close to the little one.

Rōreka needed rest as he never had before. His sick body had used all its meagre energy. He tied the mass of net to his deck-lines and relaxed, incapable of anything except sitting and watching the dolphins.

The baby lay exhausted and bleeding in the water. Two adults worked together to support her from beneath. One was still focused on the stream of silent music it was sending to the baby. Rōreka was more convinced than ever that this was a musician at work. He knew one when he saw one. Was the silent music helping in some way? Manaia had been so sure, only this morning, that their sound-vibrations had healed her.

Other dolphins disappeared and returned with clear jellies which they fed to the baby. One fed her a small squid. Dolphins caressed her with their pectoral fins and gently massaged with their rostrums. The soundless music flowed from the healer and now the baby showed signs of recovery. It used its fins a little, compensating for the damaged one, which trailed beside it, with the forward motion dragging open the wound. This baby would not be swimming far or fast for some time, he thought, but the others were already feeding it. That might save it, and dolphins were famous for speedy healing.

Rōreka too had begun to recover from the exertion of his rescue effort, but the sky had clouded over and a fresh south-easterly had sprung up. It would be a headwind all the way home. He stowed his knife and refastened his spray-skirt.

But what about the net? He couldn't leave it in the sea to snare a new victim, but this huge mess would never fit under his deck lines. He tried towing it a short distance. It was difficult. He rearranged it as best he could, so it hung a metre or so behind him, attached by its own ropes to his deck-lines. Still not great but better. He looked up the bay towards home – an easy paddle in the days when he'd been well and strong. Not much more than three kilometres. Now, it seemed impossibly far, the headwind was strengthening, and he'd be dragging this massive sea-anchor all that way. His body was still shaking in the aftermath of the effort he'd taken to rescue the dolphin.

Rōreka put his head down and set out for home, measuring his progress against the land. With all that drag, it was hard to get moving but he was making headway despite the rising headwind. If he stopped, he'd be blown backwards. He focused on technique – the best way to conserve energy, rotating from the waist, reaching with the paddle, grabbing the water to claw himself forwards. He crawled upwind. The sea was rising now. One big wave knocked him sideways and the next tried to capsize him, but with a reflex born of long experience, he leaned into it, jammed his paddle into the wave and braced, saving himself. The drag of the net handicapped him, making the waka handle oddly. It took forever to reach Jack's Point and that was less than a third of the distance he had to cover.

Tāwhiri-mātea was merciless. He blasted Rōreka with stronger gusts. Rōreka paddled on, but his burden was too great. Rainclouds swept over the waka and doused it with rain. He hardly noticed the rain, but how he wished the wind would die and change direction. It didn't. The cloud thickened. The world darkened. The sea looked grey and cruel. Why hadn't he waited on the little beach at Motukauri? Too late to turn back now. Turning downwind might entangle him in the mess behind. He struggled on but the pain from his illness grew, draining his strength. His vision darkened at the edges and it seemed that everything was fading away.

Tāwhiri-mātea sent one almighty gust. The kayak twisted and a wave took it at the wrong angle. It capsized. Normally, in a capsize, he would simply roll all the way around and pop upright again on the other side. It was a familiar action, ingrained in his reflexes. But he was uncoordinated and half-conscious in the rough sea. The unusual drag on his boat from the tow-load, worked against him too. He was trapped upside down underwater, his spray-skirt holding him inside the cockpit. His foggy brain took a few seconds to remember the grab loop on the spray-skirt. He tugged it weakly. Nothing happened. He mustered his strength and yanked harder. This time the skirt released. He slid out and surfaced alongside the waka, gasping for air.

Think! Think!

But his brain moved slowly. Where was the paddle!

He found it, still safely attached to the waka by its spiral lanyard. How would he re-board in these conditions? He'd rarely practised self-rescue because he'd always been skilled at rolling. He tried to remember the techniques now. There were weird names for them – something about a cowboy scramble or a heel-hook. Didn't you need a paddle-float though? First, he had to right the waka, get the water out of the cockpit. He flipped the boat upright, but in his weakness, failed to lift it enough to drain much water out. This was a sea kayak though, so its watertight bulkheads kept the bow and stern dry and the boat floating.

He greyed out again with one hand gripping the waka. He followed a few half-remembered instructions to get back aboard. First you had to get your body over the stern. He tried but it was too rough, and he was too weak, too cold. Pain throbbed inside him. He lay in the water, his flotation vest keeping him face-up. His eyes closed as he faded to a place where he felt no more pain, no more cold, and weakness didn't matter. His hand slipped from the boat. Rough water thrust between him and the boat, first one metre, then two, then three. Tāwhiri-mātea gambolled away to the open sea leaving a dying wind behind, but Rōreka drifted alone, lost, aware of nothing. Wind and tide carried him out towards the mouth of the bay, back the way he'd come.

One foot skimmed the strands of net as he passed, menacing filaments reaching for another victim, but he floated clear. The space between him and the net increased.

Now that Atarau was free, Elethea could move the focus from pain relief to healing, both physical and emotional injuries. Techniques included, therapeutic sounds, songs and powerful healing thoughtwaves. She gave them all to Melody and Zeta with instructions on their use.

'Keep her as still as possible,' she said, 'to avoid pressure on that cut fin. She's still dehydrated from the blood loss, so bring high-fluid food. I'll come every day to update her healing, but if she has any problems I haven't foreseen, call me in again.'

Melody and Zeta pressed against Atarau, cooperating to hold the fin-wound closed.

'Would you help the human who saved my baby now?' asked Melody. 'He's sick and may still be nearby.'

'But I healed a female human of a mind illness only recently. Ought we to heal another? There are already too many humans.'

'But I owe him everything.'

'His kind left that net in the ocean,' argued Elethea.

'This man is not cruel. He's sick, but his own kind don't heal him.'

'Perhaps they don't know how,' replied Elethea.

'This one deserves any help we can give him,' urged Melody, 'We all saw what he did for Atarau.'

'True,' replied Elethea. 'I'll try and find him. He can't have gone far in that squall.'

'Take Libran with you.'

Libran and two others went with Elethea, to find Rōreka.

Melody turned her full attention to her broken baby. She and Zeta moved Atarau slowly around the northern shore of Motukauri island, with Melody supporting the left fin, trying to keep their forward motion from dragging the cut open. The right fin had only superficial injuries and Atarau could use it normally. The cuts on her flukes were deep, but forward motion did not force them open in the same damaging way.

They found a tiny patch of soft sand in shallow water, beside a narrow channel. They placed Atarau on the sand, soothed by sleeping songs, protected from currents by sheltering rocks. There, she had only to drift gently upwards a metre or so to breathe and sink again to rest. This minimised stress on her fin injury.

Many other dolphins swam within easy call, busy collecting food for Melody, Zeta and Atarau. Melody noticed a commotion nearby. It was Elethea's group to the west. They'd found the human musician. He was in the water, his empty boat still visible further off.

Atarau was safe for the moment with Zeta and others around her so Melody shot out to towards Elethea and the unconscious man.

Elethea's group surrounded Rōreka as Melody arrived in a flurry of foam.

'Elethea, have you started working on him yet?' she asked.

'Just about to. We've only just found him.'

'He's dying,' said Melody. 'If he dies, he's sacrificed his own life to save Atarau. I can't come with you. I must stay here with Atarau, but before you start, I want to give him something. Who knows? It might help him later.'


The man would get plenty of help from Elethea but Melody herself would give him the only thing she had time to impart – the Aerdluthan chord.

She thought of the thirsty man on the raft. Sleep! Need! The thirsty man had been in need. Rōreka was comatose and in need. This chance was too good to miss.

Then Ātārangi's octopus, the first Tangles, spoke to her from deep in her memory.

'This is the one for you,' she'd said, speaking of this very man!

Melody swam close beside Rōreka and beamed the alien chord into his brain. She pretended he was a dolphin who could receive thoughtstreamed sounds. He was no dolphin, but this sound came from a planet where even the wind could talk to its world. If anything would work, it must be this.

Strangely, as she imparted the chord to Rōreka, the spectre shrunk and its colour faded, until it was hardly visible, hovering weakly.

It took nanoseconds to impart the three-second chord by thoughtstream.

Something was different this time.

The chord closed in on the mind of Rōreka. It wavered, almost tried to drift away again.

But his spirit detected something. It gave a gentle pulse – a gleam. In the presence of his need, in the presence of Melody's gratitude, in the absence of fear and hatred, a tiny flicker of spirit-energy gently tweaked his sleeping spindle neurons. These neurons detected the chord and held onto it. It changed them at one touch, enhancing them. No power on Azure could have achieved what that chord achieved in that moment. But it was not of Azure. It was of Aerdluth, the planet whose bio-communications left Azure's in the dust.

Melody did not know it. Rōreka did not know it. But the chord lodged inside him. There it lay captured, cocooned, safe. It vibrated gently, wafting along his brain fibres, glancing from neuron to neuron, sliding across the synapses between. Rōreka felt nothing. He knew nothing. He didn't even stir in his coma. But whether his life was short or long, his brain would never be the same again. A link was forged.

Melody had done all she could. She dashed back to Atarau and Zeta.

Meanwhile Elethea's group supported the barely-alive Rōreka towards Jills Bay.

Elethea saw straight away that the human was too cold to survive. His thinness provided no insulation.

She gave Libran the task of warming him.

If the temperature at Rōreka's core dropped even a degree lower, he would die. But Libran swam close, warming the sick man with specialised high frequency soundwaves. The other two males cooperated to move him through the water, gently pushing from below and behind, as though he was an ailing dolphin of their own pod.

Elethea observed Rōreka's inner organs with her ultra-sound. Again, she saw dozens of tumours, slowly growing, many of them capable of killing him soon. She would need powerful thoughtstreams to do this job properly.

But she knew the human brain was deaf to thoughtstreams. She could only use physical sounds that might stop them growing for a time, but not dissolve them.

As long as she didn't miss any of the crucial ones, he might remain stabilised for weeks. She gave him an hour of sound therapy on his slow journey home, managing as best she could without thoughtstreamed cures.

She finished and he was still far from home. There was still time to experiment.

She sent him a silent thoughtstream, expecting no response.

'Wake up!'

His eyes flicked wide open. She jumped.

'Did he hear me? But he's human. Impossible.'

'It sure looked like he heard you,' said Libran.

Rōreka drifted back to sleep.

Very carefully, making no physical sound at all, she thoughtstreamed again.

'Wake up and call out.'

Rōreka woke again. 'Help!' he cried in a feeble voice.

Again, he returned to his coma.

He had twice obeyed thoughtstreamed suggestions! Was it coincidence? Then she remembered Melody beaming something to the man, just before their journey began and saying it might help him later.

'I'll try healing thoughtstreams,' she decided. 'I still have time. They might fail but they can't harm him.'

She began to work in earnest, streaming sounds and healing data to his brain. Though some of this was sound, all of it was delivered in silence. Tens of millions of years of dolphin bio-technology had refined all this data for this purpose. Some was ordinary, some was even dull. Some was extraordinary, rare and exquisite. Much had originated in the oceans of Azure, but some had arrived from distant planets of the home galaxy, and some from galaxies beyond. But it all played a part in the healing process, just as each note has its place in a symphony. The material was so vast and complex that silent thoughtstreams were the only way to deliver it.

Down all those millennia, dolphin healers had woven these thoughtstreams into combinations that activated brain capacities, powerful enough to turn rogue cells against themselves until all tumours dissolved.

The thoughtstreams themselves did not heal. They worked by teaching the brain how to heal the body it ruled. They could not have healed a tumour in the body of a jellyfish, because the nervous system of the jellyfish has no brain.

Not even Elethea herself knew if her therapies would succeed with a human. But she worked on and on, just in case. The human brain was so different from the larger dolphin brain she was used to. Humans had fewer spindle neurons, the limbic system was primitive by comparison, and she could clearly see how the cerebral cortex lacked the convolutions and intricacies of the more evolved dolphin brain.

Still Rōreka floated face-up, his head supported above water by his flotation vest, breathing as efficiently as if he were wide awake. As always, this human ability to breathe while unconscious impressed the dolphins.

He had no idea he was receiving therapy, though nothing like it had happened before, in all the history of humankind. His own wife Manaia had been healed by dolphin therapies but only with physical sounds, not by the complex thoughtstreams Rōreka was now receiving.

Elethea's work was done by the time they reached the Jills Bay shallows. If the man woke here, he could reach the shore.

'Wake up!' she said, 'Stay awake this time.'

Rōreka's eyes opened, closed, opened again and stayed open. He looked about, still groggy. Aue! He was almost home. How did he get all the way back here?

The dolphins left him and returned to open water.

He rolled over, his legs reaching down, touching sand. He kicked his way to the shallows, tried to stand, stumbled, fell. He tried again and this time managed to keep his footing. He staggered out of the sea and onto the beach.

He looked around. There was nothing to see in the bay but the usual handful of moored boats. His waka was nowhere to be seen.

He sat on the grass for a while, drying and warming himself, recovering, trying to understand what had happened to him.

He gathered his strength at last, and headed for home, towing the empty gear trundler.

He was tottering like an old man, up through the bush track, when he met Manaia coming down.

'Oh, there you are,' she said. 'I've been worried. You've been ages. My God! You look dreadful. Are you sick? Here. Let me pull that.'

She grabbed the trundler from him, and he didn't argue.

'Sick?' he said. 'I'm lucky to be alive. I was kidnapped by dolphins, freed their tangled baby, then capsized and nearly drowned. I was way out there by Motukauri. I don't know how I got back to the beach. I was unconscious. I've lost my boat.'

'Kidnapped? By dolphins? What are you talking about?'

'They dragged me in their slipstream. I tried to escape but I failed. The tangled one was out there. They took me on purpose to save it. I'm certain of that.'

'Dolphins!' she said. 'What craziness is happening with the dolphins in this bay? I can't get them out of my head. And now they're going after you too?'

'I'm so hungry,' he mumbled. 'Just let me eat and sleep.'

He did both and his sleep was long, deep, and dreamless.


When he awoke at last and lay in bed, thinking over the previous day, there were two huge blanks in his memory. The first was music soothing a tangled baby dolphin. He'd only seen that music, not heard it, but he longed to hear it. The other blank was how he'd arrived safely home after his capsize.

I guess I'll never really know what happened, he thought, but he puzzled over it for days.

He phoned Coastguard and informed them of the missing yellow kayak and its dangerous tow-load. Coastguard judged it a hazard to shipping. They broadcast a warning to boats in the area, calculated its likely drift and sent out a boat, which quickly found the capsized kayak floating in the Te Rawhiti Inlet. They removed the net from the sea, returned the waka to the beach at Jills Bay and called Rōreka back to let him know it was there. Manaia insisted he stay at home resting. She took the trundler herself and went alone to the beach to secure the boat and retrieve the gear.

While she was out, Rōreka remembered the new song, Slipstream he'd made out there. After all that had happened, he was surprised he'd retained any of it. But he managed to create a first draft that was good enough.

A few days later he woke early and set off for a run in the cool of the morning.

'Good days and bad days,' the doctors had said. It was proving true. This was a good day – the first time for many weeks that he'd felt like running. He walked the first stretch, uphill, then turned into a short no-exit road that led through shady bush. He jogged back and forth along it a couple of times. With weak legs and shallow breathing, he ran at the pace known as the 'survival shuffle' and covered hardly more than two kilometres. Yet, because he'd been so sure he'd never run again, this shuffle-run seemed more important than any of the long effortless flights he'd once taken for granted.

# 24 – SONG FROM THE DAWN OF MUSIC

Rōreka had kept the cancer secret, locked away in a box somewhere, to worry about later. Now that Manaia was healed, he must tell her soon, but not until after he'd uploaded the new Ipipiri album. Anyway, he'd been feeling so much better lately, he'd almost forgotten about his illness.

He closed down his recording studio for the day, switching off the equipment, piece by piece. He shut the studio door and climbed the stairs, expecting to need to conceal the usual pain as he approached the kitchen. But there was little pain to conceal. It had stabilised in the last few weeks, despite his near-death experience in the waka. Perhaps the warmth of summer was keeping cancer at bay. He wasn't complaining.

Manaia was frying onions – one of his favourite smells.

Food. Funny, his appetite had returned lately too, though he still enjoyed the smells as much as the food itself.

'Power bill came,' she said, shattering his smell-spell. 'How's Ipipiri going?'

'Could be a while before any money comes in.'

'Much still to do?'

'I finished Slipstream. Happy with that. Only one more song now but I want that song to be magic.'

'Lots-of-money-for-power-bills-magic? Or obscurely-magic that no one wants to pay for?'

Ouch! It wasn't like Manaia to be harsh over money. The power bill must be a biggie.

He could hardly remember the last time he'd felt like a pre-dinner beer, but now he grabbed one from the fridge. He didn't open it straight away. He sat at the dining table and gazed north-west, out to sea. A gentle breeze ruffled the surface. He rubbed the can across his forehead – for its coldness – and to prolong his anticipation of the first sip. The shadow of death taught you to appreciate the little things.

But how to answer her question? He turned and looked towards her in the kitchen, popped the can, and took a long swallow.

He said, 'Magic enough to call up the vibrations of the universe.'

She giggled, but somehow, he hadn't been joking. He wanted a song to give his family financial security after he'd gone. One song might do that for him . . . if it was good enough. The doctors had told him how aggressive this thing was. Ipipiri, once on the market, could be his last chance.

The Powers who controlled the vibrations he spoke of, heard his summons of course, but there was no further response from the kitchen.

Far out on the bay, in the calm water close to Motukauri, Melody swam slowly with Zeta and Atarau. Atarau was healing quickly. She was not ready for any long hard swims in rough seas, but she could already swim unsupported in calm water if she kept her speed down. The dreadful gash was closing, and she'd learnt to swim cautiously, without putting too much pressure on the damaged fin.

Melody felt an inner shiver. A spirit pulse – neither pleasant nor unpleasant.

Down in the waters of Jills Bay, Tangles stopped half-way through eating a big crab. Her see-forever eyes glowed in the dim greenness as they sensed a shift to come. She turned to the koha-rock, the human creation. Whatever was coming, was huge, and it was going to happen right here, in Manawaora.

Beans, corn, broccoli, cashews – all sizzled with the onions in the pan. A pot of rice steamed gently at the back of the stove. Familiar children's voices drifted up over the deck from the lawn below; Takurua and Hinewai still playing volleyball. Rōreka heard a bark or two. Jake, the neighbours' dog, must be joining in. Rōreka took another swallow – the bitter fizz soothed and cooled.

'Vibrations of the universe, huh?' said Manaia.

'Mm! Could be.'

'And the power bill?'

'Got a gig this weekend – can we hold out till then?'

'We'll have to, I guess. Hey, you haven't done a gig for a while.'

'I've been turning them down – too busy with the album.'

He was amazed himself, to feel strong enough to perform again.

Cancer was so unpredictable. Maybe these doctors were all wrong.

'Listen Manaia, I'm happy with the album. It'll sell as well as anything we've done once it's uploaded. Remember we have overseas fans now too. Since the last compilation we've had better reviews than ever. I just need to record this one last song; get everything mixed and mastered, then we can put it out there and the money will come.'

His use of the word 'we' reminded Manaia of her own part in his musical project.

'I worked on the graphics for the album art today,' she said.

'Hand or digital?' he asked.

'Digital – photoshop. I'm not happy with the seascape as it is. It needs something to bring it alive.'

Hmmm, so . . . not the power bill after all, he thought. Artists were all the same. Their mood depended on the state of their current creative project, whether it was music, wordcraft or visual art.

Halfway through dinner, Rōreka noticed a lift in spirits, of a kind that one cold beer could not explain. The shadow hanging over him lightened.

That night he lay awake in the still heat of the closed room, naked from the waist up. The pain was less than it had been, hardly enough to remind him he should tell Manaia soon. For now, she slept deeply and peacefully beside him. He was aware, though, that his own death would hardly help to keep The Mávro at bay.

'Don't think of that, think of the song.'

He stood up, threw on a robe, crossed the dining room and lounge to the big sliders. He walked out onto the deck in the starlight. The cool air caressed him, taking him back to his teens, a night breeze on his skin. He was standing on a ledge on the cliff face. A rope hung from the huge pohutukawa tree growing above. He gripped it and leapt, flew out over the high tide, letting go at the height of the swing. The thrill of freefall, the splash and chill of the entry. He sank down, down, all the way to the bottom. He pushed off the sand, shot upwards through the velvet blackness, erupted gasping at the surface.

The memory was strangely vivid tonight – he could almost feel the water enclosing him. He looked up. The Milky Way glowed, thick with stars. Drawing in a huge breath, he whispered, 'Send me the song I need for my girls.'

The universe didn't need this second request.

A chilly wind sneaked through and rustled the leaves. It sounded to Rōreka like the patter of rain, though he knew it was not. But he thought about rain pouring from clouds, draining from hillsides, and flowing down streams into the sea. The sea! It looked closer than ever tonight. He shivered in the sudden cold, then yawned and headed for bed. He wrapped himself around Manaia, appreciating her warmth, now that he needed it, and was asleep in moments.

At around two o'clock Rōreka woke suddenly. He lay still, listening. And there it was again – a frightened wail. Hinewai was dreaming and he knew the best cure. He went to her room, muttered soothing words, and led her through to the toilet. When she'd finished, he blearily 'flushed the bad dreams away', explaining it in those words as though she was five, and right now the big nine-year-old was too sleepy to object.

He took her back to her bed and as always, she slept peacefully afterwards.

Rōreka likewise. He dozed off immediately. Lying on his stomach with his head turned to the side and one arm flung forward like a swimmer, his sleep was dreamless at first. Almost. Gentle images drifted through; water glimmering in starlight; ripples spreading on a calm surface; rain pattering on a slow current, swirling over the deep.

Far out at the mouth of the Bay, Melody swam with Atarau tucked up close in her protective slipstream. Zeta, Elethea, Libran and Antares surrounded them. It was a quiet group. Antares was on guard duty while most of the others drowsed along in the half-sleep of dolphinkind.

Melody was not sleeping. Her flukes propelled her slowly. She'd been with Rōreka since his pre-dinner conversation with Manaia, had gone with him to Hinewai's room, seen him put the child through her usual bad-dream cure. The Aerdluthan chord vibrated inside him, enhancing her view of his mind, even from this distance.

She waited while his sleep deepened, and he slipped down towards the state where sometimes even a human might greet the universe.

Still, she waited . . . watching for that perfect moment when his spirit was most free to wander. Then she plunged deep into his mind and brought him home with her to swim the starlit ocean.

Light blazed in Rōreka's eyes. My God, they're stars, he thought. Not just above but all around.

Yes. That's Scorpius low in the sky and there's Centaurus. There was nothing but water around his body and stars everywhere else. He was swimming in the dark, far from land. He must be dreaming. But in his dream, someone swam near him, a warm female. Not Manaia. He turned to look. A dolphin! No mistaking it. The strangest vibrations ran through his body.

On and on they swam together, while she gave him the song he'd requested of the universe. He sang it with her and was puzzled because he knew no instruments on earth that could have made the chords he heard.

It was The First Song – the dawn of music in the universe. There was no song, anywhere in all creation, older than this one, created over twenty million years ago by the dolphin Ripple herself. It was only a simple love song for her Cosmo, but because it was the first, it had bestowed intergalactic renown upon Azure.

Under a moonlit rainbow,
Through the flying spray,
Who did you leave behind,
When you came my way?
Carried in the midnight silk,
Of starry currents in the seas,
I listen to the rising wind,
That sings to you of galaxies.
It sings to me of you,
Stranger from the blue,
And will you take my music
To the galaxies with you?
Under a moonlit rainbow,
Through the flying spray,
What were you fleeing from,
When you came my way?

The dream faded as he woke but the song stayed deep inside him, gathering itself. It pushed upwards as he dressed; a harmonising wind, breathing through the cloudscape of his mind. Waves of melody blew from the ocean; lyrics danced like seabirds on the breeze.

He must record it now; in case it vanished like the dream. Dazed, he stumbled into the dining room, where by now the song played for him as though an orchestra was performing in the middle of the room. Manaia was drinking tea beside the window. He positioned his hands against his temples like blinkers, as though to shut everything else out of his mind.

'This is the one,' he told her as he turned down the stairs to the studio.

'Rorie, you look weird. Are you alright?' she asked.

'Put a dolphin on the graphic,' was his only reply.

'Are you going to eat?'

'Maybe later.'

'A dolphin?' she said. 'Why didn't I think of that?'

In the studio Rōreka recorded the song. It spilled out of him fluidly, finished in an hour, though he lost all track of time. As he finished, the urgency disappeared, and the song faded like his dream, leaving nothing but vague images of stars and dolphins. His final touch was to add a name. He called it Moonlight Rainbow, then put it aside. He'd review it at day's end.

He spent the rest of the day upgrading some of the other songs. These were ones he'd previously thought finished. Now he found a dozen ways to enhance every one of them.

Finally, he stopped and returned his attention to the new song. Disappointment bit like a snake as he listened to the recording. Compared to the song he'd heard in his dreams it was pitiful. But now all he wanted was food. Food! How can I be hungry, he thought, when I've just wasted the inspiration of a lifetime?

Manaia had made a potato bake, its top golden with her home-made cashew cheese.

She served it, adding steamed fresh veges to their plates and the family sat down to eat. Rōreka ate ravenously.

'You're eating better than you have in weeks,' she said. 'I was beginning to think there was something wrong with you.'

'This bake is delicious,' he mumbled around a mouthful.

'How's the new song?'

'I'm disappointed. But listen later and see what you think. How did the art go?'

'I layered transparent dolphins over the sea-and-star-scape. It's perfect. What made you suggest them?'

'Just a dream. Can't remember it now.'

After dinner, while the girls were doing homework, Manaia came down into the studio to listen to the new song. He put the headphones on her, hit play, then sat back to watch her reactions. She stood at first, eyes focused on a small painted rock sitting in an alcove on the wall. Her fingers rested thoughtfully on her chin. As she continued to listen, she dropped slowly to her knees, collapsing all the way down, until she lay flat on the floor, her eyes closed, tears escaping from the closed lashes. When it was over, she lay there unmoving, for long seconds.

She spoke at last, 'Where did it come from?'

'It was a dream; something about the sea. I haven't done the inspiration justice.'

'I always believed in you, Rōreka, but I didn't know half of it.'

She played it again and again and looked at him with different eyes. She brought the girls in to listen. They too wouldn't stop playing it, until Manaia ordered them to bed.

Rōreka and Manaia followed the girls out of the studio. Manaia skipped up the stairs in her light-footed way. He ran up after her, hardly noticing.

A few days later, one night when the girls were already asleep, Rōreka told Manaia about his cancer. Her face went grey, and she stared at him. Speechless.

'Wait! Just listen!!' he said. 'I think it's all going to be okay.'

'I was feeling awful,' he explained, 'and getting worse by the day. They said I might not have long. I didn't want to tell you because of your Mávro. But remember how sure you were that the dolphins healed your depression? I think it's happened to me too. Maybe that day … when I capsized? I was in the water that day, just like you were when they healed you. I don't need a doctor to tell me I'm getting better. I just know. I thought I'd never run again, but I went for a run the other day and I was fine. Even kayaking was becoming too hard.'

'Go back to the doctor,' she said. 'Get tests. Find out the truth. I must know.'

He did as she suggested. The doctors could barely believe what the tests told them. They passed all his scans, x-rays and case-notes back and forth, muttering 'spontaneous remission' in shared amazement.

*

Out in the sea, Melody recognised that she had changed him in mind and even given him a song. But he did not remember. He thought it was a dream, made no effort to reply. This was not communication. Communication went two ways.

I helped him, she thought. But I failed.

Her frustration increased. The spectre expanded with delight. Would she need to visit the whales again? She couldn't leave the injured Atarau, and it would be weeks before the child was ready for such a journey.

She stayed in Manawaora Bay more often now. It was more peaceful here where the new human laws had quietened the human boats. With its sheltered waters, rich food supplies, and the new tranquility, it was the perfcct placc for a young, injured dolphin to heal. Best of all, this was Rōreka's home. She'd already given him the Aerdluthan chord, and one song. But could she build on that? Could she take him further?

It was the task she'd been called to, the task she'd always detested. Yet, she felt no dread of working with this human, and it meant she could work right here in this safe bay with her baby beside her.

To combat the spectre, she banished thoughts of failure and focused on progress she'd made. There was hope now. Rōreka was her last hope. And when she worked with him, the spectre lost its chill.


One day during this time, when Rōreka was ashore, Melody, Libran and Atarau swam slowly together through the fading daylight, eastwards along the Te Rawhiti inlet, then north-east, passing between Rawhiti and Urupukapuka. The adults stopped often to let Atarau rest. Whenever Atarau rested, Melody fortified her with the latest healing songs prescribed by Elethea, while Libran hunted for them all. These waters were rich with food. He found plenty close by.

Night had fallen by the time they arrived in Maunganui Bay. But the sky was clear with a full moon. The little journey had been so restful for Atarau that she arrived feeling fresher than when she'd started. She began to play, for the first time since the entanglement, dancing with gentle bounces that would have been too painful before. But now her scarred fins swept blue phosphorescence glittering around her. It was a dance of returning health. Melody watched, hardly breathing.

'My baby is healing so rapidly. For that I thank Elethea and all the other dolphins who helped us. But before this came the greater miracle of her survival. And who caused that miracle?'

The man Rōreka!

There in the light of the full moon, with her healing baby frolicking around her, she fathomed something that gave her the biggest surprise of her life.

She'd assumed she could never love a human. But this man was different! He belonged to the species that caused all the grief she'd ever known. But he'd risked his own life to save her child. He loved music as much as any dolphin, loved the sea the way a dolphin did, and ventured among them only in peace and respect.

As this understanding dawned, a strange new warmth glowed within her. It was a rising tide, transforming the colours of her aura.

'Libran, I need solitude just now,' she said suddenly. 'Will you stay with Atarau?'

'Of course,' he said, sensing the change, and wondering if his dreams for her were coming true.

Melody swam out of Maunganui Bay, then North-east into the open sea where the great swells lifted her and lowered her, lifted her and lowered her, in the rhythms that define our planet.

The new warmth grew and spread, opposing the spectral chill she'd lived with for so long. The spectre writhed and groaned. The glow flooded her, strengthening every physical part of her. Oh, the heaven of just being warm! The spectre screamed. It diminished. It clawed at her with fangs of ice. She vanquished it with the warmth of a simple cross-species love.

Soon, there was nothing left of the spectre but the trace of a reddish gleam, harmless, like an aching flicker, in the light of her spirit. Its chill was gone, its pain a memory.

She filled the space it left behind with a vision of Ātārangi as he had been before the net, whole again, real, perfect, and happy with the aura of his freedom on Azure – a happy ghost – a healthy memory.

Then another tide began to rise in Melody. Its power silenced the ocean around her. This was the tide of music.

One red tendril escaped from the now-hidden spectre. It stole through her brain, gathering Aerdluthan traces, harmonising with her frolicking ghost child, instilling a spark of purest pain into a mighty chord. Then came notes, melodies, harmonies, and more chords, tumbling out of her, like clouds billowing before a gale.

It was a song to the memory of Ātārangi, and it rang around her until the moon reached its culmination.

The new song harmonised her need to keep her lost son close while also allowing him to be as far away as he truly was. Its rhythms and chords lulled her to deeper rest than she'd known since her last respite with the whales. It caressed her through a time of half-sleep then accelerated in tempo as she woke in a heaving sea.

The skies of this night seemed higher, the setting moon brighter, and the eastern horizon more distant than ever it had been, during her time in the cold.

The planet rolled over, letting the hills of Te Tai Tokerau prepare to welcome the sun. She sent out a thoughtcall to Libran.

'I'm coming home. I'm making music. All is well.'

She sent him the new song. He received it and listened carefully.

Libran and Atarau swam out and met Melody beside the Motukokako tunnel where the strange flash from the human light-tower shattered the starlight every few seconds. The eastern sky glowed magenta.

The ghost of Ātārangi still romped around her. Melody shared the vision with Atarau. The vision was so clear, Atarau laughed and bounced beside her dead brother as though they were both alive.

'Your old aura is back!' cried Libran.

He performed sky-leaps of delight, his own aura flaring. She joined in his play, which she'd missed for too long.

'Has the spectre gone completely?' asked Libran.

'It exists within me, reduced to an ember.'

He examined her aura closely.

'Yes, I see a trace, just a deepening of the colour, almost an enrichment.'

'Did you like my Ātārangi song?'

'Oh yes, very nice.'

'Very nice! Is that all?'

'I'm sure you'll regain your full capabilities soon. It's good that you've made a song to commemorate our lost son.'

'That's hardly the response I expected.'

The dolphin inability to lie was sometimes hard to accept and this was one of those occasions. Libran could not pretend the song enthralled him, but the next day she noticed him replaying it in his brain from time to time.

Zeta and Elethea gambolled in from the west and Melody gave them the Ātārangi song. Neither responded with much excitement and both veiled the worrying thought that Melody's music might never be the same again.

The five dolphins hunted together.

'It's so good to hunt freely with you again, Melody. We missed you.'

Again, she noticed Libran replaying the song.

'How does it sound today?'

'Hmm, perhaps there's more to it than I thought at first.'

The following day, the second since he'd received the song, he said, 'Melody, it's growing on me by the minute. It develops with every replay. I believe you're a better composer than ever before.'

Zeta and Elethea were also replaying it by now and sensing the magic emerging. Even little Atarau was catching on to the weird new sound.

Belated enthusiasm from Libran, Zeta and Elethea finally convinced

Melody to keep working. She gathered her memorised sounds from in the tunnel in Maunganui Bay to create a song for the moray who'd honoured Ātārangi and herself with affection there. Other new songs leapt to life, including many infused with traces of Aerdluth.

With every new song she shared, the pattern was the same. She delivered the music by the usual compressed thoughtstream. The dolphins listened and thanked her politely. No-one danced. Auras barely responded. They didn't understand the strange airy rhythms.

At first.

But this new music had the power to stick to the deep brain and work its way up. A day or two later, the dancing began. Dolphins worked in teams, blasting out new moves while auras shimmered and interconnected in new ways. Tendrils of light interlaced in patterns that changed by the second, carrying the music with them.

Dolphins came to thank Melody, to apologise for their delayed appreciation. But by the time they found her, she was lost in the creation of some new song. She made one after another, trying to make up for the time she'd lost. The others respected her need to work undisturbed. She didn't need their apologies. She knew by now that the impact of her new songs took time to flourish.

Once the music was flowing, Melody found she could work with Atarau close by, keeping one part of her consciousness focused on the young one, while another part created chords, melodies, harmonies, and lyrics. Soon, the closeness of her baby only served to enrich her songs.

# 25 – OCEAN MIND-BLOWN

The water was clear and shining blue. Eagle rays glided near the beach in Opunga Cove. Melody played an old song that matched their wingbeats. Its echoes remained with the rays when she and Atarau swam away.

Meanwhile at Jills Bay, Rōreka launched the waka. He followed the north-eastern coastline of Te Huruhi Bay, passed between the rocks that lay off the end of the headland and turned east into Opunga Cove, arriving a few minutes after the dolphins had left.

He paddled to the beach and along the water's edge, looking down through glass-clear water at the pebbly bottom. He saw movement, something big. He dipped the blades gently, taking care not to splash. Yes! Several eagle rays cruised in line along the edge of the water. They recognised an old friend, and glided beside him, their wingtips dancing a gentle ballet.

Then he heard a sound that matched the wingbeats of the rays. A strong fading beat that lingered like a fragrance. Like an echo.

The rays slid away under his bows and vanished into deeper water. The echo faded with them.

He ghosted on into Assassination Cove and Te Hue Bay.

There he turned and headed back the way he'd come, towards open water. Near Orokawa Bay he noticed a disturbance a few hundred metres in front of him. There it was again and this time he saw two fins. Dolphins! One big. One small. They were within 400 metres, so in respect for the rules, he secured his paddle in its groove, relaxed, lay back and prepared to wait it out.

These dolphins were moving unusually slowly. The adult and baby made straight for him and fell into place beside him. The baby had horrific scars still healing on its fins and flukes and around its head and blowhole. It could only be the one he'd disentangled. It had survived then!

He trailed his hand in the water. A minute passed, while the mother inspected the hand. He felt a vibration there. Was she scanning? Then she touched his palm with her pectoral fin, light as a ripple. It sent a wordless message, as clear as the sea around him, flowing through his body and mind.

And Rōreka returned it! Not just to this one dolphin, but to her child, her kind, the eagle rays he'd seen before, the whole marine world, the sea itself.

His brain exploded into new life. It was like the big bang that once generated a universe, spindle neurons firing impulses through every synapse to create energies unknown to humankind. His mind morphed, blending with every plant, every animal, every grain of sand, every drop of water, every breath of air – all suddenly bursting with stories to tell him. The whole marine idea-sphere invaded his consciousness, overwhelming him.

'Am I going mad? What's this chaos?' he said aloud. He wondered if the cancer had returned, this time infecting his brain. He clutched his head. His heart sped up.

Melody saw his confusion. She moved into his mind. He felt her there. She began organising the chaos as though tidying a room. To protect him, she swept away everything he wasn't ready for, leaving only what he should focus on for now, just as a mother does for her newborn when it first meets the idea-sphere. She soothed him. He stared down at her.

This dolphin, he thought, just planted some huge shemozzle into my brain and then barged in and sorted it out.

Gradually his heart calmed, his body relaxed, and with that, his curiosity grew.

What was going on here? These were the dolphins he'd helped, they had to be, but what really happened that day? What did he miss when he blacked out?

She read his thoughts. Her answers began streaming into his brain.

The closest word he had for it was movie. Yes, it was like watching a transparent movie. But he was viewing it with some kind of super-sense. It overlaid his eye-vision, as clear in every detail as a printed photograph, but its transparency let him also see the real world beyond. The movie was three dimensional and included sound, temperature, texture, colour, line and form. On top of all that, it conveyed ideas. These were dolphin thoughtstreams – mind-pictures that spoke ten thousand words.

It showed himself, leaning from his waka, straining to cut the strands. The wounded baby lay bleeding under his hands, the two females nearby pouring music into the trapped one. But now, with Melody's help, he was not just seeing the music performed, he was hearing it too. He'd longed to hear that music. Now he had the best seat at the concert and could hear every note, chord, melody, and harmony.

Dolphin music! It was so . . . he searched for words . . . alien? No. He found the word he needed at last. Not alien. It was marine.

This was music from an advanced but ancient marine culture, unknown to humankind until now. And he was the one watching the first glimmer at the dawn of human understanding.

Next, Melody showed Rōreka what had happened during his blackout that day. He saw himself floating unconscious, two dolphins pushing him homewards. Two others swam there. One generated music, the other warmth. As for the music! No choir of angels could have created it and now he understood that his tumours had begun dissolving then and there.

The dolphins were healing him.

It ended. He stared down at the dolphin beside him. Dolphin thoughtstreams!

'Teach me to do that,' he begged.

A wordless idea arrived in his brain, as though in response to his request. Tossed at him like a ball.

'Like this. Like this.'

It was a simple picture of an octopus.

She was telling him to imagine a picture? He'd obey then. He closed his eyes and pictured an eagle ray like the ones he'd seen earlier. But he wasn't good at drawing, not even in his head. Manaia was the artist. She'd do a great job of this. As he sat with his eyes closed, looking at the stingray in his brain, it suddenly wriggled, its shape and colours adjusted, its details corrected. He hadn't done that. Then he knew. The dolphin was viewing the picture and improving it for him.

This was communication. This was going two ways from her to him and from him to her.

She leapt in excitement. She popped up beside the waka and touched the coaming with her pectoral fin, then resumed her position beside the boat.

She sent him another movie. Herself as a baby, with motorboats chasing her. Her mother, a beautiful adult female, trying to protect her from the spinning propellors. The blades slicing the mother's tail, the tail spiralling down – the blood, the sharks, the death.

Then came a picture of the death-ship with its vast net astern. The net had trapped her firstborn son as well as tens of thousands of fish. Her child, and all those fish, were dying together in agony.

He had no reply to this. He sat a long time trying to think of a way to apologise on behalf of his species, but no words came to him. No words. No consolation. He was human –therefore complicit in the death of her first child.

He wished he had answers. He thought of the vegan activism he'd done online, the marches he'd attended, the petitions he'd signed, the letters he'd written to government. None of it did any good. Humans continued to rape and eat the planet as if it was infinite. Overstuffed nets continued to lumber aboard the death-ships; dairying destroyed the atmosphere; megafauna died steadily on land and sea. He knew all this as well as Melody did.

A new picture was arriving from her. She carried the decaying corpse of her child, day after day through the sea. The music became terrifying and the corpse morphed into a red fiend from hell that screeched at him. He trembled, almost capsizing the waka. He squeezed his eyes shut, trying to block the vision.

'This spectre was my burden. My grief. It tortured me for years.'

The horror faded but he'd seen it once and could not remove the memory. As a member of the human species, he deserved punishment. The dolphin swam slowly now, between his boat and her scarred baby.

He'd seen what he'd seen and did not doubt the truth of it.

With his head bowed and eyes still shut tight, he put his hands in the water and used them to propel the waka slowly forward. Mother and child kept pace with him. The movement calmed him a little.

And then the music changed its mood, starting almost like a lullaby, but building inside their shared world. Not sad this time. Happy. Could this dreadful story possibly have a happy ending?

Stars flew spinning by, as the music carried him vast distances through the universe. A planet appeared where liquid beings floated in heavy air, drinking nectar from huge blue flowers. The pictures vibrated with life and energy, beyond his understanding. But he knew things about this world that could only have come from the mind of the dolphin beside him. The flowers were friendly! And one of the floating beings was her lost firstborn, alive on a distant planet! She was happy for him. The music proved it. One day she hoped to join him there.

But for now, man and dolphin came whirling back to Manawaora Bay.

'What happened? Where did we go?'

'It was not astral travel. I sent you visions from a real astral journey from my own past.'

'How can dolphins do this when humans have no clue?'

'Humans are too distracted by clutter, to advance in mind and spirit. Your hands distract you. They lock you to the material world. If your hands wielded your paddle right now, you might not be receiving my thoughtstreams.'

'Our hands? Do they make us evil?'

He thought of guns, nets, hooks and knives, all evil things from the hand of man.

She replied, 'Sometimes. But human hands saved my baby. Human hands painted the koha-rock.'

She sent him an image of Manaia's painted rock in the setting created by the octopus.

He recognised it. 'The koha stone!' he said. 'My wife created the art and gave the stone to my daughter, Hinewai. Hinewai felt the mana of the stone. She's a water-child so she gifted it to the sea.'

He left the paddle alone, and kept ghosting along, powered only by his empty hands.

'Do you have a name?' he asked.

'Melody.'

'I'm Rōreka.'

'I know,' she said. 'Your name and mine have the same meaning.'

'I dreamed recently that I swam in the dark with a dolphin. I awoke with a song in my head as though the dolphin had given it to me. I recorded it as best I could. It's better than my other music but I didn't do it justice.'

Melody did not explain her part in that dream.

There was a silence between them. The sun beat down. Rōreka removed his T-shirt, stuffed it under his stretchy deck lines. Melody noticed the tattoo wrapping across his body. She let him feel her curiosity about it. He replied by playing the tattoo song through his mind.

Fern unfurl, seashell curl,
Feather floating free,
Unify,
Land sea and sky,

In spiral galaxy
Ripples grow, from embryo,
To waves across the sea.
Burst on sand,
Retreat from land,
Reborn as energy.

He felt her listening. Melody recognised simple beauty in the little tune and she laughed. She was like a human mother laughing with delight at the first steps of a toddler, knowing how far this new skill might take the child one day.

Rōreka grinned.

'It's not like your dolphin music, I know,' he said.

'You're only human. You still have far to go. Our music has developed over millions of years, since long before your kind evolved. I'll help you. I'm a musician too. When my son died, I lost my power to compose, but it's recently returned.'

Melody was enjoying his company. Just by being himself, Rōreka proved to her that her hatred of his species had been misplaced.

By this time, they were out in the middle of Manawaora Bay, facing south-east towards his home. His paddle still sat secure in its groove. His hands still played in the water, sometimes propelling him slowly, sometimes letting him drift.

Melody darted off to find a fish for Atarau. While she was gone, he felt waves of curiosity coming his way from the scarred baby. This was the first time Melody had allowed Atarau close to any human, and now she was alone with one. And this human had saved her from her nightmare! Atarau loved everything about him. His boat, his tattoo, his funny little song, and his gentle thoughts. She placed her scarred fin on the palm of his floating hand and let it rest there.

'Thank-you,' she said, just as Melody returned with a fish for her.

Arriving near the beach, Melody suggested he swim with her. He needed to put his boat ashore first and wished to explain that. He closed his eyes and projected an imagined movie of himself dragging his boat up the beach and then returning to swim with her. Speaking with thoughts instead of words wasn't easy but the Aerdluthan chord was helping him.

She understood and stayed nearby until he returned without the waka.

They swam towards the painted rock. He looked down, but the water was not as clear here. To see it properly he'd have to dive. He remembered the last time he'd dived, the day they'd sunk the rock. It had exhausted him.

Now he dived effortlessly and reached the painted boulder in seconds. Mclody dived beside him. Atarau stayed at the surface.

The octopus saw them coming and slithered into her ceramic cave.

Rōreka circled the rock, amazed to see its colours as bright as ever, with no trace of mud or sea growth.

'We have a full-time caretaker,' Melody explained. 'Come out, Tangles! There's no danger.'

Tangles appeared from her hidden home. Rōreka held out his hand and she stroked it, reminding him of the octopus who had shaken hands with him that day so long ago. Rōreka then shot upwards to catch a breath, wishing he could share the dolphin's lungs as well as her thoughts.

On his second dive, Tangles took him by the arm and showed him around the garden she'd created. They glided along, looking down. Its beauty dazzled him. It took him several dives to see it all.

Then Melody asked if he could do anything about the death-ships and ghost nets, noise, and other problems afflicting marine beings.

'There's little I can do on my own,' he said. 'Humans don't respect the people of the sea because they don't understand them. That might change if we could show all humans what you've shown me.'

'Is that possible?' The words of The Powers came to her mind.

'You need to reach the entire species to be effective,' they'd said.

Rōreka paused.

'I can try, but only hope the message spreads,' he said. 'Manaia is the only person in the world likely to believe what happened to me today.'

Manaia herself had experienced dolphin-power, he thought, and that might help.


Over the next week the weather allowed him to meet with Melody every day on the water. She kept working on his new thought-skills, teaching him to screen thoughts he wished to keep private, and how to control who received his thoughts and who did not. She taught him thought-etiquette. That was about avoiding eavesdropping on the private thoughts of others. It was easy once you knew how.

'Other humans don't know how to screen their thoughts,' she explained. 'You'll need to avoid invading their privacy.'

He thought of his daughters. Reading their thoughts would be worse than reading their private diaries. Ye Gods! He'd hate to become some kind of super-snoop.

During this same week, Melody took Rōreka out to sea daily, and she gradually introduced him to the dolphin idea-sphere and to the dolphins themselves.

Melody was always happy in Rōreka's company. She laughed a lot while she was with him.

His discovery of Ocean Mind was more of a culture-tsunami than a culture-shock. He felt like a toddler in a world of maestros.

*

Melody and Atarau followed Rōreka home. Atarau was fully healed now. Her worst scars would stay with her forever, but her lesser scars were fading. Keeping her daughter close, Melody stayed to see Rōreka ashore, before turning to the koha-rock. Now was the time to create the song it deserved. She studied its light and dark, its myriad spirit colours. She drank in its images of this ocean, this world, and other worlds. Then she blended sounds from the ocean, from Aerdluth, and other planets. She arranged all the sounds and rhythms to harmonise the painted river, the birds, the marine life, the dolphins, the galaxies, and the suns. She worked until every visual nuance was translated into music. Now it could be viewed by ear, by eye, or both at once.

Not even Manaia herself could have foreseen what the boulder had become.

When the song was complete, Melody sent it to Antares by long-distance thoughtstream.

'You're free to share the new sound-vision to other worlds, but wait two days before you do,' she urged. Antares responded just as Libran, Zeta and Elethea had. After the first listen, he was unimpressed. But something made him play it again . . . and again.

Two days later he understood. He and Libran melded the song to the curated koha-rock, unifying them as a single work. Then Antares took it to his astronomy group and together they shared it with sentient minds all over the galaxy.

In some receiving worlds, beings heard it once and never listened again.

Other aliens invested time until they understood – just as the dolphins of Azure had done.

But The Powers of the universe and all the musicians of the Divine Hierarchy recognised its quality at once.

The song reached Aerdluth in the end, carried there on the intergalactic grapevine. Would Aerthonn, surfing his airwaves there, hear the song? Would he feel the thrill of music created in a far galaxy by an unknown dolphin who had once been his mother?

# 26 – VEGAN CRACKPOT

Rōreka was sure Ipipiri was ready. He uploaded it.

Within a week it was the biggest selling album of his career and sales were spreading overseas. There was a gradual transition from whole-album sales to sales of individual songs. Moonlight Rainbow sold twenty times faster than Slipstream, the next strongest. But all the songs kept selling well, better than he could ever have dreamed possible. His low-budget marketing hardly explained it. This could only be happening through word of mouth.

Suddenly there was so much money coming in, he wanted to share it. He made a huge donation to his favourite conservation group – the Māui and Hector's Dolphin Defenders. He'd donated to them before but not as much. Word of the Defenders' windfall spread.

To help his friends in the sea, Rōreka had to broadcast his findings to humanity. He typed onto his social media.

'I've been talking to a dolphin.' It sounded too whacko. He deleted it.

'Dolphins have telepathic powers.' He deleted that too.

He tried several other comments about what he'd discovered but deleted them all.

Sure, the world had to know, but he'd be labelled a misinformation crackpot if he posted anything like that. He went to bed without posting anything.

The next day he posted the statements anyway. But not so baldly this time. He included a bit more description that he hoped would add authenticity. Replies were pretty much what he expected.

There were polite ones:

'Sorry mate. Love your music, but a dolphin is just a big fish.'

There were less polite ones:

'Are you out of your tiny mind, crackpot?'

There were even a few unprintable ones.

And there were the same old anti-vegan jibes he'd heard a hundred times:

'Dolphin-burger is delicious.'

Rōreka didn't take it personally. None of them knew what he knew. It was the laughter of ignorance. And it wasn't stopping them buying the music.

One reply read, 'All this about dolphins is nonsense. Everyone should ignore it.'

Manaia was stung. She replied in support of her husband.

'How would you know anything about dolphins? Have you ever met one face-to-face?'

'Yes, I'm a marine biologist,' he wrote back. 'I meet dolphins often in my research work. I know more about them than you do. There is no scientific evidence for any of your claims. Please stop spreading new-age nonsense of this kind.'

Manaia's efforts to support her husband had only made him look worse. She didn't try again.


The phone rang. TVNZ wanted a video interview with Rōreka. A good marketing opportunity and his big chance to tell thousands of people about Ocean Mind. He agreed.

When the time came, he arranged his tablet computer out on the deck so the sea and islands would form his background. He logged in. They played Moonlight Rainbow before the interview and snatches of it throughout.

The interviewer introduced him, then asked:

'What inspired the Ipipiri album?'

'Ipipiri itself. But not so much the land. It's all about the sea. I spend hours on the sea in my kayak.'

'And the Moonlight Rainbow song? What do those lyrics mean?'

'That song arrived in a dream. I woke up with it. I can't help feeling it wasn't really me who wrote it.'

'It mentions a stranger from the blue. Who is that?'

'I didn't know myself at first,' he replied, 'but I think the stranger is a dolphin. Perhaps one who died long ago – a dolphin from history.'

'How can you say this now, but not when you first wrote the song?'

Rōreka told her about the rescue of the baby dolphin, the cancer, his healing, his reception of cross-species thoughtstreams, his discovery of Ocean Mind. He also told her about marine music.

The interviewer placed a hand over her mouth as he spoke. Was she hiding a smile? He swallowed his irritation and went on.

'It jolted me,' he said, 'to accept that humans are not top dogs here. There are smarter species on this planet, and they have a lot to teach us, to our benefit. But instead of listening, we kill them and torture them.'

The interviewer was smiling again, this time openly – in fact not smiling but smirking.

'To most people, your claims about dolphins would sound…er… eccentric, to put it mildly. Do you have proof of any of this?'

'Dolphins cured my terminal cancer, for Chrissake! But don't take my word for it. Give my doctor a call.'

'We heard that you made big profits and made a large donation to a group of hippie dolphin-lovers. Why them and not some more important cause like UNICEF or the Red Cross?'

Rōreka paused. Should he just say it was because he liked the Defenders' logo? There was some truth in that after all. But he didn't hate humans and didn't want anyone to think he did.

'Saving the oceans will save humans in the end,' he said. 'If I give money to UNICEF, I might save a few people for now, but what's the point if we all die later because of ocean degradation? Māui and Hector's dolphins are facing extinction. Some of the Defenders are hippies, I suppose, but all of them care about dolphins and oceans. I've marched with them, sung for them, been to the pub with them. I know them and trust them to use the money wisely.'

'Why dolphins?'

'They think. They calculate. They make music far better than mine, better than any human. They suffer. They heal. They grieve. But it's not just dolphins. It's cephalopods, whales, sharks, rays. There are whole ocean nations who're threatened by humans.'

'Er . . . nations? In the sea?'

'Yes – whole nations of indigenous tribes, as sentient as you and me. Millions of them. Far more than we have on land.'


Comments like those, which he made often in later interviews, branded him a whacko.

The interviewers sniggered publicly. 'He makes great music,' they would say, 'but creatives can be crackpots.'

He didn't blame them. He'd have thought the same until recently. The public only forgave his crazy words because they loved his songs.

He was worried though. Music conveyed what he needed to say, better than any social media post, but even Lennon's song, Imagine, had failed to change human behaviour.

Ipipiri kept selling. Even the pittance-per-song paid out by the big online streaming services was adding up. He took financial advice, cleared the mortgage, set up a fund to cover the girls' future tertiary education and another to keep the family secure. He bought an electric van and sent the old one for recycling.

Money still poured in. What should they do with it? Buy a new house? What house could be better than this one?

He asked Manaia, 'D'you want a bigger house?'

'No thanks,' she said. 'Enough housework for both of us already with this one.'

To the neighbours' relief, he employed a landscaper to tidy up the section. They had the house repainted. None of this scratched the surface of the bank-balance. He upgraded his recording equipment to the latest and greatest and gave his perfectly good old gear to struggling newbie musicians. He bought the divers' watch he'd always wanted.

Then he ran out of ideas. So, he bought a few expensive wines. They both decided they tasted no better than cheap ones.

'We have cheap tastes,' she said. 'Thank God for that.'

Manaia's life hardly changed. She continued to wander the beaches for stones, painting them and selling them at the market, charging much less for them now that she didn't need the money. Rōreka did his best to keep his family out of the media spotlight, refusing to speak of them in interviews. But still, when Manaia arrived at the market a whisper would circulate, and the art sold out in the first few minutes to tourists who'd heard who her husband was. Her stones became the souvenir of choice for visitors to Kororareka. Cheap, exquisite, unique, and small enough to slip into a handbag or pocket.

Big marine conservation groups overseas thought the songs might help their causes. They began promoting them. Rōreka thanked them with a huge donation, big enough to really scratch the surface. So, they promoted him even more – more money flowed, so he donated again. It was a self-defeating cycle. He gave money to Earthrace and Greenpeace and WDC and any other marine conservation groups whose people he knew and trusted.

He invested in companies creating planet-friendly food choices, hoping they'd one day push products of the grazing and fishing industries off supermarket shelves.

A local game-fishing charter business asked him for financial support. He refused.

# 27 – THE DUO KAYAK

Now Manaia had lost her sea-fear, she was keen to meet the dolphins in their own deep waters.

'Today,' said Rōreka, waking one morning. 'Is the day for the double kayak.'

They put the kayak rack on the van and drove to Ruakaka to visit the Barracuda kayak factory. They tested a few of the boats in the nearby waterways, and finally settled on an AR Duo, with bright yellow decks, a white hull, two cockpits and accessories.

They named the new boat Ora. Manaia painted the name each side of the bow. They launched on the first calm morning.

He steered and paddled from the stern cockpit. She took the bow. She found her natural paddling cadence and he synchronised. The only sound was the rhythmic splash of the blades in the water. Ora ghosted in and out of the early-morning mist as they crossed the mouth of Clendon Cove.

At first the dolphins kept their distance from this new boat. But when Rōreka spoke, they recognised his voice, and began swimming towards them.

The dolphins arrived, surrounding Ora, inspecting every inch of her smooth white undersides.

Manaia laughed to see them cavorting so close. Rōreka told her their names. They bounced alongside and rolled side-on to look up into her eyes.

'They know you painted the rock,' he said. 'They send you respect and gratitude.'

Her long dark hair flowed in the wind. The sight of it fascinated the dolphins.

'Lean down,' shouted Rōreka. 'Put your hair in the water.'

She bent over the water while Rōreka counterbalanced. Atarau swam alongside, shoving her nosy little beak through the flowing strands of Manaia's hair.

'It tickles,' she announced and Rōreka passed the message to Manaia.

'How did this baby get the terrible scars?' asked Manaia.

'This is the one I rescued that day,' he reminded her. 'The one almost cut to pieces by a fishing net.'

By this time Melody had trained Rōreka in all the many shortcuts of thoughtstreaming. It was now easier for him to think to dolphins than talk to humans.

'Does anyone believe you yet?' asked Melody.

'Not when I talk or type,' he replied. 'Music works better. People believe me while they listen, but they stop believing when the song ends. They think I'm a screwball.'

'That happened to our Ripple, twenty million years ago when the world wasn't ready for her discovery,' replied Melody.

'I'd love to hear that story,' he said.

'It's the only dolphin story that humans already have. A deity of the universe gifted it some years ago, and for important reasons.'

'What's it called?'

'Ripple.'

'I'll look it up online.'

'You'll find it easily.'

Meanwhile Atarau caught a little fish and offered it to her new friend with the lovely long hair. Manaia of course declined the fish, so Atarau ate it herself. Atarau was curious about the paddle. She tasted it. Manaia passed it to her. Atarau took the blade in her mouth and towed it away.

'Hey you! Give me my paddle back?' laughed Manaia.

Atarau brought the paddle back almost within reach, but when Manaia reached out for it Atarau snatched it back at the last moment and swam away with it. This game went on for several minutes with Manaia always losing. By this time, she was laughing so hard, Rōreka was struggling to keep the boat stable.

Atarau loved the sound of Manaia's laughter. These humans were so easy to amuse. She returned the paddle at last.

Manaia locked it into its groove and trailed her hand in the water. Atarau tasted the hand, nosed at it. Manaia turned her palm upwards. Atarau placed her pectoral fin on Manaia's palm. They coasted along fin-in-hand.

Melody spoke again to Rōreka.

'It would be easier,' she said, 'if other humans could learn thoughtstreaming like you did. But so far, you're my only success with the chord.'

'The chord?'

'Remember when my pod rescued you that day?'

'I'll never forget.'

'Before they took you home, while you were unconscious, I planted a chord in your brain. It's from a planet where even the wind can talk. But humans can't receive it.'

'If humans can't receive it, how did I?'

'You were in need that day. That was important, I think. But there may be other reasons. Unlike dolphins, a human mind is too tense and fearful to receive an alien element, unless it's totally relaxed. You were unconscious.'

'I see,' he said. 'Hard to replicate that for all of humankind.'

'There may be other conditions we fulfilled by accident too,' said Melody. 'I succeeded with you. That's big progress. You just keep singing your songs and I'll keep working on it too.'

# 28 – GROWING UP AND GROWING OLD

Takurua planned to make astronomy her career. The University of Canterbury in Te Waipounamu – the South Island – had the use of the Mt John telescope at Tekapo. It had 360-degree views across the largest accredited International Dark Sky Reserve in the world.

It was perfect for her. 'And I don't even have to leave Aotearoa.'

That made her parents happy.

'But remember,' said Rōreka, 'however much astronomy you learn at UC, you'll still be a novice to dolphins.'

For Rōreka and Manaia, the years flew by too quickly, until the day Takurua left home to study in Te Waipounamu.

Two years later Hinewai also went south to study, though not as far as her sister. She wanted to study biological sciences, including marine biology and oceanography at Auckland University. She signed up for papers in anthropology too, hoping they might prepare her for future collisions with ancient cultures of the sea.

Her father knew some of those cultures already. If mankind ever chose to believe him, Hinewai would be ready to ride that wave beside him; she longed to talk to dolphins like her dad. Meanwhile though, she might as well benefit from his unique guidance. Through him she could research topics suggested by the dolphins themselves!

'Coming from this family, you'll have an unfair advantage over other students and even staff,' said Rōreka. 'Don't let it puff you up. Remember, that's just luck for you and not real superiority over them. Might be better to hide your advantage. If you try to explain it, they'll say you're a crackpot like your father.'

'I might need a hundred clones of myself to do all the research dolphins suggest,' she said. 'But who knows? It may turn out that everything we need to know is covered by dolphin science already. I'll only need to translate.'

*

The dolphins worked on, as the years passed.

Atarau was now a fully-fledged adept of humanity by vocation. With help from Melody, she studied Rōreka's mind to learn how human minds differed from dolphins'. Both Rōreka and Manaia gave the dolphins free access to examine their body and brain. When the girls were home, they also submitted. The whole family sometimes lay in the water, allowing the two dolphins to swim around them, scanning. The humans enjoyed the warm vibration.

Soon Atarau was spending more time with the humans than Melody was.

She and Melody were certain now that the Aerdluthan chord was the key to cross-species communication, but how to make the transfer was still elusive. This chord was purpose-designed by its alien inventors to open the floodgates of the mind, as it had for Rōreka. But the conditions needed for transmitting it were too difficult to replicate. Love, mutual need, relaxation, the absence of fear! It had taken all that to get the chord across to just one person. Impossible to do that for all humanity . . . surely?

Melody knew that no tool had more power over the emotions than music. Music was her own greatest skill! If only she could embed the chord into a song that carried a sense of need and love between the singer and the listener, to relax the listener as deeply as sleep itself, and to banish all fear, no matter how deep-seated. Perhaps the chord might then be accepted.

Acceptance was one thing. Retention of belief was another. The biggest problem was a human psychological quirk, very strange to dolphins. It might be described as 'short-term belief.' Humans could believe every word as they sang of peace and love but go straight back to war when the song was over.

Melody could make the music, and include the Aerdluthan chord, but even if humans received it and believed it, the belief would fade with the song. Melody and Atarau needed help with this.

In the end, they did as their famous ancestor Ripple had done. They sought help from dolphin mathematicians, those trained by their vocation, to analyse and calculate every nuance of every sound. She described the problem to Vector, the leader of the Ipipiri mathematics team.

'It's a challenge,' he replied. 'It might be achievable, but it won't be quick. We're unaccustomed to the human mind.'

'Atarau may help you there,' replied Melody. 'She's almost living inside the human mind these days.'

'That might prove useful. We'll collaborate when we need to.'

'I'll work at the music,' she said. 'When it's done, I'll give it to you. I hope you can apply your discoveries to it without compromising my song. Perhaps then, Rōreka can spread the adapted song, and we can begin to contact all humanity.'

She began to compose, choosing sounds most likely to deliver the required emotional impact. If this one song could take root in the human brain, then any number of later songs might enter by the same portal. No being in the universe was so capable of this as a dolphin musician, and Melody was top of her game. She avoided lyrics and was careful to use only sounds that Rōreka could later recreate easily with human music tools.

While waiting for Vector's crew to solve their part of the puzzle, she had time to create other songs, as inspiration came.

While Melody worked on the music, Atarau worked with the humans.

The mathematicians worked on the permanence.

They all collaborated regularly, to keep up with one another's progress.

*

Time passed. Melody and Libran grew old.

The song had been perfect and complete for years, but still Vector's team were unready. She called her piece Last Chance. Its wordless melodies and harmonies pulsed, as true as a new-born star, the chord resonating throughout. It would work. She had no doubt.

But still she waited for the mathematicians to complete their work on the permanence.

She swam one day with Vector of the mathematicians.

'My song is ready, as you know,' she said, 'but my big escape is coming.'

'We're working with subliminal rhythms to include with your song,' replied Vector, 'capable of permanently altering the subconscious. It's slow work as humans are unfamiliar to us. Great subtlety is needed because the aim is gentle influence – not mind control. We have 95% confidence of ultimate success, but only 20% confidence of completion within your own lifetime.'

'Then I ask you to work on,' she replied, 'even if I've gone. I'll give you the song now, in case I go before you finish. It's called Last Chance and contains the Aerdluthan chord. It's designed to place a listener into the perfect emotional state. If you succeed with your part of the task, those humans who believe what they hear while they listen to any subsequent song, will be able to retain that belief, if they wish to.'

She gave Last Chance to the mathematicians, and there was nothing more she could do.

Libran's life sentence on Azure approached its end now. His strength was failing. He'd achieved what he owed to his world. So, he made his last decision. He swam far out to sea alone, slowly, for two days, until a pod of transient orcas closed in at last, their empty bellies growling. Just what he needed. He sent a good-bye to Melody and their pod.

The orcas made a plan to prevent his escape. They launched into the first moves. He told them their plan was not necessary. He was ready to go and would not evade. In their gratitude for his contributions to marine culture, they gave him an ending too swift for pain.

Melody and Atarau, swimming together, took his farewell from the wind, and moments later, recognised his departure. The place he had filled in their lives, suddenly yawned, empty and hollow.


Melody worked for many days to create a song of tribute for him. It wasn't easy to express, in one song, his achievements and his impact on herself and on the oceans of Azure. But it was beautiful when it was done. It comforted the many who would miss Libran for the rest of their lives, and it helped them all to remember him.

## 29 – DANCING WITH THE TIGER

A year after Libran had gone, Melody understood that her own time approached. She began swimming alone, with the music of her life ringing around her – her own compositions and those of the revered ancients. She thought more now, of the musicians who'd lived and died before her. Songs created by Ripple twenty million years ago, still resonated more than ever today, conveying all the purity and beauty of that era, as well as its horrors.

Ripple's music took Melody back in time. The songs made her feel that she swam alongside Ripple herself, sharing the great adventures of that ancient courageous life. Melody often played Ripple's love song for Cosmo.

I play Ripple's first song, she thought, but soon I must create my own last one.

She located Atarau and swam to her.

'I'm escaping Azure soon,' said Melody.

'How soon?'

'A few days at most, but I'd like to go surfing one more time.'

'The weather adepts predict good surf at Takou Bay in two days. Big easterly swell but a westerly wind. Should be perfect.'

'Would you come with me, Atarau?'

'Of course, if you're to be there, Mother.'

Melody had not surfed since the spectre had driven her to it. Atarau had never seen her mother surfing.

The news entered the scuttlebutt. The great musician, Melody, would ride the surf for the last time at Takou Bay in two days' time.

Every dolphin wanted to be there. They arrived from every direction – bottlenose, common dolphins, and even some spinners arrived from their open-sea haunts to honour her. Vrinda and her eunivore pod of orcas were there, not surfing but watching from deeper water. Easterly swells built huge waves while the offshore wind groomed them to perfection. Phalanxes of dolphins followed Melody into the massive breakers and they all let her music ring high and deep in celebration.

After the surfing, she swam east alone as Libran had done before her.

Unlike before, when she had courted death on the beach of Whangamumu, this was the right time. No-one would stand in Melody's way now, as she moved on to her next phase.

She felt the vibrations of a predator nearby. A huge female tiger shark, gliding in menace and beauty.

Perfect. But she didn't have long. It had sensed her presence and was likely to come alone to take her in the dark. Tigers were rare now, dying finless by the thousand at the hand of man.

This shark needs my flesh more than I do, she thought. May she use it to help replace the countless lost ones of her kind.

She chose this shark as her best opportunity. Her music played on, and her thoughts turned to the life she'd lived:

I failed. Contact with the human species was my task. I contacted only one. Perhaps it will happen after I've gone but the work must be completed by others. They may never succeed. I have not earned the reward I long for.

A single word floated into her mind. Hope.

Could that be possible? Was there still hope, even now? She played a few lines of her Ātārangi song.

But her thoughts moved on…

She'd had success and fulfilment in her chosen vocation. She was grateful for that. She was grateful for her time on Azure with those she loved. And her time with the whales and other beings who had supported her life. She even felt grateful that she'd learned to love a human being, and his family. But still, she grieved for her lost mother and her beloved lost child. The oceans would all have been richer if they'd lived.

The sun was setting as the tiger shark approached, its smooth easy rhythms already linked to her in the final dance. It was hungry and she was ready.

All was as it should be.

The turning planet obscured a little of the sun, then more and more, then all of it, and Melody caught her last glimpse of the star that had fuelled her days on Azure.

'Good-bye Sol,' she said. 'Thank-you for your gift of life.'

Sol replied with a sunset that filled her with gratitude for the beauty of the world she would never see again and stimulated the creation of a final brief song – her farewell to Azure. She focused now, and the song built fluidly as she swam northeast towards the great deep and the last dance with her tiger. By the time the song was finished the great shadow was already circling below her. She streamed the song across a wide expanse of calm ocean, into the keeping of Atarau.

'This is my last. Share it as you wish and be sure to pass it on to my human musician. I go now.'

'Mother! How do you go?'

'A tiger shark. She's with me now. It will be quick. All is well.'

Melody's musical thoughtstream soared away in grace, under the light of the first stars, into the mind of her daughter.

Atarau received it as darkness settled over a quiet ocean.

The reply came back within a second. 'Good-bye Mother. Thank-you.'

Melody understood that those thanks were for more than just the song.

The movement of the shark changed. It swam faster, moving in to inspect her. She saw it by sound-vision, but her memory filled in details that the darkness hid, the faint stripes on its body, the five gill slits, the rows of serrated teeth, the jaw gaping for the strike and the wisdom in the magical eyes that could see in the dark, could almost think like a brain.

The first hit came in from the side. She felt only a massive thud. The lower teeth gripped her, and the upper ones crunched down, sawing into her as the shark shook its head to remove her flesh. She swam on, still alive but in physical shock, her blood clouding around her, her consciousness fading, her spirit stretching out long and thin towards the Divine Dimension. She was hardly aware of the second bite, the one that severed her spirit. She looked down on the body that had served her so well, as it became sustenance for the superb marine being who needed it now.

The essence of Melody drifted west before leaving Azure, seeking a final glimpse of her daughter. She found Atarau swimming among many other dolphins, with Melody's new song ringing in her mind. Atarau slowed and looked up as though she felt the passing presence. Melody bestowed a spiritual caress upon her and was gone from Azure.

She entered a phase of rest, without thought, without pain, receiving no reward, and paying no penalty. She floated, alone in the Hereafter, unaware of the passing of time.

*

Rōrcka was kayaking alone, out beyond the islands. He didn't yet know that Melody had died in the night, but he felt an emptiness he could not explain. He rested his paddle for a minute or two to watch Motuarohia disappear, as he dropped into a trough between two glassy swells. The island reappeared as the next swell raised him.

'Pouff!'

A dolphin's breath. He twisted round, to see a lone dolphin swimming closer. Terrible scars! It could only be Atarau!

'I've come to tell you that my mother has died.'

The waka dropped into another trough. It seemed dark down there. It felt like hours before the next swell bore him out of that darkness.

'How did she die?'

'Tiger shark. She allowed it to happen. She felt no pain. Her time had come.'

His shoulders started to shake. Atarau did not understand why water was streaming down his face, but she clearly read the pain in his thoughts.

'Don't feel that way!' she chided. 'My mother lives on through her music. This was her time to escape her life-sentence. All her burdens are gone now.'

Atarau paused and then added, 'She asked me to pass you this song. It's her good-bye.'

The Aerdluthan chord vibrated in Rōreka. It let him receive the song and helped him to absorb Atarau's wisdom and see this as she did. His pain vanished like mist in the wind. He would remember Melody always. If, indeed, her time was right, what was there to grieve for?

He dug in his paddle and shot across the face of a huge swell. The two of them raced on over the open sea with Melody's music playing a wild playlist of intergalactic hits at full volume around them. Gulls soared, gannets dived, and sunlight shone down on their blue world.

There was another dolphin swimming with them, an invisible one, not made of flesh and blood, but memory and music.

She stayed beside them both until their own lives ended.

# 30 – THE PERMANENCE

Only a month after Melody's death, the maths team completed the permanence rhythm. They were now certain that any song that was worth believing for the duration of the song would become permanent in the mind of a willing receiver. Permanent? Yes. But not blindly so. This was not brainwashing.

They carefully wove the permanence rhythms into the opening and closing bars of the song, Last Chance. It did not change the music. There was only an enrichment near the beginning and end, so slight only a true musician might notice.

Atarau guided Vector around Rōreka's consciousness until Vector was confident he could work within the limitations of this one human mind. Every note and nuance must be correct. Even so, it was only achievable because Rōreka had practised thoughtstreaming so much by now, he was almost as skilled as the dolphins themselves.

Vector streamed the two versions to Rōreka. One with the permanence rhythms and one without. Rōreka played them back. The two dolphins found many errors, but with their guidance, each playback came closer to perfection.

After just a few hours, the dolphins were happy with the result.

'Go now,' said Vector, 'and create versions that humans can listen to. Use the unembellished version as a control to test on Manaia first. It can't harm her.'

Rōreka went home and recorded both versions, exactly, right down to the tiniest whisper of sound he held in thought for Last Chance. The dolphins had prepared him so carefully, the task was easy.

He brought Manaia into the studio and played the unembellished version. It was alien and beautiful. It thrilled her as no music ever had before.

It took her several minutes to come back to earth after hearing it.

'Did you write this song?' she asked.

'No way!' he said. 'It was composed by our late friend Melody – the greatest dolphin composer of modern times. She called it Last Chance. There are two versions. I'll play the modified one later. But first I have to try something. Stay there and keep listening.'

He played a pretty little children's tune he'd made years ago to entertain the girls. She'd heard it often, but he'd given it new lyrics.

Kahu flies from dawn to dusk.
Ruru flies at night.
But Kahu flies in the dark tonight,
with Ruru as his guide.
Look outside. Watch the stars.
Kissing their wings with light.

'Such a strange image,' she thought. 'a hawk, flying by starlight with an owl.' While she listened, she wanted to believe that the two species might sometimes choose to fly in friendship together, the hawk guided by the powerful night vision of the owl.

'Cute lyrics,' she said. 'Kids will love it.'

'Do you believe that hawks fly at night, guided by owls?'

'Of course I don't believe it. But while I listened, the song made it seem real.'

'Next song,' said Rōreka. 'It's Last Chance again, but slightly enhanced.'

She settled down again to listen.

He played the second version. She heard no difference but somehow it thrilled her even more, transporting her out of the world.

'I never wanted it to end,' she whispered afterwards.

'You can listen to it as much as you want later,' he said. 'It carries a chord that comes from another planet, believe it or not. But now I'd like you to listen to Kahu and Ruru one more time.'

She puzzled at the contrast between the soaring chords of Last Chance and the frolicking children's nursery rhyme. But he seemed intent on presenting his weird playlist, so she humoured him and listened while he replayed the exact same children's song.

As before, the music made the images of the two raptors flying by starlight seem so real. The song ended, but the image of the birds stayed powerfully before her eyes. They were really there! Flying together! She had to see them.

She jumped out of her chair, opened the sliders onto the timber deck, scrambled outside and stared around at the sky.

'Where are they?' she said. She searched but found no sign of a hawk and an owl flying together. No bird at all anywhere.

'It's okay,' he said, 'They're not there. It's not really true. Come back inside.'

'I felt like a child,' she said. 'I wanted it to be true. I believed it, even after the song was over. Why did that happen, only after you played it the second time?'

He explained everything to her.

'And now you hold the Aerdluthan chord, just like me. You're ready to receive Ocean Mind.'

It had worked with Manaia. Now he could try it on others.

He uploaded the permanence version of Last Chance and promoted it through his own web site and social media posts. Because he published it, most people assumed he'd created it. Those few who noticed the credit, "Music created by Melody of Ipipiri," assumed it was a marketing gimmick.

'First instrumental he's done,' was a common comment.

It went viral. It quickly spread overseas, to huge worldwide markets. Rōreka neither needed this money, nor viewed it as his own. He donated every penny to marine conservation. Everyone who listened to the song received the Aerdluthan chord. Among them were scientists, marine biologists, religious zealots, politicians, fishermen and owners of shipping companies.

But one day shortly afterwards, while Manaia was busy painting, he launched the single kayak and went out alone. The sky smiled. The hills waited. The sea held her breath as his blades stroked a lazy rhythm. A single note rang in his mind, soft at first but growing louder. Then another. Many more came, tumbling together into a melody flowering over his mindscape. It was a new tune! Complete after only fifteen minutes of paddling. He kept paddling, replaying the tune, fixing it in his memory.

This time he was sure it was his own song. He was not downloading this one from Ocean Mind. But he could not un-hear marine music he'd heard, so it had marine influences.

Then words fluttered in, like butterflies seeking a place in a garden. An hour later, the lyrics were roughed out. Before any of it could slip away, he raced ashore, secured the waka, and ran home to record a first draft.

He pushed all other projects aside and over the next day or two he worked in his studio, tracking, mixing and mastering the new song, amazed at how quickly it came together.

## OCEAN MIND

The flourishing idea-sphere!
The child of Ocean Mind.
Info-highway of the seas,
where whales and dolphins share with ease,
their visions intertwined.

There is a hurricane of thought,
arising from the deepest
memories, hypotheses,
stories, schemes and fantasies
and all the ocean's secrets.

I tell the world that this is true,
not just some crazy notion
Emotions do, live in the blue,
and mindscapes in the ocean.

Their world is older than we know.
Their intellects are pure and free.
The people of the ocean hold
vocations just like we.

No hands to hand-icap their thought,
no STUFF to cause distraction.
Free to focus on ideas
with quick cerebral action.

Telepathy is easy in
a brain so undistracted.
Leave your body in the sea,
and choose to travel astrally,
all limits counteracted.

Education, medicine,
math'matical adventure,
fighters to protect the weak
and adepts of the weather.

Their scholars of ecology
are strong in oceanography.
While famous storytellers work
with gurus of divinity.

Adepts of history and science,
the wise, the weird, the worthy,
developing philosophies,
prophecies and lunacies,
magnificent or crazy.

Adepts of love and family,
geography, cosmology,
anatomy, midwifery,
audacity, bewitchery.

Without electric lights to fade
the midnight constellations,
Astronomy for dolphins
is a much-revered vocation.

No manufacturers at sea,
no marketing objectives,
no weapons in production,
no corporates corruptive.

Accountancy does not exist,
Nor industry of fashion.
No climate-changing businesses,
no church, no shack, no mansion.

I tell the world that this is true,
not just some crazy notion
Emotions do, live in the blue,
and mindscapes in the ocean

It was finished. He published Ocean Mind as a single. Then he sat back and waited. The same slow start, the same gradual building of sales, first in Aotearoa and then overseas. What could he possibly use all this money for?

Millions of listeners, including almost the entire population of Aotearoa, had received the Aerdluthan chord from the Last Chance song, including the permanence rhythms the dolphin mathematicians had developed. So, when Ocean Mind came out, they were ready. Those without the slightest wish to believe, heard the song and stayed as they were. They liked the song as much as anyone did, but the lyrics meant no more to them, than the nonsense lyrics of I am the Walrus by the Beatles.

However, those who wanted to believe, did so, with all their hearts. And their belief stayed with them, even after the song was over. This was new. They were changed – their minds opened. For some, this only lasted until someone convinced them that it had to be nonsense. But even they continued to believe it might be possible and wished at least to give Ocean Mind the benefit of the doubt.

A local billionaire, who owned large blocks of land in Ipipiri, heard the song. He played it many times. Then he donated good waterfront land in Manawaora Bay to Marine Research. Ten acres surrounding an entire small bay. It had a curving beach of golden sand with grassy slopes rising behind. There were headlands at each end of the beach. Pohutukawa trees dotted the edges of the sand. Dotterels and oystercatchers nested there. Fish jumped in the water. There were several substantial buildings on the gentle slopes beside the beach.

This new Ipipiri Marine Research Centre was a short paddle away for Rōreka. He contributed money to pay for modifying the buildings and all equipment needs. He paid contractors to install a beautiful jetty. It curved alongside the headland that jutted out to sea. The University had been mysteriously swamped with new students wishing to study marine sciences, so the new centre was vital to them. Soon, facilities sprang up at other locations on the coasts of Aotearoa. Other countries noticed. Similar centres sprang up on the coastlines of the world.

Manaia believed every word of Ocean Mind, almost before he wrote it. She was more than ready when Rōreka took her out in Ora and introduced her to the idea-sphere. She couldn't get enough of it – and quickly mastered the skills of thoughtstreaming. One day she showed the dolphins her shark scars.

'Your tropical counterpart saved my life that day,' she told them.

'Your story lives on in that scar,' they said, 'though it happened so far away and long ago. We're glad we played a part in it.'

*

It was overcast and the sea shone grey and calm. Manaia looked out to sea and saw a beam of sunlight slipping through a gap in the clouds. It created a blinding streak of silver close to the horizon, well beyond the Manawaora waters, but luminous to Manaia as she commenced her daily swim across Jacks Bay. Bubbles danced around her face, popping, and rippling in a rhythmic tune, their sounds as pretty as their patterns. How could she capture both sounds and patterns with paint alone? Impossible, she thought.

The water surged around her, and she felt a light touch on her side. Atarau!

'Not impossible,' Atarau stated. 'I can show you a good example.'

The dolphin streamed the Moondance painting into Manaia's brain. Her eyes traced the brushstrokes and followed their sweet rhythms. The colours sang, the shapes danced, and the textures throbbed. Yes! Surely, she could hear the painting as she stared at it! The artist was reaching across the universe to sing to her in silence.

'This is breath-taking!' she said. 'Where did it come from?'

'It's from a planet called Raima and was created by a species with excellent hearing, for a species with no hearing at all. My father Libran curated it, here on Azure.'

'Curated?'

'Yes, he was a curator by vocation, responsible for thousands of the images that hang in the thoughtstreamed galleries of Ocean Mind. His task was to share and protect artworks that practical astronomers discovered in space.'

'It's the first time I've seen a static image make sound, let alone music,' replied Manaia. 'But the sound is as silent as any other thoughtstream. I guess the artist discovered audio-visual telepathy.'

'Did you know that Melody made a song for the koha-rock you created? Libran curated your painting and he put song and art together on the intergalactic grapevine.' Atarau played the song for Manaia.

'Am I,' she asked Atarau, 'the first?'

'You are.' replied the dolphin. 'You are the first artist in the history of planet Azure to be inter-galactically exhibited.

Not bad, thought Manaia, for a self-taught artist selling painted pebbles to tourists. But the greater honour is to be forever associated, out there in all those stars, with the music of Melody of Ipipiri.

# 31 – NEW VOYAGES

Melody drifted alone through the hereafter, at spiritual rest. The Powers of the Universe approached, looking back towards Azure to review her work there, looking away towards Aerdluth where lived the being who had been Melody's firstborn so many years ago. Something was happening on Aerdluth which The Powers had been waiting for.

There, the liquid being, Aerthonn, surged through the atmosphere with his beloved Apsara, she who now flew the windswept reaches of Aerdluth, at his side. At that moment an understanding passed between the two windriders – the time had come to act in procreation. Her azure-blue liquid body blended with his fluid magenta, harmonising their light and colour, until they shared the same space in the rushing Aerdluthan atmosphere. They drifted in that blended state for a long creative interlude, their colours intensifying, merging, and sparkling in a blaze of energy. That was the moment The Powers chose to release new life from the spirit realms, to join the conflagration. It was an elliptical star, clean and new as it danced in from the place between the galaxies, where it had waited.

When Aerthonn and Apsara separated at last, a newly created offspring flew between them, carrying the elliptical star at its heart. As mortal beings, the star was invisible to them. They only saw their new beloved one, surfing the airwaves there between them. She was magenta like her father, but as before, a thousand fainter colours pulsed in her aura, suggesting possibilities undreamed.

In her last brief spell of fading memory, she who was once Melody, dolphin of the planet Azure, received a gift from the Divine Dimension. It was one fleeting moment of Past Life Memory. It allowed her a single flash of insight to recognise the being who'd once been her son and was now her most glorious father. They'd lived together before – somewhere blue and liquid.

Then all her memories faded – leaving only love. What else mattered? The aerial surf carried her away with her new family, on a tide of wind that swooped towards the silver mountains of Aerdluth.

*

I let my thoughts return to home oceans, to watch a new voyage of Ocean Mind beginning. After sailing the worlds of outer space for millennia, the marine ideasphere now washes ashore on its own world.

It surges gently across the beaches, slides up the cliffs, and winds its way along the coastlines. It spreads slowly for now but already I spot the evidence; a scientist looking with new eyes into my depths, a mariner removing a ghost net from the sea, a politician fighting for new marine protections, a seafood restaurant re-branding as vegan.

I notice human confusion, shock, horror, derision, regret, and rejection, already morphing into amazement and acceptance. As the flood reaches them, some refuse to believe, until the day their child is healed by marine medicine, or they accidentally hear their first marine song, or their life is changed by technology from a far world, arriving via the sea.

I just hope the backwash carries with it a new human reverence for all my children. If it does, the sea-beings will thank forever, my poor haunted dolphin, Melody of Ipipiri, whose suffering was the catalyst, and whose love was the cure.

# DIVE BACK INTO THE WORLD OF DOLPHINS

If you enjoyed *Dolphin Melody*, you may also enjoy Tui Allen's first novel *Ripple,* available in both e-book and print versions on Amazon stores world-wide.

*Ripple* is the twenty-million-year-old story of how love inspired one dolphin to an intellectual achievement that changed the universe.

# ABOUT THE AUTHOR

Tui Allen, a retired teacher, lives in Ipipiri, Aotearoa (the Bay of Islands, New Zealand). Her days are spent surrounded by the sea - writing stories, making videos, walking the shores, and kayaking when the weather allows. This close relationship with the ocean fuels her passion for marine conservation and the protection of the natural world.

As a young adventurer, Tui crossed the Pacific under sail in a very small classic wooden boat, relying solely on wind and waves, without the aid of electronics or an engine. She navigated the sea as the sea-beings do, with only a wing in the wind and a fin in the sea. In those long, solitary watches under the stars, guided only by nature, Tui came face to face with many marine beings like those who inhabit her stories. They all helped her to dream herself into Ocean Mind.

www.ingramcontent.com/pod-product-compliance
Lightning Source LLC
Chambersburg PA
CBHW051653060726
47593CB00021B/392